THE SERPENT'S CROWN

THE SERPENT'S CROWN

John J. McKeon

Walker and Company
New York

First published in the United States of America in 1991 by
Walker Publishing Company, Inc.

Published simultaneously in Canada by Thomas Allen & Son
Canada, Limited, Markham, Ontario.

Library of Congress Cataloging-in-Publication Data
McKeon, John, 1951–
The serpent's crown / John McKeon.
p.   cm.
ISBN 0-8027-1146-4
I. Title.
PS3563.C3754S47   1991
813'.54—dc20   90-22683
CIP

Printed in the United States of America

2   4   6   8   10   9   7   5   3   1

To Marie

*I wish to acknowledge with gratitude
the support and loyalty of Jay Garon
and the practical, valued guidance of Peter Rubie.*

"... but know, thou noble youth,
The serpent that did sting thy father's life
Now wears his crown."

Hamlet, Act I, Scene 5.

Monday, October 28

It took a big jet to wake her. And even then, Laura lay still, wondering why her bedroom ceiling had changed so much, and why they were flying so low this morning over her part of Manhattan. Then she heard the growing roar of another widebody and located herself.

Hyatt Regency Hotel. O'Hare Airport. Chicago.

She rose frumpily on her elbows, turned on the bedside lamp and reached for her watch. Six-thirty. Four hours sleep a night, she thought. Wouldn't Mother be pleased.

Six-thirty?

Shit.

She was out of bed and tearing off her pajamas as she dialed the phone. Baggage is due in the lobby right now, she thought. At this moment. The jet roared overhead, barely muted by the hotel's cheap walls. The hotel operator answered.

"This is Laura Madison in Four forty-two," Laura said. "What happened to my five-thirty wake-up call?"

"One moment, please," the operator replied, casting Laura into "hold." She glanced frantically around the room and reached over to her suitcase to pull out her toilet kit.

"Miss?" the operator's voice said. "That wake-up call was made on time."

"No, it wasn't," Laura said. "I've been here asleep the whole time."

"The system is computerized, miss," the operator replied. "There's no possibility of error. The computer log shows a wake-up call was made to Room Four four-two at five-thirty."

"Then why didn't I hear it?" Laura said heatedly.

"I'm sorry, miss," the operator said. "I have no idea. But I can tell you the call was made. It's in the computer."

Laura hung up the phone. No time to shower, she thought, so I'll feel just wonderful in about fourteen hours, when this day is crawling to an end.

In the hotel lobby she found pandemonium as only those half-dead of exhaustion can stage it. Knots of people stood around the lobby cloaked in cigarette smoke. Porters ferried luggage out to the two charter buses idling at the curb. The big silver Halliburton cases of the photographers and TV crews were piled together, covered with stickers and warnings and pleas for gentle handling. Their owners watched them like first-time parents. At one end of the lobby a dozen pay phones were in continual use and a forty-foot line awaited openings.

The entourage—all forty-four of them, counting press, crews, staff, herself, Cavanagh and, of course, The Candidate—had fallen into Chicago about six the night before. Her boss, Senator Gillian, had gone to a banquet organized by the American Medical Association, where he told assembled leaders of the fifty state medical societies how he felt about their terrible insurance problems. As president, he was going to do something about it.

Then there had been an hour of fun trying to figure out the driving instructions to a suburban high school where the Du Page County Republican Committee had scheduled him to appear with the local Congressional candidate.

At each stop, the TV pool crew taped everything, no matter how trivial, in the hope of catching an assassination. They were chosen by lot for this ghoulish duty, and each day they taped over the previous day's deathwatch.

There were cold Swedish meatballs for dinner, and little hot dogs in jackets of grease, courtesy of the AMA, who Laura thought should know better.

They hit the Hyatt about midnight. Most of the crowd picked up their room keys and headed for the bar. Laura and Felix Cavanagh reviewed together the faults in her AMA speech for Gillian, then went over the next day's schedule and made up unresponsive answers to the several press inquiries that had

[2]

been submitted in writing. They called it a night at one forty-five, and Laura was out cold at two.

Now, she made for the coffee shop, hoping to find Cavanagh and pretend she'd been looking for him all this while. She made her way among the tables, most of them covered with full ashtrays, crumpled napkins, and half-full coffee cups. She was about to leave when a voice called her from behind.

"Hey, Madison, how much time we got?"

At a nearby table were an ABC reporter, a guy from the *Detroit Free Press*, a chain-smoking young man doing a campaign flavor piece for *Rolling Stone*, and Mitch Rydell, who looked after the interests of the *New York Times*. It was the ABC man calling.

"No idea," she replied, coming over to the table. "The buses should be meeting the planes now, and they're not near full."

"Rydell wants to know if he's got time for a holy pilgrimage," the ABC man said.

Rydell answered Laura's quizzical look. "I want to visit the site on which John Kennedy won the presidency," he said.

"Sit down," the Detroit reporter invited, waving to the waitress for fresh coffee. "This ought to be good."

"Well," Rydell said, "legend has it that some time around two A.M. the morning after election day, 1960, one of Mayor Daley's flunkies from the Board of Elections stopped his car on the Michigan Avenue Bridge—hell, it might even have been a city car—and tossed two ballot boxes into the Chicago River. All over America at that moment, bleary-eyed patriots were sitting up late, listening to Huntley and Brinkley tell them the whole thing hinged on Illinois and it was too close to call. Daley just hadn't decided how many boxes to drown."

The *Rolling Stone* man giggled. An anecdote, Laura thought, a real live little morsel of Campaign Atmosphere.

"Anyone seen Felix?" she asked. The ABC man shook his head.

"So," Rydell said, "I wanted to go visit the spot, take a picture . . ."

"My sixth sense tells me we'll be two hours late by noon," the Detroit reporter said, stubbing out a cigarette. "But I'd better wait on the bus, even so."

He threw three dollar bills on the table, made out a restaurant receipt for eight bucks, and slipped it into his wallet as he left.

"How did you all manage last night?" Laura asked. "Meet your deadlines okay?"

"I didn't file," Rydell replied.

"He never does," the ABC man put in, while the *Rolling Stone* correspondent collected the little packages of jelly. "For what he does, he's the most overpaid man here."

"When Gillian starts making news, I'll start writing stories," Rydell said. "That's fair, isn't it?"

"You don't think the Senator is making enough news?" Laura asked. Before answering, Rydell put on a pensive look for a few seconds. Arrogant, Laura thought, but winning a Pulitzer early in your career will do that for you.

"Let me put it this way," Rydell said. "I can't begrudge Gillian what he's doing. It's hard to find anything to campaign against when Erhardt has already given the people everything they want. Gillian is doing the best he can by making terrific speeches, and people remember they never elected Erhardt, they elected King and got Erhardt when old Billy popped an artery. So while Billy King lives the life of a brussels sprout in some hospital, Erhardt runs the country like he was personally chosen by God—or rather, his handlers do. Whenever I look at Erhardt, I'm never quite sure there's anyone home."

The waitress came and refilled their cups.

"But face facts," Rydell continued. "Look what's been achieved in disarmament, in building down our Defense complex, in drunk driving, child abuse, drugs, welfare fraud, tax reform . . . Christ, they've even got the damned federal budget within one percent of showing a surplus for the first time in living memory. So what can Gillian do? Appeal to the naysayers, the civil libertarians bitching about sobriety checkpoints and TV surveillance and privacy rights? Count on people voting for the underdog just so they'll have something to watch come election night?" He shook his head.

"You don't think we have much of a chance," Laura said.

"Not a snowball's chance in hell, Laura. Here comes His Lordship."

Cavanagh was on top of them.

"Has it occurred to you, Madison, that we have two buses waiting for you?"

"We were just finishing up," the ABC man said, wiping his mouth.

"*You* are not the point," Cavanagh said. "You can sit here and drink coffee till it flows out your nose for all I care, and your bosses can foot the bill to put you on any plane you want, and good riddance to the lot of you. But I'm not making special rules for you, Madison. I'm not making any customized schedules."

"Calm down, Felix," Rydell said.

"Don't you tell me to calm down, goddammit," Cavanagh shouted, and heads turned all over the coffee shop. "You have no business telling me to calm down."

"Okay, okay. Jesus."

"I'm on my way," Laura said, fumbling in her purse for change.

"My treat," Rydell said. "You've paid enough."

The lobby was now nearly empty. They'd loaded the buses in record time. Cavanagh turned to her.

"What were you doing drinking coffee with that snake?" he said. And before Laura could answer, he continued. "Would you please try to remember who you work for?"

"They had questions about the day's schedule," Laura said.

"Well here, answer them," Cavanagh replied, shoving a sheaf of papers into her hands. "Pass out the schedule on the way to the airport."

The Senator's schedule came in two forms. There was hard copy, or typed sheets, for the stone-agers, and 3½-inch diskettes for the laptop computer generation. Each week old diskettes were collected for re-recording. The day's schedule was also among the items downloaded daily by the campaign's computer into the systems of the major newspapers and TV stations. Each day's download included news releases, digitized videotape, the texts of the day's speeches, and other information. Many of the reporters, in fact, started their days by accessing Insta-Poll, a computer service that fed them the results of the previous night's before- and after-dinner polls.

Hard copy distribution was a daily ordeal. Gillian's campaign was artfully managed, and one of its goals was to keep the news media at a comfortable distance. Certain events on each day's schedule were labeled photo opportunity, which irritated the TV people. At other times the Senator's movements were set up for the convenience of the video cameras, which annoyed the print reporters. And, in a time-honored tradition, every time Gillian made himself available for questions, he made sure there was a jet or helicopter warming up nearby, so he could feign deafness if he didn't want to answer. Laura was the target for all the resulting resentments, which seemed worst after an all-night drunk. The bus would lurch, she'd stumble, and their hands would be everywhere in that boys-will-be-boys way. She was tempted to just throw the stack of schedules at them like raw fish at bears.

Two 727s awaited them at O'Hare. The A-plane carried the candidate, his immediate staff, and one or two favored reporters, plus the pool. The pool reporter and crew were chosen by their colleagues to tape the routine stuff, arrivals and waves, and to ride the front plane for a day or a week just in case the Senator ambled back and said something newsworthy. Since declaring his candidacy nearly two years ago, Gillian had won and lost primaries, campaigned in every state, and in all that time had never ambled back and said anything. But there was always a first time, so there was always a pool.

Behind the Senator's plane came the zoo, full of reporters, photographers, technicians, gambling, partying, and complaining. Duty on the A-plane was a sentence of boredom, but the zoo was always lively, and Laura always liked it. Today the boss wanted to discuss his upcoming debate with Erhardt, however, so Laura headed for the A-plane. Rydell fell into step beside her. She cast him a glance.

"I'm in the pool," he explained, and gestured for her to precede him up the stairs.

Moving through the plane, Laura saw the TV crew already on board and made a mental note to watch for trouble. The cameraman was named George Something. He worked for Cable News Network, and every time he drew pool duty there were problems. Last time, he'd handled duplicating the tape at a local station in Dallas. The other networks had found ten-second snatches of X-rated action scattered randomly through their footage. George had thought it hilarious.

Part of the jet had been made over into a working area for the staff and a private suite for Gillian. At its entrance stood a Secret Service man with a briefcase open on a small table. The briefcase contained a small gray box, some wires and a display screen. Laura handed him her DNA card, and he passed a small scanning wand, like a bar-code reader, over it. In a fraction of a second the machine examined the digitally encoded sequence of a few thousand chemical pairings that made up a string of several hundred genes on a single strand of DNA. The genetic material had been taken from the nucleus of a cell scraped off the back of Laura's throat at the beginning of the campaign. It was an absolutely unique identification, and when the little computer had compared the data on Laura's card to the Madison file in its memory, it flashed a clearance on the screen. The agent smiled and opened the door for her.

Cavanagh was already there, spreading papers out on a table between two oversize chairs. He looked up as she came in.

"Sorry about before," he said softly.

"Quite all right."

He tossed her a small photograph attached to a piece of paper.

"How do you like that?" he said. "Don't that take the cake?"

The photo was a little blurry but easy to grasp. It was a close-up of the front of Senator Gillian's limousine, clearly showing the license plate and the driver's face. It had been taken, Laura knew at once, by a highway speed surveillance camera. Attached to it was a New York State speeding citation.

"So?" Laura said.

"So they got a lot of nerve, spying on people like that," Cavanagh said.

"It's a little late for that argument," Laura replied. "These things were approved and installed two years ago. My speech for the Bankers Association okay?"

Cavanagh took the photo back, hesitated a second, then threw it into his briefcase.

"Yeah, fine, sure," he said. "If he'll stick to it. Every time he starts ad-libbing my stomach turns and I have to go to the can." He pulled out a cigar and unwrapped it, then—perhaps sensing Laura's early-morning mood—put it back in his pocket. If the Senator were here, she thought, he'd light it, and when I turned blue he'd make some crack about little girls working in a man's world.

For all that, she liked Cavanagh. He had some rough edges, but she even liked them. He was Gillian's right-hand man because he knew everybody, on both sides, everywhere. There was no one he couldn't get on the phone and no problem he couldn't solve from an airport phone booth.

There was a bustle behind her and Laura knew Gillian had arrived. She glanced quickly out the window and saw the limousine and police escort departing.

Amos V. Gillian was a tall, patrician man who could work an opening-night crowd at the Metropolitan Opera the way other politicians worked county fairs. As it always did, even after two years, Gillian's arrival gave Laura a small, involuntary thrill.

"That little creep from the *Times* just ambushed me," he said, tossing his raincoat onto the overhead luggage rack. "How did he get on this plane?"

"Luck," Cavanagh said. "He's in the pool."

"Well, I don't like him," Gillian said.

"Nobody likes him," Cavanagh snorted. "What did he want?"

"I'm not sure I know," Gillian said, wounded. He picked up the Sunday *Chicago Tribune* and spread it across his knees. "He was raving. Something about Nazis and Arizona, and some Bund or other. I wonder if the *Times* knows about him . . ."

"Probably told him they'd start checking his expenses if he didn't come up with a scandal soon," Cavanagh said. "You look over today's stuff?"

Gillian was engrossed in something in the paper, his lower lip quivering as he read. Finally he looked up.

"Looks fine," he said. "Excellent, actually. As usual."

Cavanagh retrieved his cigar and lit it with a cheap plastic lighter.

Laura wandered to the back cabin half an hour after the plane took off. It could seat forty but carried only about a dozen people now, including Secret Service, various gofers, assistants and interns, plus one or two local politicos invited along so Gillian could flatter them for a few minutes. She found Rydell in animated conversation with a UPI reporter.

"What on earth did you do to the Senator?" she asked.

"Something unthinkable," Rydell responded. "I asked him a question. Caught him without his briefing book."

"You know the rules as well as anyone else."

"Yeah, right," Rydell said, and looked out the window. He turned back immediately. "Let's make it formal then. I want a sit-down with the Senator today or tomorrow. It's vital. We've got a major story that absolutely requires his involvement."

"What's it about?" Laura asked, a sinking feeling in her stomach.

Rydell smiled. "Impress your boss with its importance," he said, turning back to the window.

She found Gillian snoring blissfully in his reclined seat. A privilege of rank, Cavanagh would say.

"Rydell wants a formal interview," she whispered to Cavanagh. He took the cigar out of his mouth.

"Not on your life."

"He says he's got something big working. If we don't accommodate him it could come out looking worse."

"Madison," Cavanagh said. "Let me ask you a question. Are we going to carry New York City?"

"I doubt it."

"Will we carry, oh, say, Indianapolis?"

"Maybe," Laura said. "As good a chance there as anywhere."

"Now, how many people in Indianapolis read the *New York Times*? I'll tell you how many. The mayor. A couple of newspaper people, and a few other folks that moved out of New York ten years ago and claim they can finish the crossword puzzle."

"But if they break a major unfavorable story—"

"It dies with the *Times*, nine cases out of ten," Cavanagh said. "Every damn Sunday they publish two or three big investigative pieces, and only a couple ever even get mentioned on the evening news. The networks hate like hell to play catch up, so they won't even acknowledge anything important could be in the paper that isn't on the air. Unless somebody forces them to pick up the story, they ignore it. Am I wrong?"

Laura shrugged. Cavanagh leaned toward her.

"The *Times* matters, sure, but in the long run there's damned little damage Rydell can really do, no matter what he's working on. Even at the worst it can get, we won't be still dealing with it after the second day. Never happen."

A grunt from the window told them Gillian had awakened. "What's up?" he said.

"Rydell, the guy from the *Times*, wants an interview."

"Can we ignore him?"

"You might think of it as a dry run for the debate," Laura said. "He's bound to be fairly hostile."

"Good point," Gillian said.

"You sit down with that guy and you deserve what you get," Cavanagh said, and Gillian's arched eyebrow told him he'd overstepped the line. Gillian was still the boss. Cavanagh shrugged and added, "That's my opinion, anyway."

"Let's do it this way," Gillian said. He turned to Laura. "Tell him he can have ten minutes, but we need to know in advance what he wants to discuss. Get a question list from him."

"If he won't?"

Gillian held his hands out, palms up. "If his paper endorses Erhardt, we'll hand out copies at every stop we make west of the Mississippi—"

"Make that west of the Hudson," Cavanagh interjected.

"No list, no interview," Gillian said. "That's simple."

"I can handle Rydell," Laura said. "He reminds me of my ex."

Cavanagh chuckled. He'd met Laura's ex-husband once, and didn't like him, either.

"And make sure that smug SOB is off this plane before I leave," Gillian said, leaning back in his seat again. "I don't want to see him."

They flew in over Brooklyn forty minutes late, and Laura strained to see her childhood neighborhood. Tiny trains moved on the elevated lines, weaving through the patchwork of backyards and front porches. Our Lady of Good Counsel Church stood above the row houses like a medieval cathedral. Traffic on the Brooklyn-Queens Expressway was stopped, though it was ten o'clock in the morning.

Soon a small motorcade—Gillian, Cavanagh, Laura and two New York bigshots in the limo, followed by Secret Service, the press bus, and six motorcycle cops—was on its way downtown.

First stop was City Hall, where Gillian would get an in-depth briefing from the mayor on New York's transit problems. Laura, who lived on East 80th Street, knew all about New York's transit problems and doubted the mayor would touch on them too colorfully. The briefing was scheduled for a half-hour, with photo ops before and after. Then they'd ride uptown to the New York Hilton, which would take God knew how long in midday traffic.

At noon Gillian was to sit on the dais at a special lunch meeting of the New York City Investment Bankers Association. This group of men (if a single woman showed up the others would point her out as a tourist sight) thought they owned the city because they'd saved it from bankruptcy twice. It was a crucial audience, and not entirely sympathetic.

Around two it was downtown a few blocks to 42nd Street and Eighth Avenue, the heart of a sleazy urban area still resisting redevelopment, for a tour of the construction site for a new hotel. Photo op with hardhats, Laura thought. Shake hands with all the shop stewards.

Then, let's see . . . five firemen being decorated for hero-ism, short speech; opening ceremony for a new Republican district headquarters, time changed to accommodate Gillian, and he'd be late anyway; then tour the latest thing in senior citizen housing, a pricey co-op with built-in hospital, no speech required.

Finally, at six, her freedom. Gillian would sit down with the New York Republican Committee's Subcommittee on Campaign Finance. Cocktails and dinner in a private suite at the Waldorf-Astoria, because finance committees know how to live. It would take the rest of the night, and since the subject was cash, it was very private.

At City Hall Laura didn't leave the limo. She disconnected the backseat car phone from its jack and plugged in her laptop computer, then used the built-in modem to dial up the campaign mainframe a few blocks away. There, stored on optical discs, was a huge volume of information about President Erhardt, beginning with when he was a business executive and moving through his selection as running mate for William King, which was seen at the time as a sop to the business community.

The vast Erhardt file was subdivided in dozens of ways, and Laura scrolled through her on-screen menus. There were press reports, speeches, transcripts and full-motion videotape of TV appearances, personal data, even the tax-return information he'd made public when he became a candidate for vice president four years ago. There were also thick files—thick in megabytes, at least—on the handlers, the half-dozen men closest to Erhardt who, skeptics said, pushed the buttons that made the President smile, sneeze, and fart.

It was a huge amount of ammunition, and any single item in the file could be printed out almost instantly on the car's portable fax machine. She'd given up hope of having all the Erhardt data organized in time for the debate in New Orleans the next evening. She went at her work earnestly, however, manipulating the main computer from a distance for forty-five minutes, grateful for the shaded glass and the indifference of passersby.

When they arrived at the Hilton, Gillian was out the door before the car stopped, and Laura ran after him into the lobby. He strode quickly past the lobby bar with its closed-up grand piano. The waitresses, serving a few isolated Bloody Marys, looked at him with glazed eyes, not recognizing him despite the fact he'd been running for president for two years. He fixed his smile and waved, and they rode up the escalator to the ballroom level. A local television crew ran ahead of him, trying to get some arrival footage for their early news. At the top of the escalator Gillian was greeted by two association officials, and soon became mired in a choppy sea of pinstripes. Laura slipped into the ballroom.

Inside, chaos reigned. The local media had encamped right in front of the podium, six cameras on tripods, each attended by a sound man, a light man, a camera operator, and at least one other person who did nothing but couldn't be fired. Lights on high stands crowded the dais like a metal forest, and heavy bundles of cables lay taped to the carpet. The crews had moved one of the round tables out of their way and taken its chairs for themselves. Taped to the podium microphone were at least a dozen separate small mikes, each with a wire leading into a pile of portable tape recorders on the floor in the path of the waiters trying to serve soup. A few yards away stood the designated press area, complete with raised platform for the cameras and direct wiring to the podium mikes. All empty. Laura looked at the ceiling trying to contain her anger. The signs of inept advance work were everywhere, and it was far too late to do anything about it.

In the back of the room, people were shoving each other through the entrances and Gillian was making his way from table to table shaking hands. Trailing him was a pack of press photographers, each with two or three battered cameras hanging from straps and one shoulder permanently stooped from the weight of a gadget bag. The lights made the front of the room hot and uncomfortable, and on the dais the million-a-year investment bankers were loosening their ties and grumbling.

Cavanagh was at her shoulder. "This Wagner's work?" he said, referring to the absent advance man, and Laura nodded. Cavanagh let out a sigh. "I don't know," he said. "These assholes invite a presidential candidate to their lunch for the excitement, then they get pissed off. They want to be on TV but don't want to put up with TV people."

"When do you suppose was the last time they had this many people at one of their lunches?" Laura said. "They're making a tidy sum off the Senator's drawing power."

Cavanagh slapped her on the arm and winked. "Listen, it ain't the real world. It's politics. And it's almost over."

Laura heard applause and guessed that Gillian had been introduced. She stayed in the back of the hall to listen, because despite Cavanagh's complaints she loved to hear the Senator speak. And it was the usual Gillian performance, she thought. He started out slowly, self-deprecatingly, scratching his brow, looking down at his text, sometimes slipping his hands into his pockets. Ten minutes later he drew his first interruption for applause. Five minutes after that, he had eight hundred investment bankers ready to shout "Amen!" every few phrases. In another five minutes there was hushed silence, as Gillian, his voice low and confiding, drew them along to his conclusion.

[13]

Then roaring applause, a smile, a handshake for the chairman, a wave, and out the door. Tonight, Laura knew they'd all go home to Westchester or Glen Cove and tell their wives that whatever else Amos V. Gillian might be, he was certainly the best speaker they had ever heard. That, Laura realized, was why the election was a real contest.

And how she loved the campaign atmosphere! The bright lights and heat and noise reminded her of the jolts of excitement she got from listening to his speeches, being around the media, rushing from city to city, being part of events she would later see on TV.

She almost bumped into Rydell as she raced to the car. He had been sitting in the back of the hall the whole time, taking notes.

"Hey there, Hi there, Ho there, you're as welcome as can be," he said, falling into step next to her.

"Huh?"

Rydell gestured back into the ballroom. "I thought you'd welcome a Mickey Mouse metaphor. Or don't you remember Annette and little Cubby—"

"Listen, I've got your answer," Laura said. "Ten minutes, today or tomorrow, but with questions in advance."

"Bullshit," Rydell said.

"I'm not opening a negotiation, I'm telling you the terms," Laura said. "You don't have to take them."

They were racing through the lobby now. Somehow, Gillian and Cavanagh had reached the limo already and were waiting inside. Laura stopped on the curb where her bosses could see who she was talking to.

"We'll do the story either way," Rydell said. "In the interest of fairness, it's important enough to talk to Gillian that we'll probably go along with your stupid conditions, but I have to ask my editors."

"Well, when you've discussed it, voice-mail me or something so we can schedule," Laura said. "I check my electronic message box at headquarters every few hours." She got into the car.

"Well?" Gillian said.

"He said he needed to talk to you in the interest of fairness," Laura replied.

"Jesus Christ," Cavanagh said. "What'd I tell you. Salt of the earth, that guy."

"He'll provide the questions up front?" Gillian asked.

"I think so," Laura said.

The answer came quickly. As the group was wrapping up its tour of the hotel construction site, Laura dialed the campaign computer from the backseat of the limo and keyed in her private password. There was a recorded message from Rydell, telling her a messenger was bringing the question list. Moments later, a skinny teenager pedaled up on a bicycle and handed her a white envelope.

She put the package into her briefcase without looking at it. Gillian was riding down in the construction elevator with the developer and two or three others. She got out to wait at the curb. Across the street was a small picket line of Erhardt supporters, with placards advertising the President's national union endorsements and the low unemployment figures. A few yards down the sidewalk a group of homeless people—the ones Gillian called "the invisibles"—watched the entire event with amusement.

She was walking to greet the Senator. She was looking up at the reflecting steel skeleton, bright bones of sunlight. Then men were rushing by her. The Senator was carried toward the car by his elbows. One of the Secret Service agents bumped her as he raced by. Shouting, commotion. Cavanagh spun her around and pushed her violently toward the limo. There was a wino in her path, unshaved and dirty, gesturing wildly.

"He had a gun, that guy, that guy they got down over there. He had a gun, I saw it. In a brown paper bag."

They were in the limousine, nobody speaking. Gillian looked out the back window. Cavanagh unwrapped a cigar and muttered, "Another week. One more fucking week."

From clear across the newsroom, Mitchell Rydell could see the glowing red light on his terminal that meant electronic messages were waiting. He sat down with a sigh and tapped a few keys to discover there were four from his boss and four from Steve Shaw, President Erhardt's press secretary. Rydell saw his boss, the *Times'* national editor, squinting at him from a hundred yards away, at the opposite end of the cavernous, low-ceilinged newsroom. The midafternoon sunlight penetrated only a few feet into the room, and the overall atmosphere was fluorescent. Mitchell was dialing the White House when he saw the editor pick up the public address microphone.

"Mr. Rydell, please."

The White House switchboard answered and Mitchell asked for Shaw, waving a finger at his boss. One second.

Shaw came on the line immediately. "Hey, Mitch," he said, as though greeting a customer at the company picnic, "been watching and waiting for you to do something on the President's computer-literacy initiative, but nada, no dice, not a syllable."

"Well, that's how it goes sometimes, Steve, you know that."

"I know Gillian has no trouble getting into your paper," Shaw said.

"Gillian's campaign is more active than Erhardt's," Mitchell said calmly. "And we have to take a different attitude toward all these routine policy pronouncements and proposals when there's a campaign going on. You have to admit that."

"How many times have we suggested little articles, features, days-in-the-life, you name it," Shaw went on. "How many private little scoops have we sent your way, exclusive—"

"Name me one," Mitchell interrupted.

"All I'm saying is don't abuse your position," Shaw said. "You may be the biggest name in town, but you're not the only one."

"Listen, Steve, is there more of this or are you through?"

"Mr. Rydell, to the desk please!" the speakers repeated. Ed the editor was glowering long-distance through the fluorescent cave.

Mitchell waved again, held up the telephone and pointed to it, while Shaw's voice continued to emerge from the earpiece, small and tinny.

"Honest to God, Mitchell," Shaw was saying, "it's not like I lean on you all the time. You should have heard The Boss this morning. I have to take this shit, not you . . ."

No, Rydell thought, but I have to talk to Ed in another minute. The editor was standing with arms folded now, staring at him implacably.

"And that's nothing to the crap I take from Loubert," Shaw said. "A damn flunky advisor . . ."

"Steve, I gotta get going," Mitchell said. "I hate to be rude, but most people would say an incumbent president already has too much easy access to the media. All he has to do is declare war or something, and he's on every front page. Now you can certainly talk to my bosses if you think we're being unfair . . ."

"Hell, Mitch, I promised I'd call and chew you out, and that's what I did," Shaw replied amicably. He knows how far *he'll* get with Ed, Mitchell thought. "Keep in touch."

"Sure," Mitchell said, hanging up. He started across the newsroom, walking at a steady slow pace. The long, horseshoe-shaped copy desk occupied the far third of the big room, in an area known for generations as the bullpen. The chipped old mahogany and wire desktop baskets spoke of older times, of sleeve garters and ink-stained fingers, but the desktop now held a half-dozen putty-colored computer terminals displaying story drafts and page layouts.

"Nice of you to make time," Ed said when he arrived.

"Sorry," Mitchell replied. "I had to talk to Steve Shaw."

Ed looked at him over his glasses. "Would it inconvenience you too much to ask when we can run the Gillian story?"

"Not tomorrow," Mitchell replied. Ed snorted in frustration.

"Not today, not tomorrow," he said. "You remember the election? It's a week off, if I'm not mistaken. You ever hear of deadlines?"

Rydell pulled a chair over and put his foot on it. "Listen, it's simply got to have Gillian's comments, and he's not available until midday tomorrow. And I'm still uneasy about the whole thing. It's too pat. There's still a few key pieces missing."

"We've committed a lot to this story," Ed said. "The damn thing's practically in type." He raised his voice the way he did when he wanted the whole newsroom to hear a dressing-down.

"I've been straight with you about this one," Mitchell said. "It's a great story, but right now it's a collection of hearsay. And Gillian's whole career rides on it, not just this election, so we have to be sure."

"Don't lecture me," Ed said quietly. "Listen, Mitchell,

nail it down, okay? Today? There's interest at the top in this story."

Mitchell smiled. It was a cliché, used to motivate young reporters doing scut work.

"And besides," the editor went on confidentially, "word is out that we're working on something big. I even got asked about it at lunch today. You pursue something like this for a long time and don't get it, it makes you look bad. It makes you look like you chase wild geese, which the *New York Times* does not."

"Okay," Mitchell said. "I'll put off my flight to New Orleans until tomorrow morning and work on wrapping this up this afternoon and tonight. By deadline tonight you'll have a definite go or no-go—but for day after tomorrow, okay? *With* Gillian's comments?"

"Day after tomorrow will be all debate coverage," Ed said. "I'm calling it up for tomorrow morning, and you've got until six-thirty to tell me no."

"Christ, Ed . . ."

"Thank you, Mr. Rydell," the editor said. "Good afternoon."

Mitchell stalked back to his desk and stood there, hands on hips, fuming. He looked at his watch. Nearly three o'clock. Enough time to ferret out a few pieces of vital information that had eluded him for two weeks? And then to call Laura Madison and insist on talking to Gillian today? He took out his wallet and counted eighty bucks. Probably enough, he thought. He picked up the phone and dialed a number in Brooklyn. No answer, not even a machine, which irritated Mitchell. He looked up at the newsroom clock, which was clicking digitally ahead. Then he grabbed a notebook, shoved it into his pocket and headed for the elevator.

On West 43rd Street he slipped between two eighteen-wheelers delivering giant rolls of newsprint and walked to Seventh Avenue, where he hailed a cab.

"Where to?" the cabbie said. He was a short man incongruously dressed in a suit, white shirt, and silk tie.

"How do you like Brooklyn?" Mitchell said, climbing in.

"How do *you* like the subway? That's what it's for."

"Double the meter," Mitchell said. The cabbie shrugged.

"I don't know if I know Brooklyn."

"I'll guide you," Mitchell said. "I know it like it was part of the city."

They crept across town, down Second Avenue, and across the Manhattan Bridge. Traffic on the BQE was relatively light, and Rydell directed the cabbie via the Prospect Expressway to Ocean Parkway. This was the heart of Brooklyn, he reflected, the land of Willie Loman. Once stately homes lined both sides of the broad boulevard, here and there interrupted by the stone façade of a synagogue, a convenience market, or a storefront with a shingle. Cars were abandoned at the curbs, and on the park benches that lined the islands in the street old men sat reading their Hebrew newspapers.

They left Ocean Parkway and drove on through progressively more commercial areas, until the cab bogged down in traffic. Mitchell paid him off with two $20 bills and walked the rest of the way.

The local newspaper office was upstairs from a delicatessen, and the stairwell smelled richly. But at the top he found the door padlocked. Outside, Mitch surveyed the street for a public phone and saw none. Across the street was the neighborhood bar, a street-level watering hole named the Captain's Tower.

The bartender was a man his own age with a long beard, wearing a bulky crew sweater and scrubbing glassware.

"Got a phone?" Mitchell asked. The man nodded into a far corner of the gloomy bar, beyond a row of idle electronic games. Mitchell realized in an instant that the man he wanted was getting up from a stool at the end of the bar and heading for the back door. In moments Mitchell came up behind him and tapped him on the shoulder.

"Trying to avoid someone, Dennis?"

"Hey, Mitchie!" Dennis said, all joviality. "How's it hanging?" Then he lowered his voice to a harsh whisper. "What the hell are you doing here? I told you I'd call *you*."

Rydell put his arm fraternally around Dennis's shoulder and they walked along the corridor toward the men's room.

"I been sitting by the phone, old buddy," Mitchell said. "It never rang, unless you happened to call when I was in the head or something. I've been waiting for one little thing . . ."

He stopped, turned Dennis around and began to push him, very slowly, back against the wall.

"How old are you now, Dennis?" he said.

"What is this, a joke?"

"Nah, no joke. How old?"

"Thirty-five."

"You wanna live to be thirty-six, you better come up with what you promised me, in the next five minutes."

"I gave you everything I promised," Dennis said. "Listen, I'm a journalist myself."

"Yeah, the *Flatbush Clarion*," Mitchell said sarcastically. "Founded by James Gordon Bennett, or was it Leo Gorcey?"

Dennis flushed and pushed Mitchell's hands away from his chest.

"So let's talk," he said. "But not here."

Mitchell followed Dennis out the back door, through an alley where laundry hung drying above them, and across the street. The wind was picking up, blowing newspaper pages and empty paper cups along the asphalt.

Inside the newspaper office above the deli were six desks, all nearly invisible under mountains of paper. All the windows were closed, and Mitchell thought of how the wind outside would affect the decor. Dennis shoved a pile of ad makeup sheets off a chair and sat down, gesturing Rydell to do the same.

No computers, Mitchell noticed. How nice.

"Catchy name, the Captain's Tower," he said. "For a hole in the wall."

"The owner's an old druggie," Dennis explained, leaning back and putting his huge feet up on a pile of *Clarion* back numbers. He wore brown socks and police shoes, the leather creased and dry. "The name comes from a Dylan song. Remember 'Desolation Row'?"

"How evocative," Mitchell said. "Now listen to me, Dennis. My bosses are getting very impatient with the lack of conclusive proof to nail down this Nazi thing. You weren't my only source on it, not by a long shot, but you got it started, and for two weeks now you've been promising me a smoking gun."

"You got the book, the inscription, the land records . . ."

"No," Mitchell said. "I've got photocopies of all that stuff, no originals. And even originals would still be circumstantial, and you know it. You're a journalist yourself, right? Now we're a week from the election, and my boss just asked me a good question, namely, can we print this thing or not? As of now, I say not, and that makes them very unhappy."

"So what do you want from me? I'll write the fucking thing for the *Clarion* if you don't have the balls."

"Dennis, Dennis," Mitchell said. "I'm starting to get the nervous feeling you aren't going to deliver. I can practically see you holding back a smirk. The editor of the *Flatbush Clarion* put one over on the mighty *New York Times*."

"What I gave you was legit," Dennis said. He took his feet off the desktop and leaned forward. "And you did enough digging on your own to convince you, didn't you? Deep down you believe Gillian is a raving Nazi. A founding member of the True American Bund, and right-hand boy to good old Jonathan Marin himself. A classic closet Jew-baiter."

"So what?"

"So don't get cold feet now," Dennis said. "It's too near election and there's too much at stake."

"Christ, listen to you," Mitchell said. He realized, to his surprise, that his heart was pounding. "You *planted* the motherfucker, didn't you? *You're* the fucking source! You and those crazies you hang out with . . ."

"Mitch," Dennis said placatingly. "I brought you what we professional journalists call a tip. It was up to you to make something out of it. This isn't a matter of history, or legalities or moral theology. It's politics. You've got an elected president hooked up to tubes in Bethesda, and a replacement who's done great things in four years. He's promised the middle class a tranquil life, and people will swap a lot of abstractions for that. So now he's nervous because it's all at stake . . ."

"Where does this story come from, Dennis?" Mitchell demanded, getting to his feet and walking off to put distance between himself and Dennis's quiet, insinuating voice. "Don't bullshit me."

"I can't tell you," Dennis said. "I can tell you it's solid, but I can't tell you where I got it."

"You bastard," Mitchell said.

"Don't play holier-than-thou with me, just because you moved uptown."

Mitchell left him at the window, took the stairs slowly and recrossed the street to the Captain's Tower. He found the telephone and ran his key card through the scanner to get a dial tone.

"Ed, it's Rydell," he said. "That Gillian piece is a story all right, but not the story I thought."

"What are you talking about?"

"It's a plant," Rydell said. "It's concocted. It stinks all the way through. Remember Nixon's dirty tricks brigade? They're back in business."

"Can you prove it's a plant?" Ed said in his most business-like voice, an editor who knew when a B-plus story had just become an A.

Mitchell sighed. "Not by tonight, Ed. No way. And it's possible the whole thing goes no further than some small timers in Brooklyn." It has to stop here, he told himself. There's no way Erhardt or the White House is involved in this. This one is Dennis McCarthy through and through.

"Mitchell," Ed said. "Delaying the piece is *more* unfair to Gillian, not less. The closer to election, the greater the impact and the less chance for him to react to it."

Mitchell was silent, nodding to himself in agreement.

"Mitchell?"

"As of today I say no story," Mitchell said quietly. "It's not there, and I don't think it ever will be. Sorry."

Ed sighed. "You want to tell the guys upstairs, or do you expect me to do that?"

"I've got to get ready to head for New Orleans," Mitchell said.

"Well, at least we found out early we've got three extra columns to fill."

"Give it to Arts and Leisure," Mitchell said. "There's probably a young pianist playing somewhere tonight that nobody else will review. Launch a career."

"Thanks for the advice," Ed said. "I just hope you realize you've spent a lot of your reputation on this one."

Mitchell went to the bar. A month's work shot down in,

what, an hour? he thought. All just a game, just politics. Nobody has to take it too seriously.

He ordered two Heinekens from the bartender and finished the first one in a single draft. He'd take the subway back to Manhattan, get home, get in the shower. Get the dirt off.

He and Dennis had been equally idealistic young journalism students at NYU a million years ago. We were going to win Pulitzers . . . both of us, he thought. Be famous, talked about in reporter' bars from coast to coast. Grill secretaries of state on "Meet the Press."

And now what? he thought. Where's the dividing line between journalistic ethics and what Dennis calls cold feet?

He interrogated his conscience: Was the story of Senator Gillian's Nazi past true?

His conscience answered: No way. It never figured, no matter how plausible all that trumped-up evidence made it look.

Second question, a professional one: Is there, now, a story here worth pursuing?

Second answer: Probably not. Probably just a little diddling by good old Dennis. Maybe a few city or state Democratic politicos involved, but nobody that matters. Bury it.

He'd have to tell Madison, of course, and she'd be insufferable. What she'd be, he corrected himself, was a pro. As always.

He called the bartender over.

"What can you tell me about Dennis?" he asked. The bearded man wiped the bar with a rag and said nothing. Thinks I'm a cop, Mitchell realized. He put a twenty-dollar bill on the bar.

"What's my tab?"

"Four bucks."

"Keep the change? And talk to me?"

The man took the money. "What's your interest?"

"We're old buddies," Mitchell said. "I just wanted to know how he's doing."

"Seems fine," the bartender said. "Buys a lot of rounds for the house. Comes in with some tough-looking friends sometimes."

"Oh?"

"Not that they make any trouble. Dennis introduced them

[23]

as buddies from the Marines. Sometimes he comes in with just one guy and they sit in a back booth and whisper to each other. What do you think, is old Dennis straight?"

"Far as I ever knew," Mitchell said. "The other friend, what's he look like?"

"A fag, but one of those tough ones, the ones that work out a lot. Tall, black hair, very quiet. Dresses like a sailor. Slickers, and a blue cap with an anchor on it."

"Get a lot of sailor types in here?"

The bartender laughed. "That's why I noticed. The guy looks like a jerk, to tell the truth, but he also looks like the last guy in the world you'd say that to his face."

"Gotcha," Mitchell said. "Thanks."

Outside in the growing cold, he made for the subway. Cheer up, he told himself, you're headed for New Or-leeeens.

Laura leaned against the wind as she walked down East 80th Street from Lexington Avenue. Her building was halfway down the block. At the door, she put down her small bag of Chinese takeout and fumbled in her pockets for her key card. She slipped it quickly through the laser reader, and waited. Nothing. Cursing, she shoved the card through the reader again. On the eighth try the electronic system finally let her into her home.

The elevator was still out of order, so she walked up the four flights to her apartment, noting with self-approval that she was barely out of breath when she arrived. Inside, she dropped her coat and scarf on a chair and turned to her television to see what it had produced while she was out at the Chinese joint.

Before leaving, she'd keyed a number of commands into the TV. Now, the output tray next to her laser printer was filled with pages—summaries of evening newscasts, verbatim transcripts of stories about Gillian and Erhardt, and advance copies of major stories scheduled for tomorrow in the New York Times, Washington Post, and other newspapers. Once these stories had final editorial approval, the newspapers released them to electronic databases that could be accessed through cable television services like Laura's. All it took was a personal identification number.

Mixed in with all the output she'd ordered were two cable-generated reminders that she had until nine P.M. to cast her electronic vote on tonight's IQ, or Important Question:

> Should people convicted of drunk driving be allowed to vote?

Groaning, Laura pitched the reminders into the trash. She poured her Chinese food onto a paper plate and put it into the microwave, then opened the refrigerator and drew a glass of cold white wine from the aseptic box on the top shelf. So packaged, the wine lasted forever, which was a good thing considering how infrequently she tapped it.

She sat down in her easy chair and put on her headphones. A few commands tapped into her portable keypad, and the TV began to scroll through the contents of her compact disc library, until she found one she liked: *The Marriage of Figaro.* She selected it, and the overture began as she retrieved her Kung Pao Chicken.

She ate slowly, browsing through the news reports and whiling away the first act of Mozart's comedy. There was no mention, either on TV or in the early newspaper stories, of a man with a gun at the hotel site. The *Daily News* had a photo of the Senator and the union shop stewards on its front page, which would mean a happy flight to New Orleans.

The *Times* ran something about the Bankers Association speech on page nine, half a column. Not good, not bad. The next sheet, though, stopped her. It was a "news analysis" piece, scheduled for the front page, by Mitchell Rydell. Her name was in the first paragraph. She went on to read a portrayal of her own frenzied activities of that day, leading into an extensive report on the "increasingly frenetic" atmosphere of the Gillian campaign.

She read the whole piece through, then went back to the beginning to read her name again. Not bad, she thought. Wait till Dad sees my name in the *New York Times!*

If he can find the *Times* in Key West, Laura thought, and pictured her father in the cockpit of his sailboat, the *Hotspur,* moored to some marina slip she couldn't quite imagine, rolling gently in the waves that passed into the anchorage from the sea. Happy, she hoped, missing him terribly. When this is over, I'll be coming down, and I may stay a long while.

Then the other voices began. It's my job to get Gillian's name in the papers, not my own, she thought. And *favorably*, not in stories portraying our campaign as a sinking ship. Nice job, Rydell, she thought. A little ego blast leading into a big hatchet job. Cavanagh has you pegged right. A snake.

"*Ah, vengeance!*" a basso sang into her ears. "*It's a pleasure reserved for the sage!*"

Laura suddenly remembered Rydell's interview request. His question list was in her briefcase, unopened. She ripped it open and pulled out a thick sheaf of papers. There was a typewritten page, and beneath it a photocopy of a handwritten letter. No salutation, not even "to whom it may concern." Only:

> The *Times* is working on a story documenting Senator Gillian's association, in the past, with a neo-Nazi organization called the True American Bund. This organization holds as its primary goals the preservation of what it calls "the purity of the white race in America," and the extermination of the state of Israel.
>
> According to information in our possession the Bund held several secret meetings in September and October, 1980, on property in Arizona which, according to official records, was owned at that time by Senator Gillian.
>
> The Bund has since purchased that property from the Senator at a handsome price, which included both an official payment to Gillian and a number of sub-rosa cash payments to members of the Senator's family and staff. We are told, moreover, that he was present during some of the meetings on his property in 1980.
>
> It is also being charged that Senator Gillian interceded in a grand jury proceeding to prevent an indictment of Jonathan Marin, founder of the Bund. Marin has served prison time for inciting to riot and desecrating a synagogue in suburban Chicago. His present whereabouts are unknown and he is believed to be dead.
>
> Out of respect for Mr. Gillian, and his position as a candidate for president, we wish to have his answers to these questions, and possibly others:
>
> Was he ever a member of the Bund?

Why did he permit this Nazi organization to meet on his property? Did he know who they were? Did he know who they were when he accepted their money in a sale of his property? Why did he intervene in the grand jury proceedings? Has he ever supported the Bund financially? How does he regard these activities today, years later?

Attached to the question list was a photocopy of the title page of a book by Marin entitled *The Blueprint for America's Defeat*, with what looked like Gillian's handwriting all over it.

"Brilliant analysis," the writing said. "A clear message for all true Americans . . . a long overdue statement of principles . . ."

There were photocopied sheets that looked like land ownership records, with the seal of some county clerk in Arizona. And newspaper clips about Jonathan Marin, all old. In one story he was getting arrested for trying to urinate on a federal judge. If they publish this, Laura thought, we'll be lucky to carry a single state. There's still a week until the election, time enough for this story to reach every voter in every precinct in America.

She pulled off her earphones and the silence of her apartment surprised her. Even the street outside seemed quiet.

But is it true? It looks true, she thought. But it can't be. Gillian is no bigot. If anything, he's *too* open-minded.

She'd have to confront him, of course. And be convinced by his denial. But what if it were true?

She picked up the telephone to call the Waldorf, then stopped, thinking: Better face to face.

It's the end of the line, she thought. Only thing left is to survive as well as possible.

It can't be true. Gillian's been around too long, and his past has been dug into again and again. And he's too . . . too *honorable* for a sleazy association like this. Somebody's out to get him.

They got him. Face it, Laura.

Take it to Cavanagh. Let him and the Senator handle it. All may not be lost.

All is lost.

In a daze she dressed and went downstairs to hail a cab.

Gillian was dining with several finance chairmen in a suite on the twentieth floor of the Waldorf, overlooking Park Avenue. She rang the bell and a doorman in a tuxedo answered, telling her the party could not be disturbed.

"Please tell Senator Gillian, Laura Madison is here, and it's vitally important," she said. The hotel man seemed to sneer as he closed the door.

A long time passed as Laura paced the corridor. Finally the door opened again and Gillian stepped out into the hall.

"Yes, Laura?"

"Can we go somewhere private?" she said. "I have something important to show you." Gillian nodded and led her into the suite. Between the door and the dining room was a small anteroom that could be closed off entirely. When the Senator had closed the doors they were alone, and Laura wordlessly handed him Rydell's paper. The Senator's face colored as he read.

"The scuzzy little son of a bitch," Gillian said when he finished. It was the harshest language she'd ever heard him speak. He continued to stare at the paper.

"He can't get away with this," he said. "He'll have egg on his face for years."

"But what are we going to do about it?" Laura asked. Gillian handed her back the paper.

"First things first," he said. "If you're going to work for me effectively, and prevent this thing from ruining the campaign, you must believe me when I assure you, as solemnly as I possibly can, that there is no truth whatsoever to any of this."

"I do," Laura said. "Believe you."

"Do you? Considering how plausible it looks? Considering all the apparent evidence he's got?"

"Yes, I believe you," Laura said. "I'd believe you if you told me every shred of that stuff was completely fabricated."

"Good," Gillian said. "Because I'm telling you the truth, and I'm willing to swear on whatever it takes to make you believe it. This story *is* completely fabricated, though I'm damned if I know how."

He let out a long sigh and paced across the confining room.

"Truth never catches up with falsehood," he said. "People forget. If somebody said on television tonight that the Germans bombed Pearl Harbor in 1957, tomorrow morning fifty million people would believe it . . . including plenty of those who lived through the war. Damn." He fell silent for several seconds, then looked at Laura and said, "Any advice?"

"My guess is Rydell has a lot of circumstantial evidence," Laura said. "Maybe even a few of these Bund types willing to lie for their own reasons. Nazis don't mind lying, I don't think. But if he were as confident of the story as he wants us to think, he'd just write it. Dot every *i*, cross every *t*, and call at the last minute for a comment. Instead he wants an interview, and my question is, why?"

"Because he *hasn't* got it all nailed down," Gillian said. "He wants to trip me up, which shouldn't be hard considering how completely foreign all this will be to me."

"So we don't meet him," Laura said. "Not in a million years. We dare him to prove it. I call him and tell him go ahead, break a leg."

Gillian raised his eyebrows. "It might work. It's dangerous." He suddenly smiled and slapped her on the arm. "I like it," he said. "It's got guts. Like you."

He glanced at the door. "Well, time to rejoin the money men, if they've noticed my absence. Get some sleep if you can, and we'll see you in New Orleans."

Sleep, Laura thought as she rode down in the elevator. Not high on tonight's list of probabilities.

Tuesday, October 29

Gillian, Cavanagh, and Laura made their final debate preparations in a top-floor suite at the New Orleans Marriott, which they had transformed in less than an hour. A broadcast-quality video camera stood on a tripod facing a lectern, all brightly lit by floodlights on high stands. Gillian stood behind the lectern and responded to questions put to him by Cavanagh and Laura, as well as to attacks on him mounted by Louis Czerny. Czerny was a professional actor with an advanced degree in economics who made a living by coaching corporate executives in communicating on television. Czerny's advantages, Laura thought, started with the fact that he *looked* like Erhardt.

Behind the camera Laura sat in command of an electronic arsenal. From New York she had brought an optical disc drive for her computer—a single twelve-inch disc, recorded, read, and re-recorded by laser, stored libraries full of information. Laura accessed vital points through a custom-designed database management program on her laptop computer. Among the data that could be retrieved from the videodisc in split seconds was full-motion video of Erhardt himself, on the stump, in news conferences—anywhere he'd made a statement and been videotaped, that tape found its way into Laura's optical memory bank.

Cavanagh, who had always been more at home with ring binders and index cards, paced behind her and watched the proceedings with growing nervousness. Gillian had briefed him hours before on Rydell and the Nazi story.

The preparations were going well, Laura thought. Every

issue had been distilled to its basics, and Gillian had demonstrated a fingertip command of facts, phrases, and debating points. The hours had blended together until Laura's joints ached and her eyes watered. And if Rydell writes that story, she thought, all this is just exercise. We could spend the day better having lunch at K-Paul's.

The phone rang, and Laura answered. It was Frank Wade of the Associated Press.

"Ready when you are," he said.

Laura stood up. "Time for the drawing," she told the others, excusing herself.

Wade met her at the door to the press center downstairs— a huge meeting room that had been filled with tables, chairs, phones, and television monitors to serve the press covering the debate. She liked the AP man. He seemed to be without personal vanity, and because of the nature of wire-service reporting, he wrote the straightest and clearest accounts of everything.

Erhardt's press man was waiting for them, along with about a hundred noisy, jostling reporters.

They moved quickly through a formal drawing of the names of the reporters who'd question the candidates tonight. The din in the room never really subsided, and Laura was glad to get out. She was half-satisfied, too, with the results:

Anthony Canning of Cable News Network, a workmanlike reporter, no prima donna;

Melissa Lyons, ABC. She thought she was a movie star;

Jonathan Howard of the *Christian Science Monitor*. Laura knew him only by reputation, and by reputation he was a horse's ass;

And Wade.

Laura was delighted. Good questions and fair treatment, she thought.

Rydell caught her in the corridor.

"You can stop worrying about that story," he said. "*If* you were worrying."

"Oh?"

"And accept my apologies for having hassled you with it," Rydell went on. "I got suspicious about a few things and

[32]

checked them out, and the whole thing started looking less and less . . ."

He shrugged. "Let's just say it wasn't what it seemed. Frankly, it's a little embarrassing."

"And you're not used to that, are you?" Laura said. Rydell colored a little, then smiled.

"No," he said. "I guess not."

Gillian and Cavanagh, accompanied by their small cadre of security men, were coming off the elevator to check out the debate room. She joined them as they made their way down a long service corridor.

"He's backing off," Laura said to the Senator.

Gillian smiled. "Guts wins," he said. "Guts and good judgment. Thank you."

"That, and the fact the story was a fraud," she said.

When they paused at the back entrance to the grand ballroom, Laura suddenly felt a difference in the atmosphere. She might have noticed earlier if she hadn't been preoccupied. The President is on the premises, she thought. The signs were everywhere. The precautions surrounding Gillian paled compared to those involved in presidential movements. As Cavanagh said, when you start noticing tall, healthy looking thirty-year-old guys wearing hearing aids, you know. And blending into the background wasn't their objective, Laura knew. Sometimes it pays for security to be as conspicuous as possible.

After lengthy identity checks and other rigmarole, Cavanagh, Gillian, and Laura were allowed into the ballroom.

Inside, they were assaulted by a smell of fresh paint. At one end of the high-ceilinged room was a dais, with lecterns from which the Marriott logos had been removed. Behind them, a floor-to-ceiling panel of thin plastic boards had been nailed to a two-by-four framework and painted light blue. As they approached, huge banks of lights came on in sequence and bathed the area. Gillian stepped up and was directed to one of the lecterns.

About forty feet opposite, four chairs sat behind a long table draped in blue, awaiting the four official questioners. Behind them, on a raised platform, was a single TV camera. Between questioners and debater's platform was a no-man's-land of cables, wires, and cases of unused equipment, where still photographers would crouch during the debate.

There were perhaps three hundred spectator seats in the rear of the ballroom. Later, they'd be filled by invited guests, who would have a much better view if they watched on TV downstairs in the hotel bar. But they'd all put up with the heat, noise, confusion, and lousy sight lines to be in the inner sanctum.

The checkout went quickly and smoothly, Gillian finding not much to adjust or complain about. One of the healthy looking thirty-year-olds with a hearing aid escorted them to the holding room, a small meeting room about fifty yards down the hall. Instead of a luncheon table it had been furnished with spare auditorium chairs and a rolling cart on which stood several coffeepots and a plate of pastries. At the door, Laura, Cavanagh, and the Senator all ran their sore thumbtips over scanning screens and had their genes examined by computer before being admitted.

"Is the President inside?" Gillian asked.

"Yes, sir," one of the guards replied.

Gillian looked at Laura and Cavanagh and raised his eyebrows.

"Ready?"

"Abso-tively," Cavanagh replied. Gillian nodded to the agents, and they opened the door.

"Senator!" the President of the United States called as they entered. William C. Erhardt strode across the room, hand outstretched. "Pleased to see you. You're holding up well under all this nonsense, I see."

Gillian smiled and shook his hand. "Allow me to present some of my key staff," he said. "Mr. Cavanagh you know, he's my general manager, and Laura Madison handles my news media relations."

"Now *there's* a thankless job," the President said, taking Laura's hand. To her utter astonishment, he bent over and kissed her lightly on the knuckle. "I saw the profile in today's *Times*, though," he said. "You certainly seem to be a real pro." Laura realized she was flushing and tongue-tied, and simply nodded a few times and stepped back. It was the first time she had met him in person, and he seemed huge, perfectly calm, totally in control. Yet the media painted him as a puppet, dancing on strings pulled by . . .

Emile Loubert, for one, she thought, realizing that Erhardt's National Security Advisor was in the small knot of VIPs in the center of the room. She knew him from his photographs and TV appearances. And there was Steve Shaw, the President's press secretary. It's really true, she thought. There's an aura that surrounds the President . . .

"Dazzled?"

It was Cavanagh, standing next to her.

"A little, I guess."

"So am I," Cavanagh said, "and I've shaken the hand of every president since Kennedy. Ah well, soon President Gillian will cast the same spell."

Laura looked over at Shaw and saw Laura Madison, White House Press Secretary. She sipped her coffee to drive the image away. Cavanagh was starting his second cup.

"I wish they hadn't done this," he said. "For one thing, coffee makes you need to pee. For another, Erhardt's little cocktail-party patter act is taking all the edge off. Look at him, he's got the boss laughing."

Erhardt was regaling the small group with some kind of story and everyone was very jovial.

"Now watch," Cavanagh continued. "Just before we go on, Erhardt will tell his funniest, dirtiest joke. Then he'll hope the Senator remembers the punch line at the wrong time and cracks up. Damn, I hate this. They don't make prize fighters share a dressing room."

The makeup people called for Gillian at 5:45 P.M. and Erhardt at 5:50. At 5:55 they were all milling in the service corridor and could hear the noise of the crowd in the ballroom like the low growl of an animal. Finally, at exactly 5:59 the door opened and the debate chairwoman led the candidates to the platform. To Laura, as she took her reserved seat, the electricity in the room was almost frightening. The lights and the blue color scheme combined to make the platform seem like a floating island in a dark sea, and Laura saw it all again in miniature on the monitors alongside the reporters' table. Erhardt and Gillian, now all business, were shuffling notes and smoothing their shirtfronts. In front of them, the director held up ten fingers, then five, then four . . .

A red light glowed on the main camera and the moderator began speaking. Laura couldn't hear very well but could make out the introductions. Then, as challenger, Gillian made the first opening statement. Within moments Laura knew it was going to be all right. All the edge Cavanagh had spoken of was there. His voice was calm, clear, and unwavering. His command was effortless as he moved through a withering attack on Erhardt's policies, while conceding the popularity of many of his measures. A touchdown, Laura thought, on the game's first possession.

Erhardt's turn. To Laura, the President's statement was a predictable recitation of the administration's claimed achievements.

Frank Wade had the first question. He noted that Erhardt had nearly balanced the budget, but had done it by massive cuts in social programs, and asked whether it was worth it. Both candidates used the question as an excuse for canned speeches about the importance of social programs. It seemed to Laura that Gillian missed an opportunity.

Next, Melissa Lyons. The ABC reporter tossed her hair with the assurance of someone who knows exactly where the camera is and what it likes.

"Senator," she said. "Are you a Nazi?"

Laura felt her body temperature rise and her heart accelerate. Gillian merely tilted his head and seemed to chuckle. "Am I a what?"

"A Nazi," Lyons repeated. "More specifically, is it true you permitted the True American Bund to hold meetings on your property in Arizona, and that you endorsed the writings of that Nazi group's leader, Jonathan Marin?"

Gillian was reddening. "Wait a minute," he said, pointing, "I want to stop this right now. I've heard about this in the last few days, that this rumor was going around, that there was someone trying to plant this story in the media. There's no truth to it whatsoever, and I don't intend to address it again. It's a disgraceful and demeaning slander."

Lyons began shuffling through a stack of papers. "Isn't it

also true," she said, unperturbed, "that you intervened in a grand jury proceeding to prevent—"

"No, Miss Lyons, it is *not* true," Gillian said, his anger plainly visible.

". . . and that some years ago you in fact sold your Arizona property to the Bund, in part for secret cash payments to yourself—"

"Stop it," Gillian said. "It's a slander, a planted story. Don't you check these things out?"

"If you'll permit me to show you . . ." Lyons said.

"I told you I wouldn't address it," Gillian snapped. "Unless the snake that fed it to you is willing to come forward and own up to it, which I doubt."

Gillian slapped his palm on the lectern. "That's it. Next question," he said, and looked at the moderator.

As soon as the camera was off him, Gillian looked over at Laura and Cavanagh with a mixture of rage and desperation twisting his features. There were still more than forty minutes of debate time left, and Lyons was sharpening her claws for the kill. Laura stared at her. How had she come by the story Mitchell Rydell said wasn't sound enough to print? And where was the flaw in the evidence that had scared Rydell off? Whoever wanted to plant the story had found a willing ear in Lyons . . . but if the story could be conclusively proved a sham, it might even rebound to the Senator's advantage.

Lyons's next turn came while Laura was still puzzling out the possibilities. She held a sheet of paper up to the camera.

"I ask you, Senator, if this is your handwriting," she said.

"Miss Lyons," Gillian replied. "I have already said I will not address this sleazy business for one more minute. Move on to something else."

"We want an explanation, Senator," Lyons said and stared icily at Gillian. Gillian stared back, and the seconds stretched out into an eternity. Laura could hear coughing behind her in the audience, and the moderator hesitated, wondering whether to break in. Finally, after thirty seconds of impasse, she leaned toward her microphone and said, "Mr. Canning . . ."

Canning directed a question at Erhardt, but the entire room—possibly, Laura thought, the whole nation—was waiting for Lyons's next opportunity to lash out at Gillian. She got it a few minutes later, and she simply said, "I'm still waiting for your explanation, Senator. What have you got to do with the True American Bund?"

Gillian said nothing at all in reply. Another endless 30-second silence filled the hall.

Finally, it was all over. The floods went out and normal light engulfed the room like a cloud. Gillian stood at the podium shuffling papers pointlessly, consoling his hands for the fact they had nobody to punch. He reminded Laura of her father, puttering with his wife's personal things the morning after her death. In the rest of the room there was a sudden rush to the doors, reporters charging to phone in their catch-up stories. Erhardt looked over as though deciding whether to say anything, then left quickly through the service doorway. Finally, there were only Gillian, his aides, and the Secret Service in the room.

Gillian stepped down from the platform.

"How'd I do?" he said wistfully, and Cavanagh chuckled.

"Just fine," he said. "The public hates snooty lady TV reporters to begin with."

"Your anger may have been exactly the right response," Laura added. "You certainly made it clear you were not only innocent, but wronged."

They walked down the service corridor alone, their footsteps echoing.

"We need to kill that story," Cavanagh said. "Kill it so completely her network sends her out to cover hurricanes for the rest of her career."

"That would be nice," Gillian said. "Well, let's get upstairs, order a little dinner, and see what the evening news has to say." His whole posture spoke of defeat and bewilderment, two qualities Laura had never seen in the Senator before.

"I have an errand I want to run," Laura said.

She went to the press room and found bedlam. Fifty reporters were dictating stories into their phones at once, and another dozen lines rang continually. The debate had been scheduled early so the newspaper guys would have lots of time before their deadlines. Tomorrow's papers would be a nightmare. She searched the room for Rydell but couldn't see him. She did notice, however, three messages for him tacked to the wall—all from his bosses in New York.

At the hotel's front desk she rang Rydell's room and got a busy signal. When his line was still busy a minute later, she decided to go up. The elevator lobby was jammed, and two cars came and went before she could board. Finally, in frustration, she started up the stairs. She was slightly winded when she reached the eighth floor.

Rydell's door was open. Laura could hear a mechanical voice inside, repeating, "If you wish to make a call, please hang up and dial again . . ." His phone was off the hook.

Rydell had a sitting room in which she saw a suitcase propped in the corner, a laptop computer on the bed, and stacks of papers on every flat surface.

"Mitchell?" she called. "Are you here?"

The recorded voice spooked her enough that she put the phone back in its cradle. "Mitchell?" she repeated.

She stepped over to the bedroom door and glanced hesitantly inside. Nothing. Then she turned, passed the bathroom, and stopped.

Rydell sat inside on the tile floor, staring straight ahead of him. In his hand he held a pint bottle of Hennessy cognac. He looked up at her.

"Want a drink?"

"I need to talk to you," Laura said. "About that Nazi story."

"Ah, yes," Rydell said, shaking his head slowly. There's hardly any liquor missing from the bottle, Laura noticed. He didn't seem drunk. "The celebrated phony Nazi story," Rydell said. "I guess it was better than I thought. I thought it stunk all the way through. Probably not a true word in it."

"That's the point," Laura said. "I have to prove it false. It's going to decide the election otherwise."

"My sentiment exactly," Rydell said. "That's why right after they canned me . . ."

"After they *what?*"

"Shit-canned me," Mitchell said, and laughed. "I knew it would happen as soon as Lyons opened her mouth. I put them through too much garbage on this story. Spent too much of my reputation, as Ed the editor would say. So I said to myself, expose it, stick it to them, sell the whole thing to *Newsweek*. Fuck 'em good and proper."

"What did you do?"

Mitchell stifled a sob, and Laura felt a wave of alarm sweep through her.

"What did I do?" Mitchell repeated. "Why, what any good reporter would do. Go back to the beginning. For me, that was Dennis McCarthy. Old schoolmate, chum. He was the one that first put me onto the story. Passed me that stuff you saw Lyons waving around tonight. I called him, to appeal to old friendship and try to put some pieces together."

He stood up and took a long swig from the bottle, then handed it to Laura. "Here," he said, grimacing as though the liquor were poisoning him. "A bender seemed appropriate a few minutes ago, but now I'm not in the mood."

"Mitchell, what in hell is going on?" Laura said, following him into the sitting room.

"I got Dennis's mother on the phone," Mitchell said. "Dennis is dead."

Ten minutes later, Laura left Rydell staring out the plate-glass window of his suite and took the elevator to the lobby. At the end of the elevator bank, one car was sealed off from the others by a steel-pipe railing. Two Secret Service agents stood on either side of the elevator doors. They knew Laura on sight and greeted her amiably.

"I'd like to go upstairs and talk to Steve Shaw," Laura said. One of the agents relayed her request along a private phone line, and after a moment, nodded acquiescence. The elevator doors opened and Laura was carried nonstop to the eighteenth floor, an entire floor of rooms isolated from the rest of the hotel for the exclusive use of the presidential party.

She was greeted by another Secret Service man, who escorted her along the corridor to an open door. Inside the room was a mini-command post with several television sets, fax and telex machines, and a dozen or more phones. Shaw sat on a soft chair watching a videotape of the debate. He stood up when Laura entered.

"Ms. Madison," he said, holding out his hand. "We've

passed in the halls, as they say, but we've never had the pleasure."

She shook Shaw's hand and took the seat he offered, declining a cup of coffee.

"What can I do for you?"

"I need your help," Laura said. "That is, Senator Gillian needs your help."

"It's a little irregular, isn't it, for electoral opponents to ask each other for help?"

"I'm asking you not as a campaigner but as a presidential aide," Laura said. "Senator Gillian offers the President his word of honor that the allegations you heard downstairs are utterly false . . ."

"His assurance isn't necessary," Shaw said. "Everybody here has the highest regard for the Senator."

"It's important that the public know how false the story is," Laura said.

"If it's not true, it shouldn't be hard to disprove," Shaw said.

"Somebody has gone to great trouble to plant this story," Laura countered. "Proof can be manufactured, facts distorted. It's a smear campaign, designed to last just until the election. It should appall you as well as us."

"If that's all true, we're appropriately appalled," Shaw said evenly. "But I don't frankly see where it's our problem, except in the broadest philosophical sense."

"What we want, or rather what we're asking you for, is your help in tracking down the source of the story," Laura said. "We don't know where Melissa Lyons got it, and the man we think was the key to the whole thing is dead now—"

"Ms. Madison," Shaw interrupted. "Forgive me, but dirty campaigns are nothing new. In any national campaign, there's bound to be mudslinging. If the charges against Gillian are false, all he needs to do is refute them. If he can. If he can't, then the electorate judges for itself. That's how the system works."

"But the system isn't working, it's being compromised."

"I don't see that," Shaw said. "I've got no evidence one way or the other. Certainly not enough to justify undermining my own relations with the media trying to get my boss's opponent

[41]

out of a tight corner. Fair's fair, Ms. Madison. This isn't our problem, it's yours."

"But surely the President rejects dishonest campaign tactics," Laura said. "Surely he's willing to say so."

"Surely," Shaw agreed. "*When* he sees them. This may be such a case, and it may not be. Forgive me again, Miss, but we don't know firsthand that your boss *isn't* a raving Nazi."

"Oh, for Christ's sake," Laura said, but Shaw was standing up.

"If you'll excuse me . . ."

"I want to see the President," Laura said.

"He's tied up, and will be for some time," Shaw said. "We're trying to run a government here, you know, not just campaign full time."

"I'll call Senator Gillian," Laura said. "Will the President see *him*?"

"Doubtful," Shaw said.

"Doubtful!" Laura repeated, her voice rising. "Why the hell wouldn't he?"

"Come on, Ms. Madison, don't make a scene," Shaw said.

"Make a scene!"

"How else could you realistically expect us to respond?" Shaw said. "It's the real world, little girl, and this is how the game is played."

"Don't you little girl me . . ."

Shaw went back to his chair and picked up the phone. "Security," he said into the receiver.

"You're behind it, aren't you?" Laura said.

"You're out of your mind," Shaw replied. "You're taking the evening's events too hard."

" 'That's the way the game is played,' you say," Laura said, pacing to the door. "We'll see." Two Secret Service agents materialized in the corridor.

"All right, all right!" Laura said. "Send the bouncers away, Steve, you don't have to throw me out."

Shaw shrugged. "You have to be accompanied when you're up here. You know that."

Laura had to return to the ground floor to get another elevator back to Gillian's suite. But when she arrived in the lobby she heard a voice call her. It was Mitchell, changed into jeans and a leather jacket, walking away from the cashier's desk with an overnight bag in his hand.

"Going somewhere?" she said.

"There's an eight-thirty flight to New York I can still get," he said. "First thing tomorrow morning I'm on the trail of whoever killed Dennis McCarthy . . ."

"Killed him? I thought you said it was an accident."

"Yes, that's right," Mitchell replied. "Just an extraordinarily convenient and bloody car crash. Listen, can we make a pact, you and me?"

"I'm listening," Laura said.

"I'm going to dig into this one," Mitchell said. "I'm willing to share whatever I find out with you, provided you return the favor. Everything you learn about this story and where it came from, you pass to me and me alone . . . among the press, that is. And nothing gets published without my name on it."

Laura took a long breath and said nothing. Mitchell put his suitcase down and folded his arms.

"Listen, I'm not sure I can express this right," he said. "But I think we're on the same side now. I think the news media are being had, being suckered in a big way, duped into trashing a presidential election. I don't like it. I honestly don't care who wins . . . well, I do care, but that's beside the point. The point is an honest election. Which we're not getting, and it makes me mad."

Laura was still silent.

"All right, the hell with it," Mitchell said, and picked up his bag.

"No, Mitchell," Laura said, reaching out to touch his arm. "It sounds fair enough to me. I'm not sure what we can do, but we'll keep in touch."

Mitchell smiled faintly and nodded at her. "Got to catch my plane," he said. "See you in New York?"

"Maybe."

Gillian's whole attitude had changed when Laura returned to his suite. Gone was the hangdog look, the defeated slump of the shoulders. Instead, he was pacing vigorously along the glass wall of his suite, looking out over the French Quarter, while Cavanagh talked rapid-fire into two telephone handsets at once.

"We're buying a half hour on all three networks Saturday evening," Gillian said, coming across the room to her. "We've lined up a roster of prominent people to give testimonials—"

Cavanagh interjected from his telephone foxhole: "Catholic Cardinals of New York and Chicago, two former presidents, Coretta King, a former secretary general of the U.N., even the commissioner of baseball. If we could get Mother Teresa, we'd be all set."

"Each one will do one or two minutes," Gillian said.

"It'll bring tears to your eyes," Cavanagh said, returning to the phones.

"And at the end I'll lay out the facts about this Nazi nonsense. I'll call a spade a spade," Gillian said. He took Laura's hand and led her to the settee, where both sat down.

"Laura, I have never laid eyes on Jonathan Marin and I am prepared to swear to that in front of St. Peter when and if I have to. I'm going to say that to the world Friday night. I'm also going to say a few other things."

He stood up and began to pace again. "I'm going to express how revolted I am—how utterly, indescribably soiled I feel—to see an American election being conducted in this manner. I'm going to voice my outrage at being the first candidate to be slandered out of a chance to win the presidency. And I'm going to call on our dirty little friend President Erhardt to join me in denouncing these tactics, if he can."

He leaned over Laura's chair until his face was only inches from hers.

"Between now and the election you have only one job, and you can refuse it if you want to, but I hope you don't. Find out who's behind this. Do whatever it takes, but find out where this story came from."

"I'll do it," Laura said softly. "Of course I'll do it. I mean, I'll do my best . . ."

"Good," Gillian said. "We'll see that you have the money and resources you need. But at all costs, find the vampire that's doing this to me and drag him into the sunlight."

Wednesday, October 30

Laura detected the man in the ski parka following her around midmorning Wednesday, just after she left her apartment to get the papers. She had been home only about an hour, after a bleary-eyed dawn flight from New Orleans. She expected disaster in the newspapers and there it was. The *Times*, *Daily News*, and *USA Today* all carried the Gillian Nazi story in major headlines across their front page. Laura did not buy the *New York Post*, but glanced at it on the newsstand long enough to see they'd already christened the affair Nazigate. She'd seen most of the network TV coverage in New Orleans.

When she first saw the man, she stopped and stared down at the *Times* front page, surreptitiously watching him to see if he moved on. He hadn't been hard to spot—especially since Laura's sessions with the Secret Service had made her aware of the odd individual in a crowd, the one whose dress or actions just don't fit.

Now here he was again, across the street, pretending to look in the window of a butcher shop. His collar was turned up all around, and he wore a woolen cap pulled low across his brow. She began to walk slowly back toward her building and noticed him following her, across the street and about fifty yards back. He's not very good, she thought. Unless he means to be seen.

She passed the entry to her building and continued to the corner, and stood there waiting for the light. She was afraid to look back over her shoulder; instead, she stepped off the curb when the traffic lightened up, reached the middle of the street, then abruptly wheeled and headed back. Ski Parka, caught, suddenly turned and walked a few paces up the avenue. Laura passed him briskly, trying not to look at him, and when she thought she was out of sight, quickened to a trot that got her to her doorstep just before he reappeared. A hand-lettered OUT OF ORDER sign was taped to the laser key reader.

She stood just inside the door a moment, cold air filling her lungs. Leaning back against the mailboxes, she could see about forty feet of sidewalk, and after a few moments her pursuer came into view, walking purposefully toward her building. Laura tucked the newspapers under her arm and started up the stairs. She had reached the first landing when she heard the door open below her. She froze. Light footsteps approached the first flight of stairs.

Laura took the next two flights quickly, and slipped through a landing door into a narrow, badly lit corridor. She put two of the newspapers down and carefully folded the *Times* in half, holding the paper by the loose side opposite the tightest corner of the fold.

She pressed her ear to the doorway. The pursuing footsteps reached the landing, paused, then started up again. Laura could barely hear over the pounding of blood in her ears. She pushed the door open. The man was there, three steps above her, hands in pockets and collar still turned open. He spun at the creak of the door and stepped quickly down toward Laura, but she caught him flush on the temple with the rock-hard spine of the *New York Times*. His eyes widened as he teetered forward, off balance, clutching for a handhold. Laura sidestepped out of his path and shoved him, hard, against the wall. His breath burst out of his lungs and he slid down into a crouch, holding his head.

"I've got a gun," Laura lied. "You keep away from me."

But there was no sound in response, not even a groan. The man turned sideways, then slumped over, his face rapping lightly against the concrete of the landing.

Jesus! Laura thought. I didn't mean to hit him *that* hard. What if he's dead?

It took all her courage to bend over the man and feel his neck. There was a strong pulse there . . . but there was something else. Something about his face . . .

[46]

It came to her all at once. She'd seen his face in one of the news clippings Mitchell had given her to back up his story about the True American Bund. In the photo, the man in front of her was being led from a police cruiser into a courthouse. It was Jonathan Marin.

"Hooo, boy," Laura said softly. She tapped Marin on the cheek. "You okay? Hey, wake up!"

They couldn't sit on the landing all day. The morning was in full swing and people would be passing through.

Marin wasn't big or heavy but he was dead weight, and although Laura could get him upright she had a terrible time supporting him. Together they struggled up another flight of stairs, Marin sliding down, Laura tugging, heaving his body over her shoulder. Her face flushed and her skin slicked over with sweat.

She carried him awkwardly to her door and opened it. Inside, she let him fall as gently as she could onto the braided rug in the living room. Then she quickly returned to the stairs to retrieve her newspapers and check for any other evidence she might have left behind. Like blood, she thought, suddenly frightened again. I should leave him where he is and use a neighbor's phone to call the police, she thought. And tell them what? That I coldcocked a stranger on the stairs because I *thought* he was after me? But he *is* after me, she thought. There's no other reason for him to turn up at my door on this particular morning. She went back to her apartment, and a few moments later heard a groan from Marin. She pressed a wet cloth into his forehead. His temple was already purple. His eyes opened abruptly and Laura hopped back from him as though from an electric shock.

"Holy Mother of Christ," Marin said softly. He felt the side of his head gingerly with his fingertips. "It's true what they say about New York girls," he croaked.

"I'm sorry," Laura said. "I thought . . ."

Marin waved his hand feebly and tried to sit up. Against her better judgment Laura helped him. He rotated his head, wincing in pain.

"You thought I was going to rape you or something," he said. "I know. Jesus, I might have a concussion."

"We'll get you to the hospital," Laura said.

"No way, José," Marin said. "I'm not safe in hospitals. I'm barely safe on the streets, and evidently not safe at all in stairwells."

"Well," Laura said, "if you wanted to talk to me you could have walked right up on the street, with people around, and introduced yourself.

He smiled a little, weakly. "I must be losing it," he said. "My old drill instructor would string me up if he ever saw a little girl clean my clock like that."

"You'd better get to the point before you make me mad again," Laura said. Marin looked at her evenly.

"In my opinion, Miss, you owe me more consideration than that."

"I don't owe you anything," Laura said. "You start following single women up stairwells in New York and you're lucky if all you get is hit on the head. I don't happen to have a gun, but I know women who do."

"I won't argue with you," Marin said. "You sound like some kind of libber, and there's never any point arguing with them. You owe me an apology, but I'll settle for a drink. And you owe it to yourself to hear what I've got to say."

"A drink?" Laura said. It was still before noon. "The best I can do is a Sprite."

Marin pretended to gag, then said, "Mind if I use the bathroom? I want to see if I'm bleeding."

"Just turning colors," Laura said. She got a can of Sprite from the refrigerator and poured herself some orange juice, then met Marin as he came out of the bathroom.

"That doesn't look too bad," she said.

"I've had worse. Been hit harder, too."

"Not often, I hope," Laura said. "Sit down. You've got five minutes to tell me why I shouldn't throw you right out of here."

"For starters, I have never been in the same room as your boss, no matter what ABC says."

"Tell me something I didn't already know."

"What if I told you everything ABC has is a lie and a fraud?"

"I'd agree, willingly," Laura said. "But I wouldn't know why."

"Welcome to the club," Marin said. "Mind you, it ain't that I like your boss. I don't. From all I can see he's just another typical bleeding-heart liberal."

Laura felt her face flush and controlled her temper.

"What I don't understand," Marin said, "is why they're trying to steal an election they'll win easily anyway."

"Who's they?"

"Are you always this slow? Erhardt's people, who else? They planted all this bullshit about me and Gillian. If you want my opinion, they did it to discredit *me*."

"You? Most of the world thinks you're dead," Laura said. "That's as low as your reputation can get."

"They want me dead, certainly. They've been trying to kill me for a year," Marin said matter-of-factly. "I keep dodging them."

"Uh-huh," Laura said.

"Okay, so I'm paranoid. It's a healthy way to be sometimes."

"If what you say is true, there's only one way to proceed," Laura said. "We've got to set up a news conference so you can tell the world what you just told me."

"What, that Erhardt's trying to kill me?" Marin asked. "Come on, the guy's a public saint and I'm a well-known wacko."

"No, no," Laura said irritably. "That you don't know Senator Gillian, and have never had anything to do with him. That this story about him and your group is a fake."

"You don't understand the situation." Marin threw his head back and emptied his soda in one gulp. "I'm a hunted man, lady. Erhardt's people think I'm dead already. They think I got shot and carved up by some heavily armed jungle bunny in Africa six months ago. Or else they never would have put this story out. They'd have found something else. If I turn up, it would be necessary for them to eliminate me again. And there are a bunch of old warrants out for me. I'm wanted for flagrant exercise of my Constitutional rights. If I show my face in public it's even money who'd get me first, the cops or Erhardt's hit squads."

"You're right," Laura said. "You're a wacko. In fact, I don't see how we can do any business. I think you should leave."

[49]

"Saw you in the paper yesterday," Marin said, as though Laura hadn't even spoken. "Looked nice. I thought, now there's somebody I can talk to. Who knows, maybe we could even get it on . . ."

Laura stood up and went to the door, pulling it open.

"Out," she said.

"Okay, so a roll in the hay is out of the question," Marin said, shrugging. "You still ought to let me help you."

"How? Be specific and be quick," Laura said.

"It isn't enough to prove one story false," Marin said. "They'll just come up with another one. No, you've got to tie it to Erhardt. You've got to prove he sabotaged your campaign, and that ain't easy. If you do it, you win the election. If not, you may as well go to the beach."

"I can't prove it when I don't believe it," she said.

Marin grimaced in frustration. "So where do you think that story came from, all nicely tied up and delivered like that? The Leak Fairy?"

"Mr. Marin, people leak things to the press for all kinds of reasons. If it hadn't been Melissa Lyons, if it had been someone more skeptical, the story might never have gotten out—"

"Or somebody they didn't have anything on," Marin said. "Or a million things. But it's out, and it's ruining your campaign. You think that's an accident?"

Laura closed the door and returned to her chair. No, she didn't think it was an accident. Dennis McCarthy had fed the story to Mitchell, but Mitchell hadn't bought it. And McCarthy had died yesterday afternoon—how long after delivering all the same material to Melissa Lyons? The trail couldn't end with Dennis McCarthy, but Laura still refused to believe it led to the White House. That was the fantasy of a creative and somewhat imbalanced mind.

"Listen," she said to Marin. "If you won't give a news conference, will you go with me to visit one particular reporter, somebody who can give your story the circulation it needs, and give us some advice on where to go from here?"

"You refer, of course, to the peerless Mitchell Rydell," Marin said.

"How did you know?"

"He was crawling all over the Bund's former property—*my*

[50]

former property—in Arizona not long ago. And asking lots of questions at the courthouse. That's another thing," Marin said, rising. "The deed on my property out there simply vanished. I turned around one day and didn't own it anymore. Same thing happened to a bank account with forty thousand dollars in it. Disappeared from the bank's computer, without a trace. That's when I went to South Africa. I figured it wouldn't be too long before somebody erased *me* from that One Great Diskette. And they tried, boy, they tried. I've been lucky."

"Mitchell Rydell," Laura prompted. "Will you come with me to talk to him?"

"Sure, why not? But I have to be careful about moving around in daylight."

Laura dialed Rydell's number and looked over at Marin while she waited for an answer.

"You can sit tight here," she said. "Either I'll get Mitchell to come here or we'll wait until evening. Though I hate to have a whole day go by."

"You can't just hurry into print with something like this," Marin said. "You'd play right into their hands."

Laura got Mitchell's answering machine. "Mitchell, it's Laura Madison," she said. "Call me as soon as you can at 555-6578. It's vital."

Marin stood up and examined Laura's small library. Laura stared at him a moment, thinking, it's true what they say about politics making for strange bedfellows. Here's one of the country's most prominent nut cases, in my living room. And I'm taking him seriously.

"Listen, I have to go out," she said. "Over to the campaign office. I'm sure all hell is breaking loose. I'll be several hours. Can I trust you here?"

Marin smiled. "I'm at your mercy," he said. "If you put me out on the street I'm in trouble. And I sure don't want you to hit me again."

"Don't answer the phone," Laura said from the door. "I've got a machine."

She took a cab downtown to the Gillian campaign office, which was in a slick new office building on Sixth Avenue. It was one of those sites where they'd torn down a sixty-story building to build a ninety-story tower, and another was going up right next to it. She took the high-speed elevator to the eighty-first floor and was still holding her stomach as she reached the office.

If anything, it was busier than ever. The phones rang incessantly, hardly a sign of a dead campaign. She passed the table on which the out-of-town papers were displayed, and they were all predictably awful. From Boston to San Francisco, Gillian the closet Nazi was on every front page.

Her desk faced a glass wall overlooking midtown Manhattan, but Laura did not notice the view. She dialed Rydell's number from her desk but got his machine again and hung up. She called the New Orleans Marriott in the hope of catching Cavanagh, but they had already left for Chicago. After a moment, she got up and shut her office door, then sat silently, hand resting on the telephone receiver. Damn, she thought. She tapped her fingers lightly on the desktop, lifted the receiver, put it back, then lifted it again and dialed her ex-husband.

The cramped delicatessen was a block from the U.S. Courthouse at Foley Square. It was noisy and filled with cheap looking lawyers and bail bondsmen, men with shiny suits and two-pound wristwatches. David hadn't said two words to her since they'd met outside the FBI New York field office.

Now, he took a big bite out of his baked ham and swiss sandwich, chased it with a gulp of iced tea (*lots* of sugar), looked at her and said, "Well?"

"Is that all, just well?"

"I never expected to hear from you like this," David said. "Out of the clear blue sky. I thought we had both said all we had to say through our lawyers. If there's something else you want, I'd appreciate it if you just get to it and let me get back to work."

"I need help," Laura said.

"You don't need the FBI," David said. "I'm sure there's a million places you can go for help. Your boss, for instance."

"David, give me a break," Laura snapped. She paused and took a deep breath. David looked at her across the cluttered Formica-topped table.

"Listen," Laura said. "I've got to trace this Nazi story and find out where it came from. Until this morning I didn't know where to begin. Then, like you say, out of the clear blue sky, I bump into this Marin guy . . ."

David leaned forward.

"Laura," he said, "Marin is dead. He's been dead six months."

"All I want to know, before I go any further, is whether the FBI has anything on any link between him and Senator Gillian," Laura said. "I want to know if there are any real facts out there, anything to get a grip on and follow."

"Where is this guy now?" David said.

"At my apartment."

David tossed his napkin down and stared at the ceiling in annoyance.

"Now *you* listen," he said. "If it's really Marin, you're harboring a federal fugitive. There are outstanding warrants on Marin. You're committing a felony. If I had any sense I'd send someone over there right now to get him, but that would only get you in trouble."

"And you've always been such a prince about that."

"And furthermore, the guy's got a small room for rent in the attic," David went on. "He can't be trusted for a single minute. He's a thief and an extortionist at the very least, to say nothing of a raving racist. Get rid of him."

He stood up.

"Thanks a lot," Laura said, "for reminding me of why I made you my ex-husband."

"Same old Laura," David said. "You were never hard to please. The sun, moon, and stars would always do nicely. Now let's face reality for a change."

He bent over and put his hands on the edges of the table so his face was only inches from Laura's. She noted with some satisfaction that there wasn't a hint of desire stirring anywhere in her consciousness. David was finally over with.

He whispered, "I cannot and will not withhold evidence concerning a federal fugitive. For old times' sake I'll give you a little time." He looked at his watch. "Nine o'clock tonight he'd better be gone."

He dropped a twenty-dollar bill on the table.

"Enjoyed the lunch," he said, and started to leave. When

he had gotten halfway across the dining room, Laura called after him. As he turned around, she smiled at him, lifted the twenty, and tore it into little pieces.

The casket was draped in an American flag. "His buddies from the Marines brought it, this morning," Dennis's mother said to Mitchell. She was sitting in a brocaded armchair in Parlor C of the McCarthy Funeral Home on Flatbush Avenue. The undertaker, a cousin, was giving a good price.

"They thought the plain closed casket looked too bare," Mrs. McCarthy explained. "I didn't want a closed casket in the first place, but my brother, he was the one who went to identify Dennis, he said Dennis was messed up pretty good. He said people might be disturbed by it, not that I'd care, you understand. The hell with them is what I say."

The closed casket bothered Rydell. It took away his chance to say an adequate good-bye to an old, if strained, friendship. And that made him think he'd had no reason to come to Brooklyn in the first place. He didn't know anyone else in the room, though it was very crowded. There was a small group of men in uniform in the rear, but Mitchell felt no kinship at all with them, any more than with the older mourners comforting his friend's mother. After a few minutes of respectful attention to the old lady, Mitchell excused himself by saying he needed a cigarette and went downstairs to the smoking lounge. He didn't smoke, but he never knew how to fill an hour at these things.

In the downstairs lounge two old gentlemen were engaged in a lively conversation and switched to Gaelic as soon as Mitchell entered. He got a cup of water from the cooler and leafed through an old *National Geographic*, then got more water, then read a brochure on funeral pre-arrangement which, the brochure assured him, was a very thoughtful thing to do for one's family.

Ah, well, he thought, I've done my duty. Let's say good-bye to Mrs. McCarthy and hit the road.

Upstairs a woman Mitchell vaguely recognized—perhaps an old NYU classmate?—was sitting next to Mrs. McCarthy and talking in a loud voice.

"Oh, Mrs. McCarthy," she was saying. "You didn't know

your son. Sometimes mothers don't, you know. Not everything."

"Don't give me that," Mrs. McCarthy said, rearranging herself in her chair. "I knew Dennis. He kept no secrets from me. He lived at home, after all. I never saw him touch a drop, and he promised me he wouldn't."

"Well, let me tell you," the younger woman said, "when he wanted to, he could really pack it away. With the best of them. Not that that's a fault, mind you. I'm not saying he was an *alcoholic* or anything . . ."

"He did not drink," Mrs. McCarthy said emphatically. "No matter what the police say, he couldn't have been drunk."

"All right," the classmate said. "I don't mean to speak ill of the dead, anyway."

Mitchell interrupted to take his leave, and a few minutes later was walking down Flatbush Avenue. It was early afternoon of a cold, clear, and altogether beautiful day.

That was rude, he thought, and uncalled for. But truth be told, Dennis did drink a bit. We shared the odd jar, as the Irish would say. He walked on toward Nostrand Avenue, an intersection known in Brooklyn for generations as the Junction, end of the line for the IRT subway he'd take back to Manhattan.

Dennis could put it away, he remembered, hands in pockets. On the sidewalks he passed young black kids with state-of-the-art radios, and one cheap storefront after another, selling everything from stereos to bicycles, all behind heavy gratings. He remembered riding in Dennis's car one night after a ballgame at Yankee Stadium. Catfish Hunter had pitched, gotten shelled, and they'd left early. He remembered heading down the FDR Drive toward the Village to have a few more beers, and they had the top down on the convertible. He remembered the magical lights of the city passing by, and how he had put his head on the seat cushion and listened to Dennis singing "Wild Thing" at the top of his lungs, doing Jimi Hendrix on the steering wheel.

"Mitchie, baby, I sure got to whizz," Dennis had said as he wound slowly from lane to lane, staring straight ahead, fighting intoxication while cars passed on both sides, sometimes honking their horns.

That was it, Mitchell thought, stopping in midblock. *Slow.*

Dennis drank, but the Dennis I knew drove at a snail's pace when he was loaded.

He was really messed up, his mother said. Bad enough for a closed casket. He must have hit the bridge support at a pretty good speed.

He stepped out into Flatbush Avenue and searched for a cab. A few moments later a gypsy cab pulled over, and Mitchell asked for the police station with jurisdiction over the section of the Belt Parkway where Dennis had his accident. It was about a twenty-minute ride to a precinct house half-hidden under an elevated roadway. For a block in every direction even the illegal parking spaces were full.

Inside he found a small anteroom with a reception desk staffed by a middle-aged woman in civilian clothes. Mitchell was fourth on line and while he waited he stared at the photo of the mayor above the information window and at the bulletin board covered with public service reminders. Finally he stepped to the window and showed the woman his *New York Times* ID.

"I'd like to see a vehicle accident report, please," he said. "Happened yesterday on the Belt Parkway, victim Dennis McCarthy."

The woman silently gestured Mitchell to a door, and when he took the handle he heard a loud buzz as the lock snapped open.

"See the sergeant at the desk," she said, pointing.

The sergeant inspected Mitchell's press badge, shrugged, and turned to his computer terminal.

"No more written reports, you know," he said. "The cops dictate their reports into their radios, and the computer converts it and files it. I recall the smash-up, though. What's so newsworthy? Just another drunk blending into the concrete."

"So they say," Mitchell said. He watched the sergeant tapping at his keyboard with his two index fingers, one key at a time with long pauses in between.

"Damn, must not be here. Just give me a second," he said to Mitchell, and went back to the beginning to start keyboarding his commands all over again. Mitchell could plainly see the words "access denied" appearing on the screen.

"There sure *is* something going on," the sergeant finally

said, turning to Mitchell. "The report's there, but it's been sealed."

"Sealed?"

"As in I can't access it without the right password, and my password ain't the right one. Maybe there's a grand jury involved or something. You might ask downtown, cause I can't help you."

Mitchell thanked him and walked slowly back out into the street. The subway was only a block away and he rode in silence all the way home.

He pulled a bottle of Anchor Steam beer out of the refrigerator and sat down at the phone. There was a message from Laura Madison on the tape, but he had other priorities just now. Police headquarters was one of the numbers stored in the memory of his multifunction phone, so he had to push only one button.

"Jerry Moynihan, please," he said when the switchboard answered. He waited a moment, humming atonally.

"Jerry," he said. "Mitch Rydell at the *Times*. Listen, I got a quick question for you. Can your computer pull up the status of an accident report from yesterday, from Brooklyn? Happened on the Belt Parkway, with a fatality named Dennis McCarthy."

"I got a few other things to do, you know," Moynihan said.

"Come on, Jerry, you owe me one."

"You already used that one," Moynihan said. "Now you owe me. Give me five minutes."

Mitchell walked around his apartment checking for dust and examined his kitchen for signs the roaches were coming back. He was staring out the window at the street eight floors below when Moynihan called back.

"Sorry to disappoint you," he said, "but there's no such record."

"Got to be," Mitchell replied. "A fatal, you have to respond, right? Not like some minor fender-bender."

"That's the rule, and the cops log their reports from the scene, verbally. If it happened, it's in the computer."

"Well, it happened," Mitchell said. "I just came from the funeral."

"It was McCarthy, right, M-C-C-A-R-T-H-Y?"

"Right," Mitchell said. "Happened yesterday, early afternoon, on the Belt."

A long silence, then: "Sorry, Mitch. Nothing. It didn't happen."

"Of course it did," Mitchell said. "There's certainly a body at the McCarthy Funeral Home."

"A family business? I knew there was an undertaker in every Irish family somewhere."

"Seriously."

"Seriously," Moynihan said. "Have you considered the possibility that the family is, ah, being polite with the facts?"

It had occurred to Mitchell. This wouldn't be the first time somebody's pride and joy had taken a few too many little pills, or injected something naughty into his veins, and the family told the world it was an auto accident.

"How about a death certificate?"

"Vital Statistics, Mitch, not police."

"Thanks, Jerry. I *do* owe you."

Mitchell spent the next hour talking to flunkies in the Bureau of Vital Statistics, trying to find out if a death certificate had been issued the previous day for Dennis McCarthy. Then he called several hospitals near the accident scene, and came up empty. He was beginning to doubt he'd ever known a Dennis McCarthy. Then he spoke to the McCarthy Funeral Home and a rather mean-dispositioned man told him New York City death certificates no longer listed the cause of death. The certifying physician was from Manhattan, office at NYU Medical Center, but when Mitchell tried the number he got a recording saying the doctor was making hospital visits and wouldn't be back today.

The afternoon was far gone when the doorbell rang and a voice on the intercom identified itself as belonging to a police lieutenant named Maddalena. The lieutenant, when he appeared, turned out to be a nattily dressed, olive-skinned man in his middle thirties, with a leather portfolio case tucked under his arm. Mitchell thought, bet you anything he's got a master's in criminal justice.

"What can I do for you?"

Maddalena stepped into the living room at Mitchell's invitation. "Nice place."

"Thanks."

The lieutenant opened his portfolio and pulled out a thin sheaf of papers. "I'm told you were inquiring about this incident at the precinct, and again at headquarters, and the Department wasn't very helpful," he said, handing the papers to Mitchell.

On top was a computer printout of a police accident report. Attached were hand-drawn diagrams of the accident site, with a single bold line veering from the left lane of the parkway straight across into the bridge, where a heavy X marked the point of Dennis's departure from this life.

"Mind waiting while I read this?" Mitchell said.

"It's a copy."

"Why'd they send a lieutenant out on a delivery errand like this?"

Maddalena shrugged. "You've got friends, I guess. They don't want to see you waste your time."

Mitchell read the report, sitting down absently. The coroner's report said Dennis's blood alcohol was .33—plastered. The responding police officers said the smell of booze was all over the car when they pried the door open, and his shirtfront was soaked. The coroner had also discovered Dennis had a serious problem with atherosclerosis that might have killed him before be was forty.

"This certainly seems to answer my questions," Mitchell said.

"Good," Maddalena replied. "Now perhaps you'd answer a few of mine. For instance, why you've been identifying yourself on the phone as a reporter for the *Times* when they say you no longer work there. They want your ID back, by the way."

"That didn't take them long."

"So?"

"It opens doors," Mitchell said. "Makes it easier to get answers."

"What answers?"

"Mostly about Dennis being drunk," Mitchell said. "I had a hard time believing it. Dennis was a beer drinker, not whiskey. And you can't drink enough beer to bring your blood level to .33. Hell, it's hard to keep that much whiskey down without puking."

"He was a friend of yours, I take it?"

Mitchell nodded.

"And you don't think he was the type to get loaded and drive into a bridge abutment." It was a statement, not a question, so Mitchell didn't respond.

"Well," Maddalena said, rising, "take it from me. All the answers you're going to get on this case are in that report. If I were you, I'd leave it alone."

"Thanks for the advice," Mitchell said, seeing Maddalena to the door.

"Sorry about your friend," the lieutenant said as he left.

The accident report sat on the coffee table, and Mitchell stared at it. It was a photocopy, but a copy of a computer printout. The original, if you could call it that, was nothing but a bunch of little electrical charges clinging to tiny filaments of copper.

He wondered: What stake could the New York City police have in lying about the death of a small-time editor and political hack?

It was nearly dark, the days shortening rapidly toward the black city winter. From his window, Mitchell watched Maddalena climb into a city cruiser, then watched the red taillights weave down the avenue until they disappeared.

Lieutenant Carlo Maddalena arrived back at the midtown precinct house in a bad mood. He was looking at another evening of overtime, another missed dinner, another tantrum from his wife when he got home. All because of a shitty little errand they shouldn't have sent a rookie on. Driving anywhere in Manhattan in late afternoon chewed up the time, and all the work he had left on his desk two hours ago was still there. Plus some.

Plainly Rydell thought there was something wrong with the report on McCarthy's death. So what, Maddalena thought. If the truth were told, there's something wrong with just about every report that gets filed around here. There's always a patrol officer trying to make himself look good, or a witness lying through his teeth to hide an extracurricular roll in the hay, or some critical fact that gets filled in later on. You don't have time for a lot of paperwork anyway, not when it's Cops 99, Chaos 98 in the fourth quarter.

He was settling himself behind his desk with an ostentatious sigh when he was summoned to the captain's office.

Turley was the very picture of the career Irish cop, and he didn't open his mouth until Maddalena closed the door.

"So?"

"So what?" Maddalena said. "I delivered it. Anybody object if I get back to my job now?"

"What did he say?"

"Nothing."

"Nothing? Why was he so interested in one little accident report?"

Maddalena shrugged. "He said he didn't believe his buddy was that big a drinker. He said the report answered all his questions."

"Did he sound convinced?"

"No."

"Did *you* read the report? Is it questionable?"

"It looks legit," Maddalena said. "But I wasn't there. We don't send lieutenants out on accident calls. Delivery errands, yes."

"Gimme a break, Carlo," Turley said. "I wanted somebody with some smarts. The request came right from City Hall, and it never hurts to anticipate your boss. Know what I think?"

Maddalena stayed quiet. Nothing would prevent Turley from saying what he thought.

"I think maybe the thing we ought to do is follow this Rydell character for a few days . . ."

"Come on, Captain, we're stretched as it is. We can't spring a man every shift—"

"Carlo, listen," Turley interrupted. "There's something going on, and I want to know what. *Before* I hear it from downtown. So humor me, will you?"

"One guy enough, or do you want to box him?"

"One's plenty, Carlo, and don't wiseass me. I'm still your boss."

"Sorry, sir," Carlo said. "By the way, tell me something. McCarthy's blood alcohol was .33 . . ."

Turley whistled.

"Rydell said his old buddy was a beer drinker, and you can't drink enough beer to get that plastered. Can you?"

Turley laughed. "Carlo, about forty-five minutes after *I* start drinking beer I start peeing. The rest of the night, every twelve ounces going in turns into twenty-four ounces going out. You can get loaded on beer, but .33, I don't know . . ."

"I'll start on Rydell right away," Carlo said, leaving the captain's office.

His call home a few minutes later was everything Maddalena expected, and when he hung up he was angrier than he'd been before. He walked over to the bulletin board and checked the duty rosters for the evening and overnight shifts. Nearly everyone on the evening shift was out, or otherwise assigned. He picked a name off the night list: Hanna, a tenacious young cop with big ambitions. Let it drop that headquarters might be interested and Hanna would tail Mitchell Rydell into his toilet. Maddalena wrote a note to the turn-out sergeant assigning Hanna to a surveillance and noting where to pick up the target at midnight. As to the evening, Carlo had already made a decision. To hell with his old lady, he'd take the first watch on Rydell himself.

Though technically off duty, nevertheless he left word of his whereabouts at the desk and signed out an unmarked car. The rush hour was still terrible, and it took him nearly forty minutes to get back to Rydell's building. He pulled into a vacant space in front of a garage, about a hundred yards up the street from Rydell's address. From a phone booth at the corner he dialed Mitchell's number and hung up when he answered. He could see faint light through the front window of the reporter's apartment, and flickering shadows on the walls. A TV, he thought, walking back to the car.

Mental notes: Talk to the cops that filed that report. And double-check the autopsy details with the medical examiner, you never know. The McCarthy documentation was being handled as though it were bad, even if it were perfectly right. And Rydell was too smart to buy a police lieutenant hand-delivering some photocopies just as a favor.

Deduce, Maddalena thought. Reason from evidence to conclusions. Construct a logical framework, then let your gut have its say. Assume something's wrong with the McCarthy paper. What part?

That he was drunk? That no other car was involved? Was there even an accident? Was McCarthy even dead? A long time ago, Carlo had known a guy who knew a guy who had slipped out of a life of debt and boredom by getting the local police to make up an accidental death report on him, complete with autopsy. It had cost less than you might think. Last Carlo had heard, the guy was crewing on charter yachts in Australia, presumably happy as a clam.

It got close to seven, and he thought of the crummy dinner he was missing at home. He'd get a slice of pizza at the corner. Rydell seemed settled in for the night, and Carlo needed quiet and time to think, two things not on the menu at home.

Besides, waiting was something Carlo Maddalena was good at.

Laura took a cab to West 33rd Street, to a shop whose address she'd copied from the Yellow Pages. There, she rented a high-resolution hand-held video camera and a portable video-disc recorder, and bought two of the new 3½-inch laser discs, each of which would hold an hour. She used her gold American Express card for the security deposit, and had the clerk walk her through the camera's workings once to be sure she could manage it.

As she stepped out onto the sidewalk, Laura had the momentary feeling she was being followed. Her mind dismissed it as paranoia, but she walked up to 34th Street all the same and slipped through the revolving doors into Macy's. The main floor was crowded with shoppers and Laura took a roundabout route between and through them. She stopped abruptly several times and changed directions, like a browser with no special priorities, always looking, but finding no evidence of a shadow.

I'm going overboard, she thought as she approached the huge store's main doors. A security guard checked her package, and a moment later she hailed a cab outside.

The ride back to her apartment took nearly an hour and cost twenty dollars in rush-hour traffic. She ruefully wished she hadn't given in to her melodramatic inclinations and torn up David's twenty. She leaned back in her seat and rested her head against the frayed leather cushion.

The driver had the radio on and the five o'clock news was all Nazigate. In Chicago, Gillian had issued a strongly worded attack on ABC News, revealing that the *Times* had questioned him about the story and rejected it as unfounded. An ABC spokesman said they were standing by their story, which had now been picked up by nearly every major media outlet in the world.

"Christ in a sidecar," the cabbie said, honking his horn and cutting in front of a truck. "What do you make of that guy!"

Laura didn't reply. She closed her eyes and pulled the video camera closer.

When she opened the door to her apartment, Laura stood dumbfounded. Then she put down her shopping bag and began a slow inspection. Marin appeared in the kitchen doorway.

"Ta-daaa!" he said loudly. With a sweep of his arm he took in the two dozen red roses in a glass vase on the coffee table, the silver ice bucket next to it, in which rested a bottle of champagne, the crackers, Brie, fresh strawberries . . .

"There's more," Marin said. He opened the refrigerator and took out a plate carrying two cold whole lobsters on a bed of ruffled red lettuce.

"Whatever else they may say about Johnny Marin, he knows how to treat a lady," he said. Laura could almost feel her ears getting red.

"I thought you couldn't go out in daylight?" she said.

"Who has to go out?" Marin said. "A little cash goes a long way. Everybody's willing to deliver."

"What the hell do you think we're going to do here, party the night away?"

"Nah, just have fun while we do business," Marin said. "And besides, it will give you a chance to change your mind about me."

"You don't quit, do you?" Laura said. Marin pulled the champagne bottle out of the bucket and went to work on the wire.

"Never quit. Not when I see something I like."

[64]

"You call out for condoms while you were at it?" Laura said, enraged. Marin put a hurt look on his face.

"Put the bottle back," Laura said. "We have work to do."

"I'll work, you drink," Marin said as he slipped the cork out of the bottle almost noiselessly. A wisp of vapor rose at the mouth of the bottle. "I won't touch so much as a berry until I've completed all my assignments."

Laura took the champagne glass and put it down on the floor.

"Not even a sip?" Marin pouted.

"You're lucky I don't call the FBI," Laura replied. The phone jangled obtrusively at her elbow. She turned down the bell volume and the speaker volume on her answering machine, which answered after the second ring.

"Listen," Laura said. "We're going to make you a star tonight. You're going to make a statement, and I'm going to videotape it. On disc, so it's unerasable. We'll do the recording at Rydell's place if he ever calls back, otherwise we'll do it here."

"That might have been him just now," Marin said.

"I don't suppose he could have gotten through this afternoon even if he'd tried," Laura said. "Somebody was tying up the line ordering party supplies."

She rewound the tape, turned up the volume, and hit Play.

The message went by so quickly she barely had time to decipher it. Puzzled, she rewound and played it again. It was a man's voice, thin and reedy, and it said: "Channel one-oh-three, midnight, be watching."

"Channel one-oh-three?" Marin repeated. "What the hell kind of message is that?"

"A crank," Laura said. "There's a lot of them in New York. You'll fit right in. There's probably a little unscheduled smut some sewer-mouth wants to be sure I see. Here," she went on, handing Marin a yellow legal pad. "Start writing. I want you to make a point that you've never met Senator Gillian, don't know him, never have. That you've never had anything to do with him in your capacity as chief of your loony party. That you strongly deny there's ever been any link whatsoever between you and Gillian, no matter what ABC says. Plus anything else you can think of. I want it strong as hell. But none of that bullshit about Erhardt trying to kill you."

Marin mock-saluted and sat down on the floor. "I understand," he said. "A useful statement, not a true one." He began to scrawl on a pad. Laura sat down, slipped off her shoes, and took a sip of champagne. She watched Marin as he industriously covered two pages of yellow paper with his big, indistinct handwriting. Then the phone rang again, and after a moment's indecision she answered.

"Laura?" It was Mitchell.

"Listen, Mitchell," Laura said. "Can I come over to your place tonight? There's somebody you want to meet."

"I've had a long day," Mitchell said.

"So have I," Laura said, a little edge in her voice. "But it will be worth your while, I promise. And we'll bring goodies, so don't load up on dinner. Nine okay?"

"Sure."

Marin handed Laura the pad when she hung up. She skimmed and said, "Okay so far."

He went back to scrawling.

Eventually, he shoved the pad aside, saying, "That will have to do." He poured himself some champagne and, while Laura read, attacked the cheese tray.

"Tell me something," Laura said to his back. "You say you hate Gillian, one would think you'd be perfectly pleased to see him lose this election . . ."

"That's true," Marin said. "Except Gillian hasn't been trying to kill me for the past year."

"Oh, yes, that," Laura said. Marin chewed hard for a moment, then held up a finger.

"When we do this taping, I have one absolute condition . . . no, two conditions. First, the setting has to be completely nonidentifiable. I don't want anybody down at the *New York Times* jumping up and saying hey, that's Mitchie Rydell's apartment. Second, I want a safe place to stay tonight. Tomorrow I'll be out of your hair, and I'll take care of myself from then on."

"Fine," Laura said, thinking of David's nine o'clock deadline. "But I want you to call me every day. I'll give you several numbers, and don't quit until we talk. Time to go."

Marin gathered the food together while Laura slipped into her jacket. He loaded an assortment of cheeses, berries, the lobsters, and some other things into a large plastic pouch, which he slipped into the shopping bag on top of the video recorder. Then, as they were headed for the door, the phone rang again, a tiny, muffled ring, because she'd turned the volume down. She stood in the dark and listened to the rings mixing with the sound of traffic, the life of New York outside her window. Then the machine picked up.

Sewer-mouth again. "Don't forget about Channel one-oh-three. You're gonna love it," the voice said. "By the way, your boss looks great."

Click. Laura saw the red "in use" light vanish. In the ensuing darkness, nothing in the apartment looked familiar. She couldn't connect a single shadowy shape with any part of her life. She turned on the table lamp and pressed the Caller ID button on her phone to display the number from which the last incoming call had been placed. She jotted the number on a slip of paper and joined Marin in the corridor. He didn't seem to have heard anything.

"We'll walk," Laura said. "It's only about six blocks."

Neither spoke as they walked. Marin had his collar turned up high, as if dreading recognition. He can't quite live with the idea the world has forgotten about him, Laura thought. She looked at him and just knew he'd planned her seduction in detail. The thought of starring in his X-rated fantasies repelled her, as though she didn't even own her own body. I'm pretty damned horny, she thought, but not *that* horny. No way.

At the corner of Madison Avenue a young man handed them a leaflet promoting the Peace and Freedom Party's candidate for Congress. Lotsa luck, Laura thought. The incumbent hadn't gotten less than eighty percent in any of the last five elections, and that was against Republicans. They saw a man being thrown out of a restaurant, and an extraordinarily well-dressed young woman (Laura knew her to smile greetings at and assumed she was a hooker) waiting at a bus stop. Two middle-aged men, walking a silly dog, were in a shouting match across the street.

On Mitchell's block, fifty yards or so from his door, a well-dressed Puerto Rican sat in a shabby car eating pizza. His Styrofoam coffee cup cast a halo of fog on the windshield.

Rydell received them in jeans, sneakers, and a cashmere sweater, looked at Marin, and said, "Well, I'll be damned."

"I take it you recognize me," Marin said.

"From your photos," Mitchell said. "I did some research, you know."

Laura was unloading the groceries. "We owe the feast to our guest," she said. "Let me fill you in a little."

She gave Mitchell a ten-minute recap of the day's events, starting with her clobbering Marin on the stairs and ending with her second phone message.

"Channel one-oh-three," Mitchell said, leafing through his cable guide. "Here we are. It isn't normally on at midnight."

"No surprise," Laura said.

"It's an evangelical Baptist cartoon channel for Hispanic children. Iglesia Nueva. Only in New York."

"That where the guy wanted you to see the dirty movie?" Marin said.

"It's been known to happen," Laura replied.

"In fact," said Mitchell, "it's a problem for the cable operators. Remember Captain Midnight, the guy that raided HBO a few years back?"

Marin nodded.

"Well, they haven't really bothered doing anything to prevent it, since they regard it as more a nuisance than anything else. It's a game, a way for techies to amuse themselves."

Laura had the video camera out of the shopping bag and was reading the instruction booklet. Mitchell put a beer down next to her and she grunted thanks.

"Now you take Ms. Madison here, she's like me," Mitchell said. "It always took me two hours to wire my stereo speakers, and meanwhile the techies are into missiles and lasers in outer space. If you don't mind my asking, just what do you plan to do with that thing?"

"I had Hitler here write out a statement refuting the charges about Senator Gillian," Laura said. "I'm going to tape him tonight, and release it to the press tomorrow."

"Not here, you're not," Mitchell said.

"Why?" Laura demanded, her voice rising. "I'd have thought you'd jump at it."

"I would," Mitchell said. "But despite my recent unemployment I keep thinking of myself as a reporter, and every time a story like this comes anywhere near a reporter, a bell goes off and the word 'exclusive' pops up in his head like a red flag. If you're planning a general release of this thing tomorrow, count me out."

"I can't believe you're taking such a selfish attitude," Laura said. "This is the survival of our electoral process that's at stake . . ."

"And my reportorial instincts have more to do with that than you're willing to admit," Mitchell countered. "I *do* take myself and my role seriously, you know. This story hinges on judgment, my own, ABC's, Gillian's. These are people society allows to lead them. It's a responsibility, and I'm not willing to share that with the whole world. This is either my story alone, or I'm out of it completely."

"I expected better from you," Laura said hotly. "I really did. A decent, honorable man is being smeared and all you can think of is getting back onto your newspaper."

"I'm a reporter, and a newspaper is where I belong," Mitchell said. They heard Marin snickering in the corner.

"What's so funny?" Laura demanded.

"You two," Marin replied. "You know, there's nothing to prevent me from taking a hike right now, and leaving you two lovebirds to your little spat. I've managed on my own before."

Mitchell took a swallow of beer. "He's right," he said to Laura. Then, to Marin: "What are you willing to do?"

"I'll make your tape," Marin said to Laura. "But Mitch has a valid claim. He's the one who did all the work on this thing and came up empty, after all. All those hot hours in Arizona. All those phone calls to the county clerk . . ."

"So?"

"So here's the drill," Marin said. "Rydell here reports the story on tape—"

"Disc—"

"Okay, disc. He identifies me, asks questions, and I answer. Then I keep myself available only to you two for the

[69]

duration of the campaign. Day after election, all conditions are off."

"And I get all day tomorrow," Mitchell said. "Until this time tomorrow, with exclusive use of the . . . disc . . . to give to whomever I choose. I assure you it will get wide dissemination quickly. And you've still got a week until election."

Laura sighed and shook her head, too tired to argue. "I suppose so," she said.

"Can I see the statement?" Mitchell said. As he was reading, Marin and Laura picked a corner of the apartment and removed two framed prints from the wall.

"Careful with those," Mitchell called, not looking up. "They're Chagalls."

"I know," Laura said. "His production of *The Magic Flute*."

"You know Mozart?" Mitchell said, glancing at Laura.

"I went to school with his sister," she replied. She pushed an armchair into the corner and turned on all the lights in the living room.

"Probably the brightest light in Manhattan," Marin said. "Ready when you are."

Laura propped the video camera on the coffee table and carefully wired it to the videodisc recorder. She peered through the eyepiece. Mitchell sat down in the corner armchair and looked at the camera. Laura pointed a finger at him and he began to speak.

"This is Mitchell Rydell. I am a free-lance journalist in New York City. Until recently I worked for one of the newspapers here. In that capacity I was approached about two months ago by an old acquaintance who offered me what he called an exclusive story linking Senator Amos V. Gillian and the neo-Nazi organization called the True American Bund . . ."

Mitchell spoke for five minutes, summarizing all the known evidence on the story. Computerized land records in Arizona showed that Senator Gillian owned a twenty-acre parcel outside of Phoenix. Numerous sources in Phoenix, including the local police, reported that the Bund had met there on several occasions. He described the evidence that had been given to him . . . and which he had rejected, only to see it come to light through other media. He stressed that there were no eyewitnesses, no one source who could definitively connect Gillian to Marin or to the Bund.

As to Marin himself, Mitchell said, he had been rumored to be dead, and was believed dead by federal authorities. He had last been heard of in South Africa, where a small force of his self-described commandos was trying to help extreme right-wing elements in their continuing guerrilla actions against black nationalist forces.

However, Marin was not dead, Mitchell went on. "He is, in fact, sitting a few feet from me. We are at a location which I will not disclose, for obvious reasons. I want to ask him to take my place before the camera at this time."

They made the switch with the camera running.

"Mr. Marin," Mitchell said from off-camera, "have you ever met Senator Gillian?"

"No, sir," Marin replied.

"Have you ever spoken with him on the telephone?"

"No."

"Corresponded?"

"Never."

"Had any communication with him whatsoever?"

"Not for a moment," Marin said. "I do not know the gentlemen other than from the TV. From what I've heard of him, I doubt I'd like him."

"Have you ever met on property owned by him?"

"Not to my knowledge," Marin said.

"What about your meetings in Phoenix, Arizona?"

"We met on *my* property in Phoenix," Marin said. "Senator Gillian may have owned it at a different time, but it belonged to me when we met and trained there."

"When did you sell it, and to whom?"

"I did not sell it," Marin said. "The ownership record on the county computer simply changed."

"How could that be?"

"Damned if I know," Marin said. "I don't know anything about computers, except I don't like them."

There was a short silence. "Mr. Marin," Mitchell said, "are you prepared to say right now that to the full extent of your knowledge there is no truth whatsoever to the charges linking your organization to Senator Amos V. Gillian?"

"I have never had the slightest connection with the Senator in my life, and neither has anyone in the Bund," Marin said.

"You can speak for every member?"

Marin smiled. "We have discipline in the Bund. Something the rest of American society could benefit from."

"Mr. Marin," Mitchell said in a folksy voice, changing the tone of the testimony. "Aren't you supposed to be dead?"

"So they tell me," Marin said, chuckling.

"So what are you doing here? Are you a ghost?"

"Hell, you can't believe what you hear from the FBI," Marin said. "They didn't know where to find me when they had my home address. Still, I guess I'm dead on their computer," he added, dragging out the word with a sneer.

"What is your mother's maiden name?" Mitchell asked.

"O'Connor," Marin replied.

"When and where were you born?"

"I was born in Brooklyn Hospital, in New York, on August 25, 1949. I attended the New York City public schools, Erasmus Hall High School, and Fordham University. I got a B-plus in calculus my second year at Fordham, from Reverend Paul Quigley. Try me on all the details of my life. I was there for all of them."

"One last thing," Mitchell said. He lunged into the camera's view and handed Marin a newspaper. "Would you hold that newspaper up to the camera, please?"

Marin complied. It was that morning's paper, with its Nazigate headlines.

"That should do," Mitchell whispered to Laura, and she turned the camera off. She cued up the recording to review it, and Laura thought it was too dark, then realized she could not erase and re-record videodisc. "It will have to do," she said.

It was nearly eleven o'clock and Mitchell, to celebrate, brought out three beers, then switched on the television.

"News time," he announced.

"Now," Marin said, leaning forward. "As to my conditions. I'm satisfied the setting was unrecognizable. Where do I stay tonight?"

"I don't see much choice this late but for you to stay here," Mitchell said. "Us old Brooklyn boys ought to manage all right." He turned to Laura. "You going home to watch your private show, or you want to check it out here?"

"Oh," Laura said. "I'd almost forgotten." She looked at her watch. "I want to see the news, and I doubt I can make it back to my place between the end of the news and midnight."

Mitchell merely nodded and leaned back in his chair. The late news began, and as Laura expected, Gillian was the lead. She rushed to turn up the volume as the Senator was seen in the United boarding area at O'Hare Airport.

". . . absolutely untrue," he was saying. "I not only deny it categorically, I defy ABC or any other news organization to present a single witness, or a single shred of credible evidence to the contrary."

Continuing his best-defense offense, Laura thought, and doing it well. After about twelve minutes the broadcast moved on to the weather, then sports, both done in laugh-a-minute style. Laura realized she was looking around the room and smiling.

"What?" said Mitchell.

"Just thinking. What an odd group. I'm the only one of us who really cares whether Gillian wins or loses. To one of you he's a story, to the other, an old enemy . . ."

"A matter of complete indifference," Marin insisted.

"Maybe. You may think this naïve, but I do believe in him. I think he's an honorable man, with worthwhile ideas, and I think he'd be an excellent president."

"He might be, even yet," Mitchell said, but Laura shook her head.

"No, not now, no matter how this story turns out. He's been accused, and that's all that matters these days." She fell silent, the news ended, and nobody in the room moved. The room seemed somehow darker than normal, the glow and noise of the city more immediate, more threatening. A few minutes before midnight Mitchell got up and punched 103 into the channel selector. A test pattern of colored bars appeared on the screen.

"This better be good," he said. "If it's just another of Ugly George's girl-in-the-street interviews, I'll be very disappointed."

Midnight passed and the three of them sat in various poses

of fatigue, staring at the unchanging screen. Finally, Laura was about to give up when a succession of distortions raced through the image, and a typeset message appeared on the screen:

Are you watching, Madison?

"I'll be damned," Mitchell said. "Somebody's gone to some trouble."

"Shhh."

The title card stayed on the screen for more than a minute, while Laura felt her stomach grow increasingly fluttery. Then the screen went black, and moments later lit up again. The new image was a crisp color photo. The sky in the photo was deep blue, with wisps of cloud. Senator Gillian stood there in casual clothing, smiling, sun on his face and not a care in the world.

A dun-colored mesa rose behind him, over a featureless gray brown desert. His right arm dangled fraternally across the broad shoulders of Jonathan Marin.

Mitchell leaped across the room and punched on his VCR. The photo stayed on the screen for another thirty seconds while Laura stared at it dumbfounded. Then she turned to Marin.

"What the hell are you trying to pull?" she demanded.

"It's a fake!" Marin shouted, jumping up.

"Sure it is," Mitchell said, crouched in front of the TV. "Give me a break. *Look* at the damn thing, for pity's sake. The *National Enquirer* couldn't paste you two together that well. You have some explaining to do."

"I swear to you . . ." Marin began, but Mitchell hushed him. The photo had vanished, and more type had taken its place.

Senator Gillian must admit the truth.
No more evasions or denials.
This photo will be broadcast
during Monday Night Football the
night before election. Think it over.

The screen reverted to the test pattern.

"That's the Giants and the Redskins," Mitchell said. "Forty million people will be watching."

"It's like having a knife held to your throat," Laura said.

Mitchell strode across the room and pulled Marin to his feet. "You've been lying to us all night," he said. "And very persuasively, too, I might add."

"No, I haven't," Marin said. "I swear it."

"I don't believe you," Mitchell said. He turned to Laura. "Needless to say, all bets are off. I won't take this project a step further, and if *you* try to, I'll call a news conference of my own."

"Mitchell, damn it," Laura said. "Think! Doesn't this whole thing strike you as a little . . . contrived?"

Mitchell said nothing.

"If somebody had a photo like that," Laura went on, "a picture of Senator Gillian with this . . . this worm . . ."

"Hold on there," Marin interjected.

"Shut up," Mitchell said, "before I feed you your teeth."

"If such a photo existed," Laura said, "why don't they just give out prints? Why the secrecy? Why show it just to me, in such a cloak-and-dagger way? Remember, you weren't expected to see it, just me."

Mitchell frowned. "You've got a point," he said. He turned to Marin. "Out in the hall," he said. "Laura and I need to talk in private."

"I'm telling you the photo is a fraud," Marin said. "I don't know what I can do to satisfy you."

"You can't," Mitchell said. "The photo is real."

"You throw me out, I might just take off," Marin said. "And you need me."

"Don't look that way to me," Mitchell said. "How would a quick phone call to the FBI strike you, let them know you're in town?"

"Fuck you," Marin said.

"Outside," Mitchell repeated. When Marin had gone out in the hall, Mitchell came over to Laura and spoke in a low tone.

"It doesn't seem logical," he said. "Not the way to handle

[75]

a true story. Somebody should be stepping forward with proof, not sliding it under the carpet like this."

"You really think the photo is genuine?" Laura said.

"How could it not be? You saw it as well as I did. That's no cut-and-paste job. But the mere fact that the photo exists doesn't mean anything. Senators get their pictures taken all the time, with all kinds of people. He goes on a golf outing and some schmoe wants a photo for his office. So what? The main thing is, somebody's using it to blackmail a presidential candidate, and doing it very secretly, as if they can't stand too much scrutiny. Nobody in the news media was meant to see it. They—whoever they are—are trying to send it direct to Gillian by way of you. And he's got to respond. You had it right, it's like a knife held to your throat, because you don't know where they'll stop."

"Where does that leave us?"

"The blackmail is potentially a better story than the Nazi connection ever was," Mitchell replied. "But as to Gillian and you, I don't know."

"But you said yourself the photo doesn't mean anything," Laura protested.

"Not in and of itself," Mitchell said. "But Gillian has been so forceful about denying he's ever even *met* our buddy. A lot could be made of it."

Mitchell started to the door to call Marin inside, but turned to Laura with his hand on the knob.

"I'm going to get into this story as quickly as I can," he said. "But as a reporter. I don't work for Gillian."

"Understood," Laura said, and their eyes locked for a moment. "What are you going to do with him?"

"We'll see."

"There's something you should know." She filled Mitchell in quickly about her meeting with David, and the prospect that the FBI was already aware of Marin's presence in New York. Mitchell merely shrugged, equal parts indecision and annoyance. He opened the door.

"You have any baggage or anything?" he said.

"Just a sack I left in the checkroom at Penn Station," Marin said.

"We'll get it in the morning," Mitchell said. "There's a

[76]

little hotel a few blocks from here that the *Times* uses when we have people working on stories where we don't want leaks, or when we've got a source to conceal. All the rooms have little kitchens, you can stay there comfortably for quite a while. I think you should stay within call for a few days."

Laura was loading the video camera into its bag. "I'll be in touch," she told Mitchell, "when I figure out what the hell happens next."

She slipped out into the corridor, then leaned against the wall to wait for the elevator. A small ache was growing in her back. A few moments later she was walking the deserted pavement. Each street lamp cast a small circle of light, and cars were parked nose to tail. For an odd second or two she couldn't hear a sound, not even traffic. Then she glanced across the street and saw the shabby car she and Marin had passed earlier. Now, a body slumped back in the shadows of the front seat. She could see shoulders and a head, wrapped in darkness, and imagined eyes watching her as she hurried to the corner.

Mitchell threw an assortment of old clothes into an over-night bag while Marin watched from the bedroom door.

"Nice looking girl," Marin said. "Just the way I like them. Young, tight, good complexion."

Mitchell didn't respond. He took out his wallet and pulled two twenty-dollar bills from it, which he shoved into the case among the underwear.

"This should cover your immediate needs," he said. "We'll pick up your bag in the morning."

"You're a lucky guy," Marin said.

"How's that?" Mitchell replied.

"Oh, you know," Marin said. "Me, now, it's been a long time since I saw a piece of ass that nice. I've mostly been among, shall we say, darker ladies?"

"I'm reconsidering feeding you your teeth," Mitchell said.

"Hey, no offense," Marin said. "Just trying to compliment your lady."

"She's not my lady," Mitchell said.

"You could have fooled me."

Mitchell shoved the overnight case into his hands. "Listen," he said, "I may need you handy, but I won't hesitate to turn you in if you piss me off enough, and you're well on your way to pissing me off enough."

"I won't say another word," Marin said. And he didn't, all the way down in the elevator, outside as they walked to the hotel, or in the lobby as Mitchell checked him in. Mitchell showed the clerk his *Times* ID, as if that explained anything that might happen in this hotel at 1:30 in the morning. Mitchell got a single key and kept it.

Upstairs they found a plainly appointed room with a window overlooking the ventilating ducts, and a kitchenette of chipped and stained Formica.

"Sit tight," Mitchell said. "I've got a call to make." He watched Marin toss his suitcase on the bed and dismiss him with a casual wave.

Downstairs, Mitchell slipped into a phone booth and pulled his small book of numbers from his hip pocket. He dialed and waited while the phone rang eight or ten times.

Finally: "Aaaaggh, yeah?"

"Dominick?"

"What?"

"Dominick? Mitchell Rydell."

"Who?"

"Mitchell."

"It's one-fucking-thirty in the fucking morning."

"I know, I'm sorry, but it's important."

"To you, maybe," Dominick said.

"You still work for Manhattan Cable?"

"Why, your signal crap out in the middle of *Fort Lauderdale Wet Dream*? Call service in the morning."

"I just saw something on an unused channel," Mitchell said. "One of those unauthorized break-ins . . ."

"Happens all the time. Don't tell me you're offended."

"I just want to know how it's done," Mitchell said. "You guys must have figured it out."

"Does it have to be now?" Dominick said. He sounded fully awake.

"No, but it has to be soon, tomorrow morning," Mitchell said. "It's important."

"So you said. I'm heading for the Island first thing in the morning," Dominick said.

"I'll come out," Mitchell said. "I'll bring lunch."

"Whatever you say. Can I go back to sleep now?"

Mitchell, chuckling, got out of the phone booth. He'd rent a car in the morning and be on Sapphire Island by noon or so. He'd stop for goodies along the way. Youthful memories of bikinis and beer swam through his mind, memories of fucking on blankets, and picking sand out of his crotch. Now, he thought, to tuck in our little Nazi safe and sound. He rode back upstairs and let himself into the room.

Marin was gone. The suitcase lay unopened on the bed. The wrinkles were still there where Marin had been sitting. The window was closed, and the single bedside lamp still burned.

Checking in, Maddalena thought. He was standing on the corner diagonally opposite the hotel, in the shadows. Rydell and another man had disappeared into the hotel lobby five minutes before. Probably time enough, he thought, and started across the street.

He'd brace the clerk. Rydell might use his own name checking in, or another. They might have gotten separate rooms. They might have said something strange to the clerk. You could never tell. Something might be learned.

Maddalena was crossing a small alleyway between the hotel and an office building when a tiny movement caught his eye. He pressed himself against the stone corner and watched. In the alley, lights out, was a white car. Two men emerged from a back door of the hotel, lugging a large package slung over their shoulders. One of them opened the trunk, and a small light flashed on. Carlo saw the license plate and mentally noted the number. The men dumped their bundle into the trunk and shut it quietly, then checked up and down the alley. Carlo stepped back around the corner, holding his breath. Beneath his coat his hand closed on his sidearm. He heard the engine start up, and when he looked again the car was pulling away. He watched for a moment, then went in to talk to the desk clerk.

Thursday, October 31

At eight the next morning the ringing phone woke Laura up. The light coming in the window was gray and wet and she heard the slipping hiss of car tires below. Rain, she thought, reaching for the receiver.

"Well, good morning," Cavanagh's voice said. "Nice to find you in."

"I was going to call you," Laura said.

"When?" Cavanagh said. "You'd have missed me. I'm out a lot. I work on a presidential campaign, you know."

"Felix—" Laura began.

"All I called for," Cavanagh interrupted, "was to find out what you were up to. I tried several times last night."

"There were no messages," Laura said.

"I don't talk to robots," Cavanagh replied. "Anyway we're moving right along on Saturday's parade of saints. We've gotten quite a little list of testimonials . . ."

"Felix, I'd go easy if I were you," Laura said, sitting up and pulling her pajamas around her to ward off the chill.

"Didn't you get Marin on tape?"

"I got it," Laura said. "A nice strong statement."

"So, what could be wrong with that?"

"Gillian and Marin have met, and there's a photo to prove it," Laura said.

"Photo? What photo? Show me," Cavanagh said.

"I can't," Laura replied. "I don't have it. It was shown to me, and I was warned that if the Senator doesn't come clean they'll spread it all over the airwaves before the election."

[81]

"Who's they?"

"I don't know," Laura said. "They."

"You don't know!" Cavanagh shouted. "Who showed you the picture?"

"Nobody, nobody in particular," Laura said. "Listen, it was broadcast on cable last night, on an unused channel, with the warning. I was alerted to tune in by an anonymous phone call. The photo could have been transmitted from anywhere, for all I know, clear across the country. Senator Gillian is standing out in a desert someplace, like maybe that Arizona site they're talking about, and he's got his arm over Marin's shoulders."

"You're sure it was Marin?"

"Felix, the genuine article was sitting six feet from me at the time."

"And where is he now?"

"Holed up in a hotel," Laura said. "Rydell is riding herd on him."

"Well, we can't ask all those people to give their little spiels for the boss with this hanging over our heads," Cavanagh said.

"Clearly not."

"What's your solution? You always have all the answers."

Laura looked out the window from her bed. The rain pelted the glass.

"The photo itself won't prove anything. It could have been taken at a golf outing or something. The Senator may not even have known who he was posing with. If he comes clean now, admits he may have met Marin, he might be able to defuse the photo as a weapon, but otherwise it's going to be devastating. Unless . . ."

"Unless?"

"Unless I can find the people doing this between now and the election," Laura said. "Can you call somebody at the phone company and get the location of the phone from which that call was made?" She fetched the piece of paper from her bag and read it to Cavanagh.

There was a long silence on the line. "You realize," Cavanagh said at last, "that our friends are about as anonymous as you can get these days? Nothing covers your tracks like a little technology."

[82]

Laura was silent, agreeing with Cavanagh. She watched the rain course down the windowpane like tears of frustration.

"The media are really camped on our doorsteps now," Cavanagh said. "A regular death watch. Some idiot editorialist on the local TV last night even compared the boss to Josef Mengele. The old menace lurking in our midst all these years, et cetera, et cetera. It was enough to make you puke."

"That's how they think," Laura said. "It's the only way they know. Pick a slogan that fits. Racism, anti-Semitism, you name it . . ."

There was another long silence, until Laura said, "Listen, I'll be in touch, okay?" and hung up. She had barely put the phone down when it rang again. She let it ring three times while she put on her bathrobe and slippers.

"He's gone," a voice said when she answered.

"Mitchell?"

"Our old buddy, he flew the coop," Mitchell said. "Just thought I'd let you know."

"What the hell are you talking about?"

"I took him to the hotel and checked him in," Mitchell said. "Then I went to use the phone in the lobby for five minutes, and when I went back upstairs he was gone. Without a trace, as they say."

"Without a trace?" Laura said, her voice rising. "You let him out of your sight after all he said last night about bolting?"

"I was in the damn lobby, Laura, and he didn't go out that way," Mitchell said. "And what was it, two minutes?"

"Why did you leave him in the first place?"

"What did you think I was going to do, sleep with him?"

"Great," Laura said. "Just peachy."

"Listen, he came to you in the first place," Mitchell said. "He won't go far now. He'll be in touch."

"And I'm supposed to just sit by the phone? Goddammit, I ask you to do one simple thing—"

"*You* ask *me* to do—" Mitchell said, his voice jumping an octave. "Listen, Miss Bigshot, I don't work for you, thank God. And Marin was your bundle from the beginning . . ."

"Were you this effective on the *Times*?" Laura snapped. "No wonder they fired you."

"Whoa, I can see I misjudged you," Mitchell said. "Well,

[83]

let me ask you a favor, Laura—or excuse me, *Ms.* Madison. Take your pinstripe suits, your briefcase, your problem and your whole ball-busting attitude, and go to hell." The phone slammed in Laura's ear. None of that was right, she thought, fighting the urge to hurl the phone across the room. Not a word of that came out the way it was supposed to. Jesus H. Christ, I'm barely awake ten minutes. How would it be if I just curled up in the closet?

She made coffee in a trance. Cavanagh's a professional martyr, she thought, Marin's crazy, David's so cold it's scary and he hates my guts besides, and Mitchell's . . . whatever he is. Funny, isn't it? The slightest little departure from adulation and they go right into their "ball-bustin' bitch" routine. Yeah, funny is what it is. A scream. And my pinstripe suits and my briefcase.

So Marin's gone, off for parts unknown. Rydell's taking his bruised ego back to his cave to recuperate. You're on your own again, girl. Well, there's something to be said for having yourself for company. At least *I'm* not offended by my pinstripe suits.

While she was in the shower the phone rang again. It was Cavanagh. Laura stood wrapped in a towel, making a small puddle on her polished wood floor.

"That number," Cavanagh said. "It's a public booth at the corner of Eightieth and Park Avenue."

"Jesus," said Laura. "That's practically right downstairs."

She took a cab to the New York Public Library. The rain was stopping indecisively, and the morning mist seemed to be lifting a little, so there was more sky above her moment by moment.

During the ride, she put herself once more through her list of options.

One: Find the photographer who had taken the picture of Gillian and Marin, or the lab that had processed it. But the scenic background of the photo suggested only the Southwest, and that was a big area. Even if she started with Arizona, since that was where Marin's property was supposed to be, there was no assurance either the photographer or the lab was local. How many commercial photo labs were there in Arizona, New Mexico, Nevada?

Besides, she didn't want to shelve herself in Arizona when people were watching her apartment from across the street, following her every move . . .

Two: Pin down the cable broadcast. She'd called Iglesia Nueva, the church group assigned to channel 103, before leaving her apartment. They spoke little English and neither knew nor cared what happened on their channel when they were off the air. Manhattan Cable had told her Iglesia Nueva shared a transmitter in Westchester County with about thirty other organizations, but that nothing had been sent from that transmitter on channel 103 after 8:02 the previous night.

Could the signal have come from somewhere else? She hoped to pursue that question in the library.

Three: Make whoever was responsible show themselves. Rattle them. But how was she going to rattle someone who was holding all the cards and staying safely anonymous?

Four: Go back to Rydell. He had the reporter's instincts and the contacts to pursue these and other avenues. That will be a cold day in hell, Laura thought as she paid the driver.

The lights were on inside the huge old building, and it looked more inviting than anywhere Laura had been in days. She almost ran up the steps.

In Microfilm she searched back issues of the *Times* for accounts of Captain Midnight's intrusion into the HBO cable channel a few years earlier. It was slow going because she didn't know the date and had to check every year's index under several headings, but she finally had the story on the screen. It confirmed what she had suspected: It wasn't particularly hard to break into a cable channel. The pirate signal could have come from just about anywhere.

She searched the indexes for information on Jonathan Marin.

There wasn't much, *Times* policy being to ignore what it considered political extremists. But there was a Sunday supplement story almost six years old about the paramilitary training camp Marin was then running in Arizona. The scenery was what she remembered from the photo on TV. There was Marin, in the embrace of a noted Afrikaner militia leader. The South

African was taller than Marin by nearly a foot, and looked fierce in combat fatigues.

The photo she'd seen had been taken—or faked—on Marin's property, Laura was sure. Where was that land? Marin said the deed had vanished from the clerk's office. The True American Bund's training camp had turned back into unmarked desert.

In the street she hailed a cab and went to ABC headquarters. People were streaming through the lobby and Laura moved against the flow to the security desk, where she asked for Melissa Lyons and was told the reporter was in Iowa with the campaign. She asked to speak to the managing editor of the evening news. After the guard dialed the phone again, he handed the handset to her. She waited a long time.

"Stuart McDonald, how can I help you?"

"This is Laura Madison, with Senator Gillian's campaign. I'm in the lobby and I'd like to talk to you."

"Go ahead." The voice conceded nothing.

"Would it be possible for me to come upstairs?"

"Actually, it's a little hectic up here just now," McDonald said. "We could make an appointment for tomorrow . . ."

"No, this is okay," Laura said. "I don't need much of your time."

"Should you be talking to a reporter?" McDonald said. "Melissa Lyons, perhaps?"

"I understand she's in Iowa," Laura replied, "and this is urgent."

McDonald said nothing. Laura went on, "It's about the Jonathan Marin story."

"You have a statement from the Senator?"

"No, a request," Laura said. "We'd like to get in touch with whoever led Ms. Lyons to that story."

"I hope you're not asking her to reveal a source," McDonald said. "Because she won't tell, and I don't know."

"I don't want to know who it is, I just want them to get in touch with us. We want to talk to them."

"I'll pass on the message," McDonald said. "It will be up to Melissa how far she's willing to go with it. There's a condition . . . as soon as the Senator is willing to talk about this, we get it exclusively."

"I don't see how we can promise you exclusivity on something like that," Laura said.

"First crack, then, with general release to follow," McDonald insisted.

"Okay," Laura said. She gave McDonald her home phone number, then left the lobby. It was midafternoon, gray and cold, and she decided to walk home. Her nose and ears stung by the time she reached her building, and the stairs were daunting, she was so tired.

She came finally to her door, and unlocked it. Then, as she reached for the wall switch to turn on a light, the reading lamp across the room came on.

Instantaneous thoughts: The spray can of Mace in her pocketbook. Jump back out into the hall.

Then she caught her breath.

"David," she said. Her ex-husband was sitting cross-legged in her reading chair, comfortable as could be. "Isn't breaking and entering illegal, even for the FBI?"

"We've got a lot to talk about, babe," David said.

"Not now, David," Laura said. "I'm in the middle of a tough day."

"I believe it," David said. "For a while there I thought you had flown the coop entirely."

"David, just what is it you want?"

"I want to talk about Johnny Marin, of course," David said. He stood up and came over to Laura.

"Well, I don't want to talk about him," Laura said. "I have nothing to say. Try Rydell."

"Oh, we will, if and when we find him," David said. "Funny, his disappearing and your going off at the same time . . ."

"I was at the library, David, the damned library."

"We almost jumped to the conclusion you two were, ah, together."

Laura smiled at him and brushed by into the kitchen, where she put a kettle of water on the range.

"Has it occurred to you that maybe, just maybe, another agent would be better on this case than you?" she said.

"Case?" David repeated. "There's a case? That's good to

hear, Laura. You at least seem to realize something unusual is going on."

"David, I'm making water for *one* cup of tea. When it's ready I intend to sit down in *my* armchair and enjoy it. You'll be gone by then, so if you're heading for a point, you'd better get there quickly."

"Marin's dead, dear heart," David said, relishing Laura's reaction. "In kind of an odd way, to tell the truth. We found his body in the front seat of a rented car in a very bad neighborhood, full of bullet holes. Maybe the darkies he loved so much finally took offense in a meaningful way."

"I don't believe you," Laura said.

"Want to see? His body is still at the ME's office. It ain't pretty, but if you need convincing, it'll do the trick."

"It just doesn't make any sense," Laura said, too tired to think.

"What kind of intrigue were you two cooking up?" David said.

"Cooking up?"

"Obviously, Marin was supposed to refute this Nazi story in some way. You had to be planning to use him to rescue Gillian's campaign. So what happened, he turn on you? Try to shake you down?"

"He came to me, David. We never sought him out."

"I know, I know," David said. "Try this on for size. Marin comes to you, and you think it's a gift from heaven. Here's one of the principals in the story willing to disavow it entirely. So you go with that for a while, then when he starts naming his price, it's way out of line. But it turns out he's also ready to back up every sentence of the ABC report, if they'll meet the price tag. And he figures he can get the dough from Erhardt easy. They've got lots of money. So you put all your heads together and decide there's only one thing to do."

"David, you've been reading too many Travis McGee books," Laura said. "How about hitting the road now?"

"Okay," David said, shrugging. "Maybe you figured nobody would worry too much over anything that happens to a sleaze-ball like Marin. But you *were* the last to see him alive."

"Next to last."

"Ah, Rydell," David said. "We'll find him, eventually. In

[88]

any case, you are now what we law-enforcement professionals call a key witness, maybe even a suspect, so much as I hate to use an old cliché, I have to ask you not to leave town for the next few days."

"Come off it, David, I work on a presidential campaign. I have to travel." Her kettle was whistling.

"Don't make it hard on yourself."

"Look," Laura said. "If you don't want me to leave New York, go get a court order. And the Senator's lawyers will fight it. Meanwhile, get out of here."

David smiled, bowed, and left without another word. Alone, Laura looked at her watch. Did she dare call Rydell, now that it was a sure bet her phone was tapped? Would *they* call? She thought of Marin on a slab at the medical examiner's office. He had vanished from the hotel at, what, one-thirty? David hadn't said when the body was found. *They* acted fast. Refute Marin's denial, then shuffle Marin himself offstage. And last night's call had come from a phone barely a hundred yards from where she sat. No two ways about it anymore, she thought. I've got to get hold of Rydell.

The car rental attendant brought up a dark blue Dodge, parked it in the lot entrance, and sprinted back to the office with his jacket pulled up over his head. The rain was angling down hard and cold, and the attendant's hand felt clammy when he handed Mitchell the keys.

"When you gonna bring it back?"

"Tonight sometime."

"You do, you bring it here to park, okay? Don't leave it on the street."

Mitchell signed the papers and looked uncertainly out at the rain. The office windows were fogged over and he could hear the steady tattoo of icy pellets hitting the pavement. The attendant was waiting for the small computer terminal on his desk to clear Mitchell's rental. The system automatically scanned police records of all fifty states for stolen drivers' licenses, drunk driving convictions, insurance revocations, and recent moving violations. All this data could be conveyed to subscribers in about forty-five seconds. The computer whirred a little and presented the attendant with a clearance code. He smiled at Rydell.

"Lovely day," he said. "Where you headed?" Mitchell started to reply, stopped himself, then laughed at his own paranoia.

"Sapphire Island," he said. "Looks like a beach day to me." He nodded at the attendant and ran across the driveway, splashing through deep puddles until his shoes and socks were squishy. In the driver's seat he shook water from his hands and wiped his face, muttering vague curses. He was still seething at Madison, his anger compounded by the weather and the prospect of an interminable drive through Long Island traffic.

He'd tried to reach Dominick at home in Manhattan, thinking he may have reconsidered going to the Island, but there was no answer. So we drink inside instead of on the porch, Mitchell thought as he pulled out into crosstown traffic.

He turned south on Second Avenue and inched down to the Midtown Tunnel, then into Queens. After an hour he had gotten past the 1964 World's Fair Grounds, with some of its monuments still intact and others inexorably crumbling to earth. At each tollgate on the expressway, he slipped his Cash Card through the laser reader, which automatically debited the amount of his toll from his checking account. He kept the car dutifully to 55, both because of the rain and in deference to the "seeing eyes," the cameras mounted on posts every hundred yards or so, activated by radar signals to take photos of speeders for automatic ticketing by mail. If I were more of a civil libertarian, or just had the spare time, I'd speed past every one of the damn things and take them to court, Mitchell thought.

By the time he reached Glen Cove the rain had settled into an all-day pour, traffic had lightened, and he was accustomed to the car's oversteer and slippery handling. Living in the city, Mitchell didn't drive much. Despite the rain and fog he recognized landmarks along the road. He spotted a liquor market and stopped for two six-packs and two bags of potato chips. A mile or two further along he picked up a large bucket of fried chicken. A beach feast, the traditional way, he thought, as the smell of fried fat filled the car and steamed the windows.

The ferry, to Mitchell's relief, was running despite the

weather. He waited on the loading ramp for ten minutes, then saw it appear out of the fog like a ghost ship. It was empty, and the ferryman huddled over the drive controls in oilcloth foul-weather gear. Charon on the River Styx, Mitchell thought, looking east toward the whitecaps that glinted against the black water of Orient Harbor, repeating endlessly into the gray-white void.

The ferryman tied up to the pilings on either side of the ramp and opened the chain gate. He stepped aside as the Dodge slid onto the metal deck. Mitchell pulled to the center as directed, then rolled his window down a few inches.

The hooded figure bent over until Mitchell saw a nose and a pair of eyeglasses within.

"Three bucks."

The rain sliced into the car as Mitchell handed over the money.

"You sure there *is* another side?" he said, but the ferryman was already gone.

He had the ferry to himself when they cast off a few minutes later. Soon both shores were invisible, and he watched the choppy waves that crested above the ferry deck. To Mitchell's astonishment, gulls swooped low over the water, battling for headway into the wind. He leaned forward, nose only inches from the windshield, and watched the gray wall of mist until he thought he saw the island. First came the word "Lite" in red neon, then the dark shape of the dockside grill, more of a shack than anything else. Then foliage composed itself in the grayness, and a darker streak that turned into the road leading to the ferry slip. There was nobody waiting.

The ferry slid smoothly into the ramp and the ferryman went about his tying-up ritual. Mitchell waved, unacknowledged, and drove onto Sapphire Island.

Dominick's house was raised on pilings facing the water, the last of a row of nearly identical wood-sided cottages partially obscured by tall hedges overgrown with beach grass. Modest dunes separated the houses from the deserted stretch of beach. Dom was waiting on the enclosed porch when Mitchell pulled in.

"You showed up," he said, pushing the screen door open. "You must be desperate for company."

"If I'll settle for you, I must be," Mitchell said. He shook water from his clothing. The porch was cluttered with rattan and iron furniture, collapsing but comfortable. Dom was inspecting the contents of the bag.

"Ah," he said happily, pulling out the sour cream and onion-flavored potato chips, "nutrition! These are some of my favorite chemicals. And the staff of life! Breakfast in a can!"

Mitchell laughed as he clapped his arms against his sides, trying to stay warm. "What?"

Dom held up a six-pack. "Look at this label," he said. "Barley, malts, hops. The stuff is liquid granola."

"The Germans do call it liquid bread," Mitchell said.

It was too cold to eat on the porch. Inside was full of the musty smell of a house that's been closed for a long time. Dom had gotten a fire started in the great stone fireplace in the living room, and Mitchell moved to it instinctively, letting the flames drive the dampness out of him. Behind him, Dom was spreading their feast on the coffee table.

"Hell of a house," Mitchell said. "I always thought so."

"One of the first beach houses on the Island, actually," Dom replied. "It's a lot bigger and better built than the huts they're getting four hundred thousand for today. It was kind of nice of my grandparents to leave it to me, though it pisses my folks off to have to make an appointment to use it."

"Some day I may rent it from you and write that novel I've always talked about," Mitchell said.

They gorged noisily on the fried chicken, potato chips, and beer for a half hour, barely talking except to comment on the quality of the lunch. Then, opening another beer and wiping his mouth on his sleeve, Dom leaned back against the sofa and said, "So, what's the story?"

Mitchell finished chewing. "As I said, I saw something on the cable last night, and I'd sure like to know how it got there."

"What was it, a sex film?"

"I'd rather not say."

Dom searched among the debris for an uneaten wing. "This for a story?"

"Yeah," Mitchell said. "But that's all I'll tell you. For your own safety. People connected with this story have been getting . . . hurt, lately."

"Well," Dom said, "let me tell you there's no big secret to getting onto a cable channel. The basic equipment you need is pretty expensive, but the technology itself is simple. As technology goes these days."

"You need a backyard dish antenna or something?"

"Not really," Dom said. "The antennas you see sprouting up on people's rooftops are receive-only dishes. You aim them at a satellite, as long as you've got unbroken line of sight, then tune to the right frequency and whatever the satellite is sending on that frequency comes in through your antenna. That includes TV programming—a mind-boggling variety of TV programming. But to broadcast your own signal takes a more sophisticated setup. Probably eighty to a hundred thou in equipment alone, plus installation."

"Don't you have to be licensed?"

"In theory," Dom conceded. "But in reality, who's policing it? The feds can barely keep up with routine relicensing of radio stations. How are they supposed to search the countryside for unauthorized broadcast antennas? Even if they caught you, they'd move against you with typical lightning speed . . . twelve, sixteen weeks, court orders, continuances . . ."

"If I saw something on Manhattan Cable, where could it have come from?"

"Not legit, right? I mean you assume it isn't coming from the Manhattan Cable system itself?"

"I assume."

"Then spread out a map."

"It's that bad?"

Dom nodded. "The commercial satellites are in geosynchronous orbit about twenty-two thousand miles out. That means they go around the earth at the same speed and in the same direction the earth turns, so they're always in the same spot relative to the earth surface. Their positions are well known. They're published. And those positions are selected expressly to give the satellites maximum visibility from all over North America. Anywhere you can receive from a satellite, you can also send to that satellite."

"Could the unauthorized signal be inserted in the programming on earth, instead of in the satellite link?"

"Sure," Dom said. "But oddly enough, it might be easier

to do it in space. Once you allow for appropriate equipment, it's not hard to break into a satellite link. For one thing, you don't have security guards and locked doors between you and the satellite. It's just lying there with its legs open."

"But don't they scramble signals? Wouldn't you need to know a code of some kind?" Mitchell asked.

Dom chuckled. "For one of the big premium services maybe, one of the channels that people pay extra for. But apart from that, almost nothing that goes through the commercial satellites is scrambled. This thing you saw, it wasn't on one of the big channels, was it?"

"No," Mitchell said. "In fact, the channel in question wasn't even supposed to be broadcasting at that hour."

"Well, that tells you several things," Dom said. "For one thing, it tells you the people who own the satellite probably don't have a hand in the broadcast."

"Why's that?"

Dom pulled another beer out of the brown paper bag and felt it with his cheek. "They're getting warm, buddy," he said. Mitchell collected the remaining cans and took them to the fridge.

"It's like this," Dom said when he returned. "If you know the right frequency to broadcast on, and the location of the satellite, you can aim your signal at the satellite and it will be received. If there's another signal coming in at the same time, yours has to be stronger—louder, if you will—to override it. Now, a military satellite or a dedicated machine like a weather satellite would have safeguards against unauthorized access, codes, and the like. But not on a commercial satellite. They're built for throughput, maximum traffic, and encoding and decoding slow things down drastically. Hell, virtually everything you see today goes by satellite, even the local programs. They send a reporter ten miles down the road to cover a fire, and it's faster and cheaper to bounce his broadcast off a satellite than transmit it any other way."

"The networks all use satellites?"

"Sure. But they all have at least one, sometimes two backups—satellite capacity they lease without using, available on demand. Something happens to their primary link, they go right to the backup. If you want to broadcast something uninterrupted, you pick a channel with a weak signal, or one that's off the air part of the day. Of course, you make sure your audience knows what's going on."

"If it were *your* channel, and you wanted to catch someone breaking into it, where would you look?"

"I'd have to have a lot of money at stake before it would even be worth the effort," Dom said. "Maybe if I were HBO or something, but otherwise, forget it. Put it out of your mind."

"Impossible?"

"Might as well be. For all practical purposes, it could come from any dish in North America. They're all supposed to be registered, but we know better. You could spend the rest of your life tracking it down, and if the sender never repeated the program you'd be up the creek."

"I doubt this program will be repeated," Mitchell said softly, musing. "But wouldn't you need a studio, a professional setup, cameras and all?"

"Mitchie, come clean," Dom said. "I can handle it. What the hell did you see, some movie of your old lady doing the bump with the Giants' offensive line?"

Mitchell took a deep breath and let it out in an explosive sigh. "Listen, Dom," he said, "I wasn't supposed to see this broadcast, but I did. It's connected with a major news story, and I really think at least one person has been killed as a result of knowing too much about it. Maybe more. I didn't come out here to buy you that kind of trouble."

Dom shrugged. "What did you see? At least give me a hint. Was it a movie, a videotape?"

"It was a still photo, in color, and a card with type on it. Somewhere, somebody has to have that print, and a camera to aim at it."

Dom was shaking his head vigorously and waving his hand. "Hold it," he said. "Now listen to me. I don't want to know any more. You were never here, we never talked, right?"

"Absolutely."

"Okay, now pay attention," Dom said. "I'm no dope. I know there's only one news story right now. At least only one that would bring you all the way out here in the rain. If you thought you were in deep shit before, you ain't heard nothing yet. You're thinking in terms of photo prints and cameras.

That's quaint, Mitchie. You're living in the stone age. This is a digital world. Reality is assembled today, then perceived. It doesn't have to exist. It's all little electrons in patterns, held together by basic universal forces nobody understands."

"What are you talking about?"

"A photo like you describe doesn't even have to exist," Dom said. "There's technology to create it, laying around on the street. It isn't even considered advanced anymore."

"Dom, this was no fake, I saw it . . ."

"What's a fake? Something you see that isn't there? Something that's there and wrongly perceived? If I take a picture of somebody wearing a red jacket then change the jacket to blue, does that make the photo a fake? Your definitions are all obsolete, friend."

Dom got up and went over to a magazine bin next to the fireplace, storage for potential kindling. He rummaged until he found a thick, tattered magazine, then opened it and handed it to Mitchell.

Mitchell was looking at a photograph of Central Park. It was a meadow, and beyond it was a stand of trees. The trees on the left were midsummer green, but on the right they were in full fall color. Above the trees towered a skyline, but not Manhattan, Mitchell realized. It included buildings from all over. The Sears Tower from Chicago stood in the center, flanked by the towers of the World Trade Center. To their right was the well-known pyramid top of San Francisco's Trans-America building.

In the foreground a man stood pushing a wheelbarrow, weighted down with a six-foot strawberry. Mitchell stared at the page incredulously. Everything about it was right. All the sunlight and shadows fell just right. The mismatched images blended together perfectly. A person with no preconceived notions might be skeptical about a six-foot strawberry, but nothing else in the photo would appear the least bit amiss.

"Pretty neat, huh?" Dom said, smiling. "And that's just what they do for fun."

"How do they do it?"

"Expensive but simple," Dom said. "It's called Digital Image Assembly, or any number of other names. It isn't even all that expensive—half a million or so for a system with all the bells and whistles. The system breaks each image down into tiny spots of light called pixels. Depending on the resolution, you can get pretty damned fine. Then you can manipulate each pixel, or groups of pixels with the same characteristics, like color. If you said you liked the grass better red, a technician could push three keys and get you red grass that looked so real you'd think you were crazy for ever believing grass was green."

"Well, I'll be damned," Mitchell said softly. "Who knows about this?"

Dom laughed. "Jesus, everybody," he said. "It's in the trade magazines, after all. It isn't even new anymore. Major printers, big publishers, big-time ad agencies, large-volume color separators, they're all into this stuff in a big way. An ad agency, for instance. They can work with an ad until they get an approved final version, then just phone it or beam it off a satellite to a dozen magazine production plants. No more film, no more proofs, no more delivery charges, no more adding three days to the production process for delivery.

"It's the latest, old buddy, and everybody knows new technology is a boon by definition. The public's barely aware of it, of course, but what *is* the public aware of these days?"

"But how do you change the negatives? What do you do with the original photo?"

"Mitchell, come on," Dom said, grinning. "You burn the frigging negatives, for all anybody cares. Especially if you don't want your new image traced to its original sources. Once you've digitized it you never need a piece of film again. You never dip this thing in a tub of chemicals. You just convert originals into computer memory, then combine, overlay, adjust. And when you've got it the way you like it, you phone up the magazine and send it by modem."

"Or you transmit it to a satellite," Mitchell said.

"Bingo." Dom's face was very serious all of a sudden, and they sat in silence for a moment. "Now, how much worse does that make your story?"

"Immeasurably," Mitchell said.

"Here, flip the page," Dom said, reaching. On the next page were two photos, side by side, of the same woman's face. On the left she had freckles and blue eyes. On the right, no freckles, and sunglasses shading eyes that were distinctly brown.

"Which was what you would call the original?" Dom said. "Does she have freckles or not? What color *are* her eyes? Are her ears really pierced?"

Mitchell looked again. He hadn't even noticed the ears.

"The sixty-four-thousand-dollar question," Dom said. "Does it matter anymore which was the original? Was *either* of them the original, or are they both composed?"

"You know, you could fuck things up royally with this system if you were of a mind to," Mitchell said.

"Sounds like somebody already has," Dom said.

"Still, this could make the source of the photo easier to trace," Mitchell said. "There can't be too many of these things out there."

"Thousands," Dom said.

"Thousands?"

"They've got them at *Time* and *Newsweek*. Hell, you've got them at the *New York Times*. Anywhere you want to compose a lot of color pages in a short time, and don't want to wait for color proofs and film processes. What could have taken all day the old-fashioned way is done in ten minutes now, on this kind of system. That's all industry is after—speed, efficiency, a chance to break the typographers' union, Apple Pie, and Motherhood. The true techies are miles further down the road. The true techies are already working on making these images move."

"A movie, with real people?"

"Complex but do-able," Dom said. "These publishing systems are a rudimentary application of an extraordinarily sophisticated technology. Link this kind of system to a big enough computer memory and there's no limit to what you can do."

"Well thanks, Dom," Mitchell said lightly. "I'll sure sleep better tonight."

"But that's what we have people like you for," Dom said. "To do our worrying for us, and point out the snake pits on all sides of our hassle-free path through life. What the politicians love to call negative reporting, which really only amounts to occasionally pointing at the emperor's bare ass."

Dom was holding the edge of a beer against his lower lip but not drinking. He was staring at Mitchell, and now he tapped a finger on the can.

"Mitch, you have to forgive me, but my brain is working overtime here, and one stupid idea is leading to another. This story you're working on . . . it's the story I think it is, right?"

Mitchell said nothing. Dom shrugged and put the beer down.

"Okay, don't answer. But let me throw this out to you, for what it's worth. The system that made those images is called a Loubex 3000, made by a company called Loubex Imaging. They're one of about six outfits that make similar machines. The founder was Emile Loubert."

"No shit," Mitchell said, sitting up.

"Before he reincarnated himself as National Security Advisor, Emile Loubert was a pioneer in electronic page assembly. He built his company the traditional American way, based on good old-fashioned Japanese values, from a garage operation to five hundred million dollars in sales in about four years. Then he sold out. You remember, he sold to ConTech, Consolidated Technologies. That, in turn, leads us to—"

"Oh my God."

Friday, November 1

The phone again.

Laura snapped awake, and realized she'd been hearing it for some moments, piercing her dreams. The bell was shatteringly loud in the darkness, and she thought: Dad.

When the phone rings at . . . (she checked the bedside clock) . . . three in the morning, it's never good news.

She pulled the receiver off its cradle, thinking, I can be in Key West by midmorning if that's what it is. And that would be the end of all this, too. Ms. Madison is not in this morning, world. She's bereaved. And then she thought, sorry Dad, to dispatch you for my convenience.

The voice was Rydell's.

"Laura, thank God."

"Mitchell?"

"I almost gave up," he said. "I was starting to think you were out of town."

"Mitchell, it's three in the morning."

"I know, listen. I cannot, absolutely cannot, go into this on the phone. But I need your help, I need it bad and I need it now."

The urgency of his voice drove away the last mists of sleepiness.

"What?"

"Do you have a car?"

"No."

"Get one, fast. Take the Long Island Expressway to Great Neck . . ."

Laura turned on her bedside lamp, grabbed a pencil and paper, and jotted notes as Mitchell ran through a complex series of directions.

"You'll be driving alongside a golf course," he said, finally. "Slow down and watch the right shoulder. Flash your brights, and I'll flag you down."

"I don't know how long it will take to get there," Laura said.

"Move fast but quiet," he responded. "And bring me some clothes."

"Clothes?"

"Yeah, pants, sweater, a coat, anything I can cover up with, I'm practically naked."

"Mitchell, what's going on?" Laura said.

"Can't say. But be careful. We're in more danger than we thought."

He hung up without waiting for a reply.

Naked on a golf course in Great Neck? Laura turned her light back out and slowly counted to ten, then reached down beneath her bed, where she kept a flashlight. In the dark she made her way to the window and drew the drapes. Then, with the flashlight, she retrieved the clothes she wanted from her closet. Jeans, a flannel shirt, navy sweater, her hiking shoes with the high sides. And her New York Yankees cap. Summer days at the stadium, a million years ago.

She dressed quickly in the flashlight beam, leaving the shoes to put on later, downstairs. Mitchell obviously thought the phone was tapped, and Laura knew it for sure. But by whom? Her best chance was speed and stealth. She pulled a nylon gym bag from the upper shelf and, after a moment's thought, shoved into it a pair of her old jeans that had grown too large for her—you're losing weight, kid—a pullover sweatshirt, and a pair of skiing socks, extra large and extra warm. They'd be the best she could do, since she had no shoes that would come close to fitting a man.

She stepped back into the closet and took an old pair of slippers from the topmost shelf. In the toe of one slipper she found ten twenty-dollar bills, which she shoved into her pocket.

In the living room she paused to pick up the telephone.

After a second's thought she dialed the information number at the Metropolitan Opera, where she knew a recorded message ran twenty-four hours a day. She waited for the recording to answer, then put the receiver down on the end table next to the console, thinking, that will hold them a few minutes, whoever they are. She took the flashlight, shouldered the gym bag, and silently slipped out the door into the hall.

She made her way down the stairs to the lobby and paused, listening to the night sounds of the apartment building. Floorboards groaned and bedsprings squeaked somewhere in three A.M. ardor. A radio was playing upstairs, and in the distance she heard a car horn honk. She sat on the bottom step and pulled on her hiking shoes. Then, flashlight in hand, she took the last flight of steps to the basement.

There was an English-style below-street apartment in front, and a boiler/utility room in the back, with living quarters for the super, who would be either out or drunk. Laura moved as quietly as she could through the utility room and the residents' storage cages, then let herself out the double-bolted door to the backyard.

Once, she thought, this was an elegant little urban retreat, perhaps with climbing roses and wrought-iron furniture. Now, it was a rectangular wasteland, made even gloomier by the faint light reaching it from the overcast sky above.

At the opposite end of the yard was a low brick wall, perhaps eight feet high. As quietly as she could, Laura brought a garbage can from alongside the building over to the wall to use as a step stool. She lifted herself up, slid over the top on her belly, and dropped roughly into an identical rectangle of dead grass and cracked concrete, facing another tall façade of dark windows and rusted fire escapes.

Seconds later she was in the street, alone, shivering despite her warm clothes. She trotted to the avenue, then south, praying for a cruising cab, a phone booth, an all-night drugstore, anywhere she could find out the best place to rent a car after three in the morning.

She walked all the way to the Waldorf-Astoria, nearly thirty blocks, in less than ten minutes. There may be a cab line in front, she thought, even at this hour.

The lobby was dark and empty, the elevators vacant, their

doors open. Peacock Alley was sealed with a steel cage door. A lone security guard leaned on the wall near the empty registration desk and watched her warily, and she heard muffled voices from the dimly lighted office behind the cashier windows.

She went out the Park Avenue entrance and found a yellow cab, its driver engrossed in the last edition of the *Daily News*. She startled him by opening the passenger door.

"On duty?" she said.

"Yeah, sure," the driver replied. "Not that I get any fares at this hour. Where to?"

"Where can I rent a car?"

"What, now?"

"No, next Tuesday sometime. Of course, now."

"Could try the airport." the cabbie said hopefully, thinking of a big fare. It made sense, and Laura nodded.

"Let's roll."

The drive to JFK took only twenty minutes on the empty highways. The airport roads were deserted, too, except for maintenance vehicles and an occasional police car. Laura was relieved to see lights burning in the first of the auto rental offices, and the driver entered the drop-off area. He let her off at the curb. Inside the building a young man sat alone behind a counter, head down, probably reading. She paused a moment and watched the taxi's taillights disappear. Then she was surrounded by silence.

The clerk was startled when Laura opened the door.

"You're open," she said. "Thank God."

"Twenty-four hours," the clerk replied. "We call it convenience, and it must work, because lo and behold, here's a customer."

Laura smiled. "It's an emergency. This was the only place I could think of where I could rent a car at this hour."

"No problem," the clerk said. The paperwork took a few minutes, and they waited together in silence until the computer beeped its approval of her squeaky clean record.

"You're a model citizen," the clerk said sarcastically.

"Well, not quite," Laura said, smiling.

"I was hoping not," the clerk said. "Laura, is it?"

She nodded and offered her Visa card. The clerk offered to escort her to her car, and she accepted. She could almost feel him composing opening lines in his mind. They reached her car too soon for him, so all he could do was hand her the keys.

"Good luck," he said. "With your emergency, I mean."

She pulled out and drove away, searching her mirror for anyone following her. The clerk was still standing in the parking lot when she circled back on the main exit road. She used an emergency cut in the center divider for a quick, illegal U-turn, and was soon outward bound. Great Neck was fifteen minutes more.

Mitchell had said they were in danger, great danger. Laura thought it through as she drove, sharing the highway with a few trucks and fewer cars.

Danger as a result of nosing into the Nazi story, she thought. The same kind of danger that had happened to Dennis McCarthy and Jonathan Marin.

It didn't make sense. Why try to steal an election you'd win anyway? Why kill to protect a bogus story when even its revelation wouldn't hurt you that much?

Was she buying Marin's paranoid view of the world, where Erhardt was behind it all and all motives were venal? What was the alternative? No third party was going to intrude on an election this way, not with a favorable outcome only a few days off, come what may.

As she got into Great Neck, Mitchell's directions became more complicated, and Laura wasn't even sure she'd gotten them right on the phone. She held the paper against the hub of the steering wheel and searched for Mitchell's landmarks.

She turned, turned again, glanced at her watch, then realized the black emptiness alongside her had to be the golf course. She slowed and flashed her lights, drove the length of the open field, and passed the entry of a private club. At the end of the road she made a U-turn and retraced her route, flashing her lights again.

Something white moved in the hedges, a hand, waving briefly. She pulled to the curb and shut off her lights. The passenger door swung open and Mitchell leaped in.

"Move," he said. "Fast!"

Lights out, she pulled away, glancing over at him. He was, indeed, almost naked—he had on only a hospital nightshirt, cut above the knee and open down the back, held together by a few flimsy ties. On his right leg a long, jagged stain of dried blood reached from his thigh almost to his ankle.

"Where did you get that outfit?" she said, trying to mask her anxiety with lightheartedness.

"Promise not to look?" Mitchell said.

"I'm driving," she replied. "I have to watch the road."

Mitchell reached into the backseat and got Laura's bundle of clothing. Then, to her astonishment, he ripped off the nightshirt. Watch me get stopped by a cop right now, she thought.

In a moment he had pulled on her old sweater and winced as he pulled one pants leg up over his left leg. His right leg remained exposed, and in the light of the passing street lamps Laura saw a jagged wound on his thigh.

Mitchell tore the hospital gown into long strips, then balled one of the strips up tightly and pressed it against the wound.

"It's going to bleed again now that it's warming up," he said. "They say flesh wounds always look and feel worse than they really are."

He reached over and turned up the car's heat. "Let me tell you, it's been a cold night."

"Am I going anywhere special?" Laura asked.

"The beach," Mitchell said. "I think you make one of these rights."

They rode on in silence, Laura glancing in her mirror every few seconds.

"I thought I was going to die there, on the ninth hole," Mitchell said. "The first foursome of the morning would find me huddled, frozen stiff, in a sand trap. I missed you the first time you went by. Thank God you tried again. Were you followed?"

"I don't think so," Laura said. They came to the edge of Long Island Sound, and she parked in a marina lot. The sky was growing lighter. When she looked at Mitchell again she saw large, discolored bruises on his temple and cheek, and a deep, red-black cut closed by stitches across the point of his chin. He was still pressing his makeshift compress onto the wound on his thigh.

"My God," she said.

"Yeah," Mitchell echoed. "They tried their best. Sorry to expose you, but it confirms all I suspected."

"Is that what I think it is?" Laura said, gesturing at his thigh.

"Just grazed me," Mitchell said. "They didn't get a good shot. It was dark and I was moving. I think I lost them in the woods between fairways, just before you came along."

"Somebody heard you on my phone," she said.

"Yes. I was afraid they would. Both our phones are tapped. I figured my only hope was to elude them until you arrived, and the golf course was my best bet."

Mitchell recounted his day—his trip to Sapphire Island, his conversation with Dominick, all he had learned about Loubex and its founder.

"So the photo could have been faked?" Laura asked when Mitchell paused. They were still sitting in the car as dawn came up.

"Right now I'd bet my left nut on it, if it hasn't shriveled away."

"And Loubex was bought out?"

"By Consolidated Technologies," Mitchell said significantly, but Laura didn't get the point and said so.

"ConTech," Mitchell repeated. "Who was CEO of ConTech until he put all his assets in trust to run for vice president?"

"Oh," Laura said quietly, then added: "Jesus."

"I see the light of understanding has dawned," Mitchell said.

"But he wouldn't . . . *why* would he?" Laura stammered.

"*Somebody* did," Mitchell said. "Either Erhardt or somebody working on his behalf, with his blessing. And they've taken pains to keep their activities quiet. Whoever faked that photo also iced Dennis . . ."

"And Marin," Laura said.

"What?"

She told him of David's visit. "Mitchell," she concluded, "David thinks we killed Marin to keep him quiet. They're looking for you . . . for us, now."

"Christ."

"So who beat you up?"

"I was coming back from Dominick's, and it was still

raining. I got as far as Great Neck on the expressway, when all of a sudden this car next to me swerves into my lane. I gave him the horn, hit the brakes, and he pulled up ahead. Then he starts slowing down, and I figure I'd better get past this drunk before he really causes trouble, but the second I get abreast of him he swerves again. This time I floor it, which was a joke in my little rented Dodge. When you push the gas pedal all the way down the engine gets a lot louder, but that's it.

"So I'm cruising along in the driving rain at sixty miles an hour, and this bastard is right next to me, still swerving into me. He hit me a couple of times, glancing blows.

"Then we're coming to an exit ramp and I figure to get off the highway, get onto a narrower street where either he won't follow or I can force him to stop. But he cuts in front of me and cuts off the exit lane. Then he slides over onto the shoulder. I moved all the way over to the left lane, and he comes swinging clear across and broadsides me. Drove me onto the shoulder.

"Next thing I know I'm coming to in the hospital. In Great Neck Medical Center, to be precise. And I hurt all over, but I'm okay. The cops were there and I told them the whole story, but they didn't believe me. They took blood for a drug and alcohol test. Which, just between us, I was unlikely to pass. Then they left me alone and I fell asleep. That was about eight last night."

"You get a look at the other driver?" Laura said.

Mitchell shook his head. "Between the twilight and the wet windows, all I could see was a shape. Seemed tall, dark haired, black jacket."

"And you got all those bruises in the wreck?"

"I was lucky. I got luckier later. I woke up when I wasn't supposed to. There was a nurse bending over me with a syringe. 'What's that?' I say. 'Your insulin,' she says. 'I don't take insulin.' 'Yes, you do,' she says. 'The dosage and schedule were on your Life Card, thank goodness.' *Thank goodness*, she says, can you believe it?"

"What happened?"

"I coldcocked her and hit the road. In my fetching hospital attire, at two-thirty in the morning. Found a phone booth and called you. Thank God my credit card number is engraved on my brain."

"What's a Life Card?"

"I don't carry one. It's a little wallet-sized card with all your medical and other vital information encoded on it digitally, even complete X rays. If you're unconscious, they help doctors treat you right. A good idea, actually, except if the card says you're a diabetic when you're not.

"It was a full syringe," Mitchell went on. "I hope you'd have come to my funeral."

He removed the wad of bloodstained cotton from his leg. The blood still oozed into a six-inch-long rip in his skin, but to Laura it looked better than it had before. Mitchell silently made another compress, and used a long strip torn from the hospital gown to tie it in place. Then he slowly, painfully slipped his right leg into her old pants. They didn't quite close around his waist.

Laura got out of the car and walked over to the edge of the water. A long pier reached out into the sound, with sailboats in slips on either side, all protected by a large, heavily locked gate. Thin sheets of ice had formed on some of the boats, and icicles hung from the shrouds and halyards. She heard Mitchell come to stand just behind her, balancing a little uncertainly on his good leg.

"What's the matter?" he said.

"I don't know," she said and turned to face him. The morning was arising as gray and bleak as the day before. "I feel . . . I can't say why, I just feel dirty. Like somebody is violating me."

"I understand," Mitchell said.

"I wonder."

She began to walk along the pilings, within a few feet of the water's edge, and Mitchell followed slowly, at a distance, which pleased her. She glanced at him, sorting things out. She wanted him there, but not too close, not now. She took a few minutes, then slowed and let him fall in step beside her, his heavy wool socks already soaked and covered with damp sand.

"You're not supposed to be able to do this kind of thing," she said. "This is supposed to be America."

"Maybe you don't live in the same country they do," Mitchell said.

"Whoever *they* are. They won't show themselves and we can't lure them out. They just hide and lie and kill. As much as I disliked Marin, we always used to think America had room for his kind, and lots of others. He may have been a bastard, but he was telling the truth about Senator Gillian, and he must have been telling the truth about Erhardt."

"But he's a Nazi," Mitchell said. "That's enough for most people. He's in the same league as drug pushers and drunk drivers. Nothing you do to the likes of him is going to strike people as wrong. That's the dark side of Erhardt's Golden Age. One of the dark sides."

They walked in silence until a hurricane fence blocked their way. Beyond it was an electric power substation.

"What about you?" Laura said. "They've tried to kill you. Is this all still just a story?"

"Don't say 'just' a story like I was a plumber and this was another clogged drain," Mitchell said. "Dominick said something yesterday that I was thinking a lot about in the car, before the . . . accident. I commented on how much a bad guy could screw things up with the right technology, how out of hand things could get. He said, 'That's what we have you for.' He meant the press. It's our job to keep things honest, if that doesn't sound too pompous. Whether it's Nixon burglarizing his opponent's campaign headquarters, or Reagan arming the Contras at the expense of the Iranians, or some county executive routing school contracts to his brother-in-law. It's up to us."

"I can see where that job would require a healthy ego," Laura said.

"Ego isn't how I'd put it, either," Mitchell said, shaking his head. He hunched his shoulders and shivered a little.

"How would you put it?"

He thought a second, searching for just the right words. "I guess it's a sense of where you belong in the scheme of things, and a feeling that you're the right person for the job. Surgeons have to have it, and jet pilots, and concert pianists, and presidential candidates . . . and journalists."

"I shouldn't be making you walk," Laura said.

"If I don't, it will only stiffen up and be worse tomorrow. As it is, it will probably be sore but okay. Years from now I'll tell people it's a dueling scar."

"Should you get it stitched?"

"You want to suggest where?"

He had a point, Laura realized. "I don't even know if I can go home now."

"I wouldn't advise it," Mitchell said. "We're on the lam, doll. You sorry I called?"

"No," Laura said. "Are you?"

"No."

"Mitchell?"

"Yes."

"We've got to beat them."

"I know."

"We've got to find a way. Senator Gillian said it was up to me to find the vampire that's doing this and drag him out into the sunlight."

"Are you prepared to find a pretty big, fat vampire?" Mitchell said. "You really ready for that?"

"I guess I have to be."

Mitchell slipped his arm around Laura's waist. She held back a moment, then relented and did the same to him. There was a line of brighter gray along the horizon, even a little clear blue sky, and a stiff wind blew the low-lying clouds out to sea.

"You know," she said, "you're a sight in those raggedy clothes."

Lieutenant Maddalena looked out the window, a cup of bad station-house coffee getting cold in his hand. Outside it was dark; inside, the night shift was signing off. He turned back to his desk. "One more time," he said.

Patrolman Hanna riffled once more through his battered pocket notebook. It was his first plainclothes assignment and he wanted Maddalena to know how well he'd done.

"I stayed on Rydell all day, just as instructed," he said. "Put a lot of miles on the city's car, too, mostly in other people's jurisdiction. Rydell rented a car from Avis at Second Avenue and Seventieth. Blue Dodge Aries. I returned to the rental agency later and found out he'd said he intended to bring the car back tonight. They'd run their little computer screen on him and come up with nothing."

"He's clean," Maddalena said.

"He drove out to the Sapphire Island ferry, stopped along the way at a party market and bought some junk food. I didn't want to be conspicuous, so I waited for the next ferry. I drove all over the island and found the Aries parked in the driveway at this address." He handed Maddalena a slip of paper. "I took up a surveillance from about three hundred yards away. It was raining pretty bad. Finally, Rydell comes out about five and heads straight back to the ferry. This time I rode over with him, 'cause I figured once he gets on the expressway I'll never catch up with him, whereas on the island there's only one way on or off, and the ferry was it."

Carlo nodded. So far, so good.

"We were practically back to Great Neck when the fun started."

"When this other sedan ran him off the road?"

"Yes, sir."

"White car?"

"Yes, sir, big Oldsmobile, about an 'eighty-nine."

"Distinguishing features?"

"None. No dents, no bumper stickers, nothing."

"Tags?"

Hanna handed over another slip of paper. "I ran a trace," he said, anticipating his boss. Carlo smiled.

"And?"

"It ain't supposed to be a white Olds. The tags belong on a blue Volvo, about four years old. Registered to something called Love Bytes, which it turns out is a company with a telephone answering machine and an address that looks like a maildrop. I called the machine and got a message saying the office was closed. Click. No call back later, no other numbers, just closed."

Carlo paced. "No doubt about what you saw?"

"No, sir," Hanna replied. "And frankly, it didn't seem open to too many interpretations. The white car deliberately drove Rydell into the bridge abutment. I'd call it attempted murder."

"But Rydell's alive."

"His car had an air bag. Believe me, the car was totaled. I stopped, as a witness, but didn't tell anybody I was a cop. Rydell was unconscious but the paramedics said he wasn't too badly hurt. Lots of bruises. They took him to Great Neck Medical Center. I followed along to see how he was doing, and when they said they were going to keep him overnight, I came back here."

"Any other witnesses?"

"Nobody stopped," Hanna said. "It was pouring at the time, and this *is* Long Island we're talking about."

"Now, if you were a detective, what would you do next?"

"Check for a stolen car or stolen tags report on the Volvo," Hanna said.

He's on a roll, Carlo thought. At the moment, he's got all the answers. "And there is none?" he said, though it wasn't really a question.

"How'd you guess?"

"Just lucky," Carlo said. He poured the remainder of his coffee into a plant on his desk. "You're gonna have to get with the Nassau police. Don't let on you were doing an undercover on their turf without telling them. Tell them this car was seen leaving the scene of an armed robbery. Tell them it got a couple of dents in a sideswipe with a parked car. Ask them to put all body shops, junkyards, used-car dealers, etc., on alert for the next few days. If that car turns up . . . hell, if the plates should turn up on the beach somewhere, we want to know."

Hanna gave him a sharp salute and left him. Maddalena returned to the window and looked out at the dark city street. He took out his wallet and removed another slip of paper, bearing the tag number he'd memorized from a large white sedan in an alley next to a small hotel. Number for number, he thought, the same car. The same tags, anyway, don't jump to conclusions.

Unrelated facts, he thought. They're only unrelated when you don't know the relationship. Somebody tried to kill Mitchell Rydell on the Long Island Expressway yesterday. Tried to run him into a bridge abutment. A very similar exit from this life had been taken three days ago by one Dennis McCarthy, about whom Rydell had been asking a lot of questions.

If you assume foul play in the McCarthy case, then covering it up is important enough to justify killing Rydell, too. And that bundle dumped into the trunk of the white car in the alley. Without a close look, Carlo knew it was a body. Two men had gone into the hotel . . . Rydell and a stranger, heavily clothed. Rydell had registered under his own name, charging the room to the *New York Times*.

So they tried to kill Rydell to prevent him from learning who had killed McCarthy, Carlo thought, watching the beginnings of rush-hour traffic in the street. Why did they call McCarthy?

Did someone kill McCarthy? The assault on Rydell supported that theory, but McCarthy had been drunk, after all. He might not have needed anybody's help in finding his way into that concrete tower.

That's another thing, Carlo thought. That blood alcohol count. For Christ's sake, .33? You know how much and how fast you gotta drink to get up that high?

He pulled his copy of the McCarthy accident report from his briefcase and noted the cops' names. He'd check with them this morning to see if they could add anything to the bureaucratic garbage of the report. There was always something.

He picked up the phone, scanned the dozens of numbers he'd recorded, under Scotch tape, on his dictation shelf, then dialed the police impoundment lot. There was no answer.

"Come on, guys," he said out loud. "Let's break up the card game and answer the phone."

Finally, a voice. Carlo identified himself.

"You should still have a vehicle there that was involved in a fatal in Brooklyn, Tuesday," he said. "Blue Pontiac, tags XV-7244." He waited through another interminable delay while the clerk checked the records.

"Yup," the clerk said at last. "Still here. Waiting for the paperwork so we can bale it."

"I'll be out there in an hour," Carlo said. "I want to take a close look at it."

What the hell, he thought as he hung up. It beats going home.

"Dominick didn't seem particularly alarmed," Laura said. She was brewing tea in the kitchen of the house on Sapphire Island.

[114]

"That's Dom," Mitchell replied. "Somebody tells him he doesn't want to know something, he believes it. Minds his own business, is the old-fashioned way of saying it."

"Are we safe here?"

"I don't know."

Mitchell sat in the armchair opposite the fireplace, where he'd told Laura not to start a fire for fear the smoke would reveal there were people in the house. Dominick had told the neighbors he was leaving early, and made a big show of shutting the windows and locking all the doors. Laura's rental car was parked in tall scrub grass a half mile away, and the license plates were on the kitchen table. Mitchell had changed into a sweatshirt he'd found in Dominick's closet, plus a pair of basketball shorts. Now, with a towel under him to catch the blood, he was gingerly removing the makeshift dressing from his leg wound.

"We moved fast," he said, wincing. "I don't think they tailed us, and I doubt they'd expect us to come right back here. We may have bought ourselves a day or two, but who knows?"

"Let me see that," Laura said. She crouched at Mitchell's side as he raised and turned his leg to show her the gash.

"It's stopped bleeding at least," Laura said. She took a close look. The wound was about four inches long but not very deep, and about a half inch wide. The skin was gone and the exposed flesh was raw, beginning to crust over with clotting blood. On either side, his unharmed skin stretched smooth, lightly tanned.

"Stay like that," she ordered, and went to rummage in the bathroom. In short order she found a small box of gauze pads, some antiseptic cream, and a roll of adhesive tape. She went to the kitchen and filled a bowl with warm water, then washed out a sponge and returned to the living room. Mitchell had put his head back and seemed almost asleep.

"Hold still, now," she said. She dabbed gently at the wound, then patted it dry and began unwrapping the gauze pads. A few moments later she had coated several pads with antiseptic, and pressed them into the damaged flesh, covering them with dry pads, then securing the dressing with several circuits of tape.

"You should have been a nurse," Mitchell said.

[115]

"My father always wanted me to go to medical school," Laura replied. "I don't have the temperament to be a nurse. I'd punch some grouchy patient in the nose."

She surprised herself with a yawn.

"Yeah," Mitchell said. "Sleep is a high priority for both of us. I'll take the guest room."

Laura looked at her watch. "It's nearly ten," she said, surprised.

"The day is young," Mitchell said. "Let's sleep until mid-afternoon, then talk."

Laura nodded, then found her way into the larger bedroom. She lay down on top of the bedclothes, pulled a quilt over her legs, and was asleep before she had time to think.

When she woke she smelled garlic, and the bedside clock told her it was nearly five. She peered between the heavy curtains on the bedroom window and saw that it was rapidly getting dark outside, a gray, forbidding darkness that promised more rain, maybe even snow. There were no lights on in the next house up the road.

She found Mitchell limping around the kitchen, with a large pot of spaghetti boiling vigorously, sauce and meatballs heating in another pan, and two neat places set at the small pine table in the dining room.

"Dom was well provisioned," he said. "Lots of nonperishables like sauce in jars, pasta, even a little lettuce, but no salad dressing."

"No dressing? What kind of joint is this?"

Mitchell found a bottle of red wine and put it on the table, and Laura dug a corkscrew out of the utensil drawer to open it.

"This is unexpectedly luxurious," she said as she poured. Mitchell drained the spaghetti. In a few more moments they had brought all of dinner's components to the table.

"From now on, we ought to think of every meal as our last," Mitchell said. "And unless we figure out what the hell is going on, it might be."

"Let's start with some key facts," Laura said. "Such as, there have been two attempts on your life, but none on mine. Why?"

[116]

"You've done nothing since the story broke that threatens them."

"Whereas, clearly you have," she said. "What about Marin?"

"Even there, they got Marin, not me. I haven't been a threat—until recently, anyway."

"You're assuming Erhardt's behind it all?"

"He's almost got to be, or else people working on his behalf. He's probably insulated himself from it, but whoever is doing these things obviously has access to some pretty heavy technology. They've known what we were doing almost as soon as we knew."

"Nobody could have known Marin was at my place unless they were listening in on my phone."

"Then when you think about that Loubex computer system that fakes photos so well . . ."

"And your phony Life Card in the hospital," Laura said. "Of course they believed it, people are conditioned to accept these things as accurate. They come out of a computer, after all. We're looking at a technological conspiracy of almost unbelievable scope. And what's affecting us is only one tiny little corner of the spiderweb, most of which will never come to light under any imaginable circumstances."

"If I came to me with this story I'd have myself thrown out of the newsroom. Makings of a first-rate case of pure paranoia," Mitchell said.

"I used to think so, too," Laura said. "But if you think about your life, if you look at all the little electronic footprints you leave everywhere you go . . ."

They ate in silence for a few minutes. Dominick's clothes were a little too big for Mitchell, she thought, and the billowy look that resulted made him look like a little boy. She tried to connect the man across the table with the Pulitzer Prize–winning reporter, the arrogant *New York Times*man Cavanagh called "that snake," but couldn't. When she looked at Mitchell, she saw a good looking, still young man who had been forced off a highway, attacked with a lethal syringe, and shot at, all within a few hours, and whose self-confidence might not be quite up to dealing with that kind of attention.

[117]

And her own words came back to her, from the early morning.

You're not supposed to be able to do this kind of thing. This is supposed to be America.

"It isn't just the technology, though," Mitchell said. "Most of these systems have been around for ages. They've always had the potential to be abused. The point is, you have to wait for a social climate that licenses abuse."

That's the dark side of Erhardt's Golden Age. One of the dark sides.

"It's the old bit about how if you have nothing to hide, you have nothing to fear," Mitchell said. "As long as it keeps happening to other people, the bad guys, drug pushers and Nazis. You tell the cops, do what's necessary to stop drunk driving, and the cops set up roadblocks, and anyone who quibbles is shouted down. This is a crisis, after all. A scourge. And years later you don't have much of a drunk driving problem, but you still have the roadblocks. Do you realize something like eighty percent of all Americans agree with mandatory drug testing for everyone? And there are already ten states that have legislated the death penalty for selling cocaine. It's a crisis, after all. Keep us safe, no matter what. You can't argue with it. You can't argue with the mother of a kid lying dead in the highway."

"Anyway," Laura said, "the difference between us is Dennis McCarthy. It was your questions about him that made them try to kill you and not me. Run me one more time through all you know about his connection with the Nazi story."

Mitchell rattled off the familiar facts again, and Laura tried to hear them in new ways, tried to find some angle in the story that she hadn't recognized before. McCarthy had been the original source. He'd given Mitchell the phone numbers, dates, everything needed to build an impressive but circumstantial case. Yet he'd failed to produce the conclusive evidence.

"I'm still coming up empty," she said. "And they've got us cornered now. You get rid of McCarthy and Marin, and what's left? Just a recently fired reporter trying to show up his bosses and a frustrated early-middle-aged divorcée with stars in her eyes. Not the world's two most credible characters."

The spaghetti was gone, but they still had half a bottle of wine, and they sipped quietly for a few minutes.

"Is that what you are?" Mitchell said, finally. "A frustrated early-middle-aged divorcée?"

"Every word fits," Laura replied.

"But surely you have a rewarding career," Mitchell said. "Apart from all this nonsense."

"You mean, other than that, Mrs. Lincoln, how'd you like the play?"

Mitchell smiled.

"Yes," Laura said after a moment. "I did . . . I do like my job. It's varied, exciting. Responsible. I hadn't given much thought to what I'd do for a living after the election was over. I doubt there will be a spot for me at the White House.

Mitchell looked around the dining room. "I always liked this house," he said. "Since I used to come out here with Dom and his parents when we were teenagers. We always talked about my renting it from him for a year and writing a novel. Well, you know, every newspaper hack has a novel burning in him. But I never wanted to commit an act of literature. I'll make it a thriller."

"How about a plot to steal a presidential election, with a mismatched pair of protagonists?" Laura said. "Sound plausible?"

"Plausibility is overrated," Mitchell said. After a pause, he added: "Well, there are lots of good memories here. Maybe I will move out here for a while. After."

He fell silent again, and Laura watched him in the half-light of the dining room. He had closed his eyes, and his fingers rested loosely around the stem of his wineglass. For a moment she had a sense of perfect peace, then suddenly knew what she wanted, where she needed to go. It came to her complete, with all the gaps and holes filled in, a gift-wrapped feeling much too strong to put aside.

But she let the silence lengthen, testing it, probing her mind, but it came out the same way every time. It would be much more than just scratching an itch, she told herself, though the physical desire was strong. She had felt it growing within her for the past several hours. Was it the combination of the danger, the darkness, the wine?

Well, all of that, she thought, and more. There was the commitment, the decision to take another person into her life for the first time in a great while. She became more certain as she sat, and Mitchell kept his head back, eyes closed. She let the moment lead her.

"Mitchell," she said, and his eyes opened and met hers. "Would you do something for me . . . with me?"

"Hmmm," he said, nodding a little.

"Would you make love to me? Could we make love? It's what I want."

For an answer, Mitchell rose slowly and came around the table to her. He lifted her hand in his, and she stood up. Slowly, gently, their lips came together, but they kept their bodies apart and stood that way for a long moment, joined only at the lips and fingertips.

Then he put his palms against her cheeks and kissed her long and hard, pulling her toward him, and she went willingly, eagerly.

"Come," she said, stepping back and taking his hand, leading him to the bedroom.

He stopped as they passed the fireplace and pulled back against her. She turned to him quizzically.

"Come," she said, squeezing his hand. But he shook his head fiercely and held a finger to his lips. He moved stealthily to the shuttered living room windows, listening intensely.

"You hear something?" he whispered. Then he bolted toward her and the world dissolved in noise. A deafening staccato tore through the living room, and bits of paneling flew from the wall opposite the window. Mitchell shoved her onto the floor, covering her with his body, and forced her to inch toward the basement stairs. Bullets, she thought, machine gun bullets hitting the wall. As they dived for the cover of the basement the last thing she saw was a blinding burst of yellow light as flames engulfed the living room.

They hit the basement floor together, and Mitchell dragged her quickly through the darkness. The images and sensations ran together. They were rushing out a basement door to the rear carport, facing the beach. Above them flames were consuming the main floor. Damp night air hit her in the face. Mitchell was ahead of her, crawling on his belly to the top of the grass-covered dune. She followed, the cold sand sliding up her sleeves and into her hair. She parted the grass in front of her and stayed low, expecting at any moment to hear the bark of machine guns again and feel the impact in her back.

From the top of the dune they rolled over and over onto the beach. Now they huddled in the deep grass perhaps fifty yards from the house, the heat and light from the fire sweeping over them. People were running in the street far above them.

"There are too many people out now," Mitchell said. "Whoever did this is watching from a distance."

Then a concussive shock reached them, and a searing moment of heat. A rising globe of white fire burst out of the collapsing house and headed for the sky.

"The propane tank's gone up," Mitchell said. "That ought to satisfy them. Nobody could be alive in there now."

Laura looked at his face, softened by the flickering yellow glow.

"I guess my proposition was rather badly timed," she said.

"At least we'd have died happy," he said. "Now, we crawl. Stay low and in the grass for another hundred yards or so, then down to the water's edge and run for your life."

The fire's intensity bought them time. They ran awkwardly along the waterline, at Mitchell's pace because of his bad leg. Above them the gray black sky reflected flames. They paused often, once to look back at the fire from a half mile away. Then they picked their way through nearly impenetrable brush up to a highway and hobbled along the shoulder. Laura blessed her years of daily jogging, fought off the pains in her sides, and struggled on.

Finally they stopped, behind a grocery store a few blocks from the ferry. Mitchell leaned against the wall, hair wildly disarrayed, mouth agape. He grimaced as he bent to knead his thigh, and Laura could see a bloodstain forming on his gray sweat pants.

"We should rest," Laura said.

"No time now," Mitchell answered. "We have to get off the island before they realize we aren't still in that house."

"What if they're watching the ferry?"

Mitchell panted and ran a hand through his hair.

"I don't know," he said quietly. Limping badly, he led her through the alley behind the short street of stores, until they had a vantage point from which they could observe the ferry slip. The boat was heading in and there were four cars lined up to cross.

"No telling," he said. "Maybe there aren't enough of them. Maybe it's a small operation."

"And maybe they really do think we're burning up," Laura said.

Mitchell crouched against a tree trunk, eyes closed, finally catching his breath.

"You got any cash?" he said faintly. Laura checked her jeans pocket and found her little wad of twenties.

"We'll need it," Mitchell said. "My wallet, money, driver's license, ID, everything, is all still back at the hospital."

He pulled himself up to watch the line of cars board the ferry two hundred yards away. The ferryman waited a few more minutes, then cast off. When the slip was empty, another car drove up and the driver got out to sit on his front fender and wait. It was getting colder.

"What now?"

"We take the next boat," Mitchell said. "I think it will be several hours before they can examine the wreckage closely, and I'm betting they'll want evidence that we're dead. We need the time to get to my apartment."

"I don't think . . ."

"There are crucial things there," Mitchell said. "Marin's claim check, for one. I want to get a look at his luggage. For another thing, I need some other clothes, and some money."

"Can you get in?"

Mitchell nodded. "Whether I can do it unobserved is another matter. Once they realize we're alive, they'll be all over our old haunts. Another reason to move fast."

Laura straightened up and looked toward the landing. The ferry had disappeared into the darkness. As she watched, a white sedan pulled up, then parked off to the side along the waterline. Two men got out and stood looking over the sound. The taller man wore a white nylon windbreaker and a sailor's cap, and when he took the cap off, Laura watched him run his fingers through thick black hair.

"Mitchell . . ."

Rydell pulled himself up onto his knees, holding his wounded leg straight out. He took a glance over the shrubbery and fell back against the tree.

"That's the car," he said.

"The one from the expressway?" Laura said. Mitchell nodded.

"They must know we got out," Laura said. She looked back inland and saw the sky still alight with the reflection of flames. "But it's still burning like crazy," she said. "How could they know?"

"The ferry is the only way off the island," Mitchell said. "They may be just staking it out. Or waiting for someone. We can't go down and ask them."

"Sit tight," Laura said, and slipped away through the darkness.

She came up onto the main road about fifty yards away, out of sight of the ferry, and surveyed the storefronts in both directions. Between her and the water was a big restaurant in a Victorian house, bright and warm. Almost directly opposite her was a bar, the Harbor House, and that was where she headed.

Inside, there was a fog of cigarette smoke, and Sinatra on the jukebox. A dozen men lined the bar and gathered around the pool table in the rear. Laura had no trouble getting the bartender's attention.

"What can I do for you?"

"Help, I hope," Laura said. She leaned over, and the bartender did the same.

"I've got to get to the mainland and I can't wait for the next ferry," she said. "My . . . my father in Syosset has had a heart attack."

"I'm sorry to hear that, miss."

"The ferry's liable to be another hour . . ."

"Oh, not that long," the bartender said. Laura reached into her pocket and pulled out the wad of bills.

[123]

"I just can't stand the wait," she said. "I'm willing to pay fifty bucks if somebody here has a boat and is willing to take me over. Somebody you trust."

The bartender walked to the other end of the bar. Laura saw him talk to a beefy young man, and then to a thinner one. The second man shrugged, nodded, and came toward her.

"Larry Meecham," he said, not offering his hand. "You're ready now, I guess."

Meecham had an old station wagon in the parking lot and began to turn inland when Laura stopped him.

"We need to pick up my brother," she said. "He's down by the ferry slip."

Meecham grimaced in annoyance, but turned the car around on the empty road. Laura stopped him again when he was in front of Mitchell's hiding place.

"Be right back," she said. Meecham's annoyance turned to suspicion when Mitchell was in the backseat, sweat pants stained with blood. He turned off the engine and looked at Laura.

"He's hurt," she said.

"So I see."

"We've got to get to the mainland and can't wait for the ferry," Laura said simply. "What do you want?"

"More than fifty bucks," Meecham said.

"Listen, pal," Mitchell said. "There's nothing crooked going on here. No trouble to get into. Just some easy money from doing strangers a favor."

"It's important to us," Laura said. "A hundred is as high as I can go."

"In advance," Meecham said.

"No way," Mitchell objected.

Meecham sat intransigently, arms resting on the steering wheel.

"The ferry will be back by the time you make up your mind," Mitchell said. "Then we'll get on it and you'll blow the hundred."

"I don't think you're getting on the ferry," Meecham said. "No matter when it comes in."

"I'll give you the hundred once we're on the water," Laura said.

[124]

Meecham shrugged, then cranked the ignition. It was a short and silent ride to a small boat yard that stank of diesel fuel. Meecham led them to his slip, and jumped down onto a skiff equipped with an outboard engine. He offered Laura his hand but she boarded without his help, then turned to help Mitchell aboard. Without a word Meecham started the engine and, keeping it revved low, slowly made his way out of the slip and through the marina. He barely made a wake. Mitchell sat on the middle seat, his leg stretched out, shivering in the cold as Meecham, clear of the boat yard, throttled steadily upward. The nose of the boat rose out of the water and a small bow wave appeared. The wind scraped their faces. Meecham was steering them straight into blackness. Laura looked for stars above her, remembering what her father had told her about navigating on the open seas. There were no celestial landmarks, and all Laura could do was watch the lights of the island slip farther and farther away. They could see the fire easily from more than a mile offshore. The flames were dying, and she thought the house must be all gone. She thought she could see Meecham looking at the flames, too, then at her and Mitchell, then back at the flames. She put a hand on Mitchell's shoulder.

"You okay?"

"Just wondering how I'm going to explain this to Dom," he said. "Jesus, Dominick! If they follow him . . ."

"You warned him to be careful," Laura said. Mitchell shrugged and glanced back toward Meecham, putting a finger to his lips.

They neared the Long Island shore. A quarter mile off, they could make out the running lights of the ferry as it started back to Sapphire Island. Meecham cut the throttle about two hundred yards from shore, and Laura handed him the money without a word. He counted it, stuck it in his pocket, and gestured toward the shore.

"Where do you want to get off?"

"Not too near the ferry slip," Laura said. She could tell by Meecham's glance that he wasn't surprised. He's probably got us pegged as fugitive killers, she thought, but since we pay in cash he doesn't care.

Meecham maneuvered up to the shore. There was a spit of

[125]

public beach lining the sound, houses beyond. He took the boat in as close as he could, then signaled them off. Laura and Mitchell were wading through knee-deep water when Meecham roared back into the night.

"Well," Mitchell said as they walked up the beach. "That was . . . interesting. Was that really all your cash?"

"Damn near." They reached a narrow walkway between houses, installed to guide the public to its beach while keeping them off private property. They followed the walkway, their feet wet and cold, to the county road, and walked along the road in silence.

"Look at it this way," Mitchell said. "You could be home watching *Casablanca* for the hundredth time."

"Knowing you *has* been exciting, I admit." Laura smiled. Her fatigue was catching up with her.

"Laura?"

"Yes?"

"Just before all the fun started, you had an interesting idea."

Laura felt herself blush and was thankful for the darkness. It seemed like days ago that she had started toward the bedroom with Mitchell.

"I remember," she said. Mitchell spoke without looking at her.

"All I wanted to say was, I hope it will occur to you again."

"If it doesn't, remind me."

Saturday, November 2

It was pushing four in the morning by the time Laura and Mitchell got back into Manhattan. Their trip had been a series of walks, short hitchhikes, and long waits for subway trains into the city. Mitchell's leg was giving him obvious pain, but he kept up the brisk pace. Now he led Laura down a side street not far from his apartment. A huge church occupied the entire block.

"St. Ignatius Loyola," Mitchell said. "Lair of the Jesuits."

Behind the church was a school, separated from the rectory by a small alley. Mitchell entered the alley and scanned the brick wall, then started counting bricks.

"Just my luck if they've repaired it," he said. He found a particular brick and scratched at its edges with his fingertips. "Still loose," he said. He pried it out of its place. "I discovered this quite by accident a few years ago and thought it was perfect. In a nice safe suburb I'd keep a spare key in a flower-pot," he said. He reached into the recess left by the missing brick and pulled out a key.

"It always pays to have one squirreled away," Mitchell said. "There are two more, but I'm not saying where."

"Do you consider that obsessive?" Laura asked. "Or merely thorough?"

He chuckled and put his arm around her waist. The night had gotten very cold and they were severely underdressed.

At Mitchell's building they used the back door and the stairs instead of the elevator, which Mitchell said would wake the whole building. He silently let them into his apartment and walked around the whole suite in the dark, then drew the curtains closed and turned on the smallest light in the living room.

He slipped out of the sweat pants and inspected his wound. The bleeding had stopped again and a scab was starting to form. "It's going to heal in spite of me," Mitchell said. Then he painfully pulled on new pants, dry socks, and shoes. He came over to where Laura was sitting at the kitchen table, head resting on her hands.

"Here," he said, putting Marin's claim check on the table. "I think you should go to the station. For one thing, you run faster than me."

Laura shoved the claim check into her pocket. Mitchell was looking through an envelope full of money. "You have enough cash to get by?" he said.

"I have no idea," Laura replied truthfully. Mitchell handed her five twenty-dollar bills.

"That at least covers what you gave that little cretin for the boat ride," he said. He folded the envelope in half and shoved it into his back pocket.

"Well, I guess that's it," he said. He looked around the apartment, a little wistfully.

"Things will straighten out," Laura said. "Someday you'll be watching TV in your living room again."

Mitchell's face clouded a moment, and he went over to his answering machine. He seemed to freeze, looking at the phone.

"What?" Laura said, coming to his side.

"Look," Mitchell replied. He pressed the redial button and a number scrolled across the digital display.

"It's Dom's number," Mitchell said. "The machine stored it. Would have held it forever, if need be."

"I don't understand," Laura said.

"It's an electronic footprint," Mitchell said. "We leave them everywhere. Like Life Cards in our wallets. For anybody who knows the tricks and has the right equipment, we're easy to find, easy to follow, and easy to kill."

Laura read about her own death in the *Daily News*, as she sipped coffee in a bar off the main waiting room at Penn Station. A few yards away the morning rush was in full swing.

Inside the bar there were only four other patrons, all hitting the hard stuff at seven A.M.

She hid her face behind the paper and thought of her father, hearing the national news and believing his daughter was dead. Top aide to Senator Gillian killed, the story said, along with a former *New York Times* reporter, a Pulitzer Prize winner.

She looked out across the waiting room and saw a small line of people at the baggage check counter. She'd been waiting for the line to disappear, but that didn't seem likely.

Then she thought: Whoever attacked us last night must have known very soon afterward that we weren't in the house. They could have faked evidence of our deaths to satisfy some hick town coroner, but they know better. They know we're out. And we can't call anyone without them knowing. I can't even get word to Dad.

Who could she trust? She'd never get near Gillian without being stopped and identified. And Cavanagh presented the same risk. Anything she or Mitchell did that revealed their whereabouts invited their deaths.

If only she could talk to Dad, he'd straighten everything out, she thought. Then she told herself: This is the grown-up world, where Daddy can't always make the trouble go away. But if she could only talk to him. She ought to go straight to Key West and say, "Daddy, I'm in trouble." She imagined him again, hearing on the radio about the fire on Sapphire Island that had killed his little girl. Where would he go to get over that? A man who had not yet, after eight years, quite accepted the loss of his wife.

She paid for her coffee with a twenty, which made the bartender pout. Then she stepped into the waiting room. Rather than cross the traffic flow to the checkroom, she followed the crowd, then walked along the far wall, among passengers coming up from the tracks. Finally she presented Marin's stub at the counter, and a few moments later was handed an oversize nylon sports bag, its corners reinforced with thick gray duct tape. The bag was heavy; she slung it awkwardly over her shoulder and headed for the ladies room.

Inside she found a row of rental changing stalls, slid a dollar's worth of quarters into the slots and let herself in. She dropped Marin's bag on the bench and opened it.

She pulled out two woolen sweaters before she found the gun. It was wrapped in newspaper, taped all over, and sealed inside a plastic bag. She left the bag and wrappings in a pile on the bench and fingered the pistol uneasily. She wondered if it was loaded and realized she didn't know how to check. The gun fit her hand but felt cold and oily. She slipped it into the pocket of her ski parka—Mitchell's ski parka.

Her next discovery was a small packet of United States passports, held together by rubber bands. There were four of them—Marin's photo was in each, with different names.

The bottom of the bag was filled with the dead man's underwear, brightly colored nylon briefs and ribbed shirts, and Laura nearly giggled. She was embarrassed to touch them, let along take them out. She started to put the other clothing back, but her hand brushed against the underwear and it struck her as odd. Stiff, crinkly somehow. She lifted a waistband and peered at the $50 designation in the upper corner of a bill. One of a stack.

Five minutes later she emerged from the ladies room, her heart still pounding. Not a bad haul, she thought. A handgun, four U.S. passports, some slinky drawers, and about $4,000 in cash, assorted bills, mostly well used.

In his robe and slippers, head still aching from too little sleep and too much arguing with his wife, Lieutenant Carlo Maddalena opened the door of his apartment in a once desirable building on the Grand Concourse in the Bronx and picked up his *Daily News*.

Behind him Maria appeared in the kitchen, cigarette in hand, and sullenly mixed herself an instant coffee. Maddalena tossed the paper on the Formica tabletop and began to make a cup of his own, then stopped. He came back to the paper. On the front page was a photo of a house engulfed in flames. Below it, in half-inch type, there was a headline: GILLIAN AIDE, EX-REPORTER PERISH. Story on page five.

"I don't suppose you'd care to give me a hint," his wife said, "just a rough guess, as to whether you'll be home for dinner tonight."

"I dunno," he replied, turning the pages and scanning the story. "I doubt it."

Tragedy, the newspaper said, struck the already troubled presidential campaign of Senator Amos V. Gillian yesterday, when senior media relations aide Laura Madison, along with former *New York Times* reporter Mitchell Rydell, died in a raging fire in a Sapphire Island beach house.

"Why should tonight be any different?" Maria said. "I keep forgetting *you* have a *job*. Maybe I'll just go out to dinner myself. It's about time I got out a little."

"Shut up, will you?" Carlo mumbled. There was a positive identification from some personal effects that survived the fire, the paper said. Remains unidentifiable, but the medical examiner was working on it. Officials said the propane tank exploded, cause unknown.

"Shut up?" Maria said. "That's great. Do yourself a favor, Carlo, go live at the station. You might as well, for all the ass you're ever gonna get again."

"Mari-aaaaa!" Carlo moaned. "Will you for Christ's sweet sake shut up!" He grabbed the paper and went to lock himself in the bathroom.

He sat on the edge of the tub and scanned the story again, thinking, they got him. Some innocent campaign girl, too. Whatever the hell *she* was doing there. Propane tank exploded, yeah, I'll bet. My oh my, is this ever starting to smell.

Maria pounded on the bathroom door. "What the hell are you doing in there?"

"Jerking off," he replied. Maria's rejoinder didn't register in his mind, because the wheels were already turning. The beach house—he'd bet cash money it was the same one Hanna had told him Rydell had visited. How did he get out of the hospital? Why return to that house? Who else had been following him lately? Most of all, *why*? What the hell was so wrong about the McCarthy death that it cost Rydell his life?

After a few minutes Maria fell silent, and Maddalena chanced to open the door. The apartment was empty. Gone shopping, he thought, or to her mother's. Fine. They'll have a good time bitching about me.

In his suit pocket from the previous day he found the address of the house Hanna had given him. He checked it against the story in the *News*. No surprise. He dialed his precinct and asked for the desk sergeant.

[131]

"Wanna do me a favor, Mike? Get me the name of the owner of record for this address," Maddalena said. "And other addresses, if any, like a place in the city."

In only a few minutes he had a name, phone number, and an address in Brooklyn. He told the desk sergeant he was on surveillance, then showered and dressed quickly.

Flatbush Avenue, he thought. That's barely on the same planet as the Grand Concourse. He devoted the long, long drive to thinking, but it didn't help.

He didn't know what to expect from this Dominick D'Anselmo, but so far nothing else was making sense, so it was worth a shot. His visit to the impound lot had turned up McCarthy's car, so badly twisted he couldn't sort out the dents in a hundred years. Still, there were crinkles in the driver's side door that didn't seem logical in a head-on crash. No paint scrapings, though, and the smell of whiskey was still strong inside the car, after all this time.

He still had to talk to the officers who'd filed the McCarthy accident report. And maybe interview the Nassau cops, too, if he could do it without drawing too much attention.

D'Anselmo lived in a semi-detached house on Avenue L, two blocks from Flatbush Avenue. Maddalena found it easily and approached the front porch, where two men were waiting for him. One was lounging in a steel chair, feet up on the porch rail. The other stood squarely in the doorway, hands in the pockets of his long black overcoat.

"Who might you be?" the second man asked Carlo, as the lieutenant mounted the steps. About thirty, Carlo guessed, with typical Guido looks, right down to the silk tie and the rough shadow of beard.

"I might be Eugene V. Debs," Carlo replied. "Who are you?"

"Well, Mr. Debs," Guido replied seriously, "state your business."

"You Dominick?"

"He don't live here."

"So you're not him?"

"You're quick," the young man said. "Real sharp. Now hit the road."

[132]

"You don't mind if I try the bell?" Carlo said. "Just to satisfy my curious nature?"

He started to reach for the doorbell, but the man stepped into his path. The older man was still sitting, watching it all with an idle smile. Guido let the front of his overcoat drop open so Carlo could see the revolver in a waistband holster.

Carlo smiled and turned away from the door.

"That's right," Guido said. "Don't make trouble . . ."

In an instant, Carlo slapped upward at Guido's chin and hit him, hard, with his right middle knuckle on just the right spot behind the ear. The young man reeled forward and Carlo grabbed the shoulders of his overcoat and pulled them down until the coat was around his waist, imprisoning his arms. The older man leaped to his feet, but a second late. Carlo greeted him with his badge, shoved into his face.

"Now," Carlo said, "it would please me a lot if you would let Mr. D'Anselmo know that Lieutenant Carlo Maddalena, NYPD, would like to talk to him. Could you do that, please?"

The older man nodded and opened the front door. Maddalena pushed Guido upright, straightened out his coat, and reached inside for the revolver.

"You got a permit for this, right?"

"Yeah, right," Guido replied.

"Of course," Carlo said, and gave him back the gun. The front door opened and he stepped inside. In the back of the house, down a narrow hallway, Dominick sat at the kitchen table. Maddalena walked back and showed his badge.

"You got lots of security," he said.

"Not too good, though, it looks like," Dom replied.

"What are you afraid of?"

"I think somebody might want to hurt me," Dom said. "I'd rather they didn't. Those guys outside work for my uncle. He's in the import business, and sometimes people want to hurt him, too."

Carlo smiled. Dom seemed like a straight enough guy, with no pretenses of being tougher than he really was, which Carlo guessed was plenty tough. He stepped further into the kitchen, and noted through the window that there were two more thugs in the backyard.

"Your concerns," he said. "Would they be connected with

[133]

the death of Mitchell Rydell in a fire at your beach house last night?"

"This an official New York police inquiry?" Dom asked.

Carlo nodded. Dom stretched his back a little, looked down at the floor, and seemed to be debating how much to tell.

"Mitchie and I go back a ways," he said at last. "We went to high school together. He came by to see me Thursday, about lunch time."

"He brought fried chicken and beer?"

Dom raised his eyebrows. "You were following him?"

"I had a man," Carlo said.

"Then he came back yesterday morning looking like he'd been through a war," Dom went on. "He was convinced somebody was trying to kill him. He must have been right."

"What did he tell you?"

"Some car had tried to drive him off the road on the expressway, he'd gotten banged up. And they tried to get him again in the hospital."

"How?"

"A phony Life Card," Dom said. "You know what that is?"

"A little wallet card with medical information on it, right?"

"More sophisticated," Dom said. "It's a laser-encoded memory, all digital. Mitchell said somebody read from his Life Card that he was a diabetic and needed a big shot of insulin. It would have killed him, probably, if he hadn't woken up just as they were giving it to him."

"Did Rydell seem in command of himself when he was telling you this?"

"How do you mean?"

"Was he upset? Frightened, panicky?"

"None of the above," Dom said. "He's not the type."

"Did you believe him?"

Dom thought a moment before answering. "Yes," he said. "I did."

Carlo drummed his fingers on his knee. "This may strike you as an odd question," he said, "but has anyone else asked you about these events? The police out on the island, for instance?"

Dom was shaking his head in amusement. "You guys are great," he said. "Don't you ever talk to each other?"

Carlo gave him a questioning look and a shrug.

"Listen," Dom said, "your big brothers the feds came by Thursday, barely an hour after Mitch left. Why don't you go ask them what I told them?"

"Bear with me," Carlo said. "What feds?"

"Guy from the Secret Service, complete with ID. I thought he was pretty well dressed for a spook."

"And what did he want?"

"Wanted to know what Mitchie and me talked about," Dom said. "I told him, pussy, mutual funds, the holes in the Giants' secondary . . ."

"Stonewalled him, in short."

"Should I be getting a lawyer?" Dom asked. "I'm trying to be helpful, but it's getting a little hot around here, if you know what I mean."

"I don't think you need a lawyer," Carlo said. "But I do think you need your uncle's friends outside."

Dom stared at Carlo for a long moment, and neither man spoke. He's deciding whether to trust me, Carlo thought. Finally Dom stood up and stretched.

"You want some coffee?"

"Is it any good?" Carlo asked.

"Best in Brooklyn," Dom said. "My mother taught me."

"Okay, then," Carlo said. "I'll stick around."

Dom busied himself at the gas range. When he had the coffeepot heating, he looked out the window.

"Look at me," he said. "I'm living like a fucking fugitive. Believe me when I tell you, I'm not used to this. I work for the fucking cable system."

He turned to Carlo.

"You after the guys that got Mitchie?"

Carlo nodded.

"You know who they are?"

Carlo shook his head.

"Now be honest with me," Dom said. "Are you prepared to follow this wherever it might lead . . . I mean *wherever*, because it might lead to some bad places."

Carlo nodded slowly, keeping his eyes fixed on Dominick.

[135]

"I think maybe I can help," Dom said. Carlo pulled out a notebook.

"Why don't you start by telling me what you and Rydell talked about on Thursday?" he said.

New rules, the lieutenant thought.

He was driving circuitously through Brooklyn—partly an accident, since he did not know the borough. But also partly by design, just like his repeated glances in the rearview mirror. And the way he had discreetly released the safety on his revolver.

Your new rules are paranoid, he thought. You haven't heard a fact all morning, not a piece of evidence that would stand up in court.

But it wasn't the kind of case that ever got to court. It was the kind of case Carlo had learned on: Leaning on one sleaze to snitch off another, then finding a key guy you could muscle hard enough to chase him out of town. Maybe not legal, but effective.

He found Senator Street by accident, circling a block for the third time. It was one-way, so he parked in the next block and walked. His jacket fell open as he got out of the car and he let his hand rest on the handle of his gun as he surveyed the street. There was no sign he was being followed, but rules were rules. There were already too many dead people.

McCarthy's mother lived in a six-story brick apartment building with the fire escapes out front. The elevator was out of order. The stairwell smelled of cigars.

A radio was playing on the fourth floor, where Mrs. McCarthy lived, and a baby cried continuously. The radio's owner, competing, turned the volume up still higher. Carlo pounded loudly on Mrs. McCarthy's door and barely heard her voice ask who was there.

"Lieutenant Maddalena, New York Police," he said. He heard clinks and rattles as several chains were undone. The door opened on a smallish woman in a housecoat, smoking. A few untied strands of gray white hair hung across her forehead.

"Yes?"

"I'd like to express my sympathy for your loss, Mrs. McCarthy," Carlo said.

"So what is this, a condolence call?" Mrs. McCarthy said. "You catch the guys that did this, that would be a consolation."

"We have no evidence of foul play, Mrs. McCarthy," Carlo said, thinking: You haven't believed that yourself in quite a while. "I'd like to ask you a few questions, if you don't mind."

"Again?"

"Police have been here before?" Carlo said, surprised.

"It ain't as if anything is going to be done," the woman replied. "Besides waste my time, I mean. It's a closed case, after all. The precinct captain said so."

Carlo noticed she was fighting back tears and trying to stop her voice from wavering.

"So what are you going to do, reopen it?" she said after a moment.

"I don't know, in all honesty," Carlo said. "But if the evidence warrants it, I promise I'll reopen the investigation."

"So what can I tell you?"

"May I come in?"

The old woman stepped aside and left the door open. Carlo closed it behind him. The front room was the kitchen, and she had a foul pot bubbling on the stove. The clock showed late lunch time. Carlo followed Mrs. McCarthy through the dinette—where a huge table covered with papers and boxes filled the room—to the living room, and took the seat she showed him.

"Mrs. McCarthy," Carlo began, "this is a little difficult . . ."

"For you?" Mrs. McCarthy said. "Yeah."

"I understand there was a discussion at your son's funeral concerning his drinking habits."

"Simple enough discussion. Dennis did not drink."

"But his blood alcohol level was enormous, according to the medical examiner," Carlo said.

"Then the medical examiner is full of shit," Mrs. McCarthy said. "Dennis wasn't a drinker. Maybe a beer now and then, but that ain't the same."

"Was he keeping company with any new people that you know of? Changing his habits?"

"Dennis didn't have a whole world of friends," his mother

said. "And that suited him. A lot of the friends he made at that hoity-toity high school his father sent him to . . ."

"Xaverian?"

"Right. A lot of those guys went on up to Wall Street to become crooks, or they became lawyers, or priests . . ."

"Left him, in short," Carlo said. "High and dry."

"Dennis wanted to stay right here," Mrs. McCarthy said, slapping the arm of her chair. "He didn't want to conquer the world. He liked Brooklyn. He liked Bay Ridge. He had just as much brains as any of them, and a hell of lot more sense of duty."

"He stayed close by you, then?"

"Right there," Mrs. McCarthy said, gesturing toward a door at the end of a narrow hallway. "That's where he belonged, and where he wanted to be."

"May I see Dennis's room, please?"

The effort of getting up seemed to daunt her. She started, paused, then waved.

"Help yourself," she said. "You don't need me."

McCarthy's room was tiny and spotless. I'll bet a drill sergeant could bounce a quarter on that bed, Carlo thought. Next to the bed was a small desk with a bookcase hung on the wall above. Six books by John LeCarré and *The Phenomenon of Man*, by Pierre Teilhard de Chardin.

Whoever that was, Carlo thought.

He sat at the dead man's desk. Its top was empty except for a fancy telephone and an answering machine. On top of the phone was a list of memory-dial numbers, but each number was identified only by an initial. Carlo lifted the receiver and idly thumbed the "redial" button. A Long Island number scrolled across the display, and Carlo hurriedly jotted it down in his notebook. Next, he pressed the button that redialed the number of the last incoming call . . . same number. He replaced the receiver and began touching the memory buttons one at a time. Each one displayed a number, and on the fourth try he found a match, keyed to the letter *S*. He jotted that next to the number in his notebook. The last calls McCarthy had received, and made, before his death, Carlo thought.

Carlo turned in the chair and looked around the room. On

top of the dresser were a small jewelry box and a photograph of two young men in uniform. Had McCarthy been in the service?

He pulled out the lower left drawer of the desk and inspected its contents: Some empty file folders, mundane office supplies, and a thick stack of recent *Newsweek* magazines. He moved on to the center drawer, which was empty, and then to the right.

Resting on top of a pile of manuscript paper was a copy of *The Blueprint for America's Defeat*, by Jonathan Marin.

"I'll be damned," Carlo said slowly. He took the book out and turned it over in his hands. Inside the front cover he found a yellowing newspaper clipping with the headline "American Nazi Leader Reported Killed."

The brief story told of rumors that Marin had been assassinated in South Africa. A second slip of paper fell out of the book, and Carlo bent over to retrieve it. "This is the guy," the handwriting said. "Presumed dead, which is thoughtful of him."

It was signed "S."

"Shouldn't you have a warrant?"

Carlo jumped guiltily at Mrs. McCarthy's voice.

"You're right," he said. "I apologize."

"Huh."

"I'm just trying to learn about Dennis. Get a feel for his life, a starting point . . ."

"Starting point for what?"

"I still don't really know, Ma'am. Did Dennis have any friends whose names began with S?"

"Shit, I don't know," the old lady said, dismissing him with a wave. "If he had any friends at all, I didn't know about them."

"No drinking buddies, even?"

"Dennis . . ."

". . . didn't drink," Carlo echoed. He gestured at the photo on the dresser.

"That your son?"

She nodded.

"He was in the service, then."

"Marines," Mrs. McCarthy said. "The photo was taken in Berlin, a long time ago."

[139]

Carlo picked up the picture. "Pardon my ignorance, but I don't know what your son looked like. Which is he?"

Mrs. McCarthy came over and pointed to the shorter of the men in the picture, thicker around the middle than his buddy and staring implacably into the camera. A man with a grudge, Carlo thought, squinting at the image from long ago.

"He was a . . . captain?"

"Lieutenant."

"Who's this with him?"

"I don't remember," Mrs. McCarthy said. "If I ever knew."

"When did he join the Marines?"

"Right after college. Right after NYU, when all his buddies were going off to medical school."

That would have been what, fifteen years ago? Carlo thought. And he'd become a lieutenant, so he'd done a fairly long stint.

"You remember what he was doing in Berlin?" he asked.

"Embassy," she replied. "He was in charge of a security shift at the American embassy there. He met the president once. Before that, the same kind of job in Beirut."

"He hated it?" Carlo said.

"Yes, how did you know?"

"Just a guess," Carlo said, looking at the staring young man in the picture.

"He said so in his letters," Mrs. McCarthy said.

"Would you happen to have any of his letters, Mrs. McCarthy?" Carlo said.

"Yes, but you can't have them," she replied. "You want to pry anymore, you go get a subpoena."

"I'd rather not have to do that," Carlo said, and thought: I'd also rather not ask for subpoenas on the basis of a hunch.

"His letters wouldn't tell you anything anyway," the old lady went on. "They were so censored you practically couldn't read them. Big black blots, three out of every four words, almost."

"Mail coming out of embassies, they read it pretty carefully," Carlo said.

"What business do they have reading an American's mail in the first place?" Mrs. McCarthy seemed enraged even by the memory.

[140]

"When he got out of the Marines, Mrs. McCarthy . . . when was that, by the way?"

"Seven, eight years ago."

"What did he do?"

"Started the paper."

"That would be the . . ."

"*Clarion.*"

"Must have cost a bundle."

"He'd saved quite a bit during his time in the service."

"Did Dennis travel much?"

She seemed startled by the question. "Of course," she replied. "He was a newspaper editor, he had to travel to cover the news."

"National news? In the *Flatbush Clarion*?"

She shrugged. "It was deductible, he said."

Carlo chuckled. The woman stood up straight and stared at him.

"Dennis was a good man, Lieutenant," she said. "He wasn't a cheat and he wasn't a drunkard, no matter what anybody said. He did his duty, which is a forgotten thing these days. He got medals, even, and a letter of commendation."

"May I see that?" Carlo said.

"What?"

"The letter of commendation," Carlo repeated. "Do you still have it?"

Mrs. McCarthy hesitated, then left the room, saying over her shoulder, "All right, but then you really must leave, and get a warrant if you want to come back."

She returned in a few moments with the family Bible, and from its back pages she took a folded letter, which she handed over to Carlo.

It was on the letterhead of the United States embassy in Berlin, U.S. Marine Corps detachment, Lieutenant Colonel Sam Peterson Mochrie commanding.

> As you leave the Corps for further challenges in your civilian life, I want you to know how grateful we all are for your courageous and invaluable service during the past year.
>
> I'm sure that, if they but knew it, your fellow citizens

would share in this sense of gratitude. While you will not have the satisfaction of public acknowledgment, you will have the great personal reward of knowing you stood your watch well, and that your crewmates are proud of you.

There is an old Japanese saying: "Who must do the hard things? He who can."

In your service to your country, you could, and you did. Thank you.

It was signed simply "Skip."

Mitchell and Laura checked into the Plaza Hotel. They brought only Marin's sports bag for luggage and paid in cash for a $350-a-night suite on the twelfth floor overlooking Central Park. The desk clerk's obvious suspicion delighted Laura. As soon as they were in their suite she called room service for a bottle of champagne.

"Are you sure about all this?" Mitchell asked her.

"Yes," she replied. "We've been thinking wrong. We've been thinking that if we revealed our whereabouts they'd come and kill us. But in fact what we have to do is *bring* them out. Make them show themselves. And we won't be caught by surprise again."

"So we act conspicuous."

"That's just for fun," Laura said. "We hardly need to. While we waited at the desk they probably ran both our names through the national hotel database to see if we ever trashed a room or ran out on a bill anywhere else, then checked us out on the FBI public-access network for criminal convictions . . . hell, within three or four minutes they probably knew all about us."

"How long before they come after us?"

Laura turned serious. "No idea," she said. "But we'd better be ready."

She put Marin's sack on the sitting room sofa and began searching through the underwear for ammunition. The pistol was still in her parka pocket. Mitchell reached in and took it out. He seemed to know it, Laura thought, as he popped the chamber and shook a full load of bullets onto the coffee table. Laura found more in the bag. As she put them down next to the loose cartridges Mitchell took her by the wrist and turned her to him.

All at once they were kissing as though their very lives depended on it. Laura clutched Mitchell's body to her, feeling the desperation of his desire, as though he wanted to wipe her out, to consume her completely. She broke her lips from his and gasped for breath.

"Oh God, Mitchell," she moaned, and in answer he kissed her again and again. They staggered together into the bedroom and Mitchell sat Laura down on the foot of the bed. Then he stepped back and quickly, businesslike, began removing his clothing. Laura leaned on her elbow and smiled at him.

"What's so amusing?" he said, pulling off his shirt.

"I've slept with three other men in my life," Laura said quietly. "There's the first of my secrets revealed. And each one got me completely naked before *he'd* removed a stitch."

Mitchell grinned and started on his pants.

"You want to hear another one?" Laura said. Mitchell stepped out of his pants, nodding.

"This is also the first time, with a new guy, that I haven't felt I had to pretend not to want it."

She let herself enjoy the moment, and Mitchell stood basking in her gaze. She lingered on his chest, the finely defined muscles, the roundness of his shoulders, his flat, thin waist, the tiny blue veins standing out in relief on the shaft of his beautiful, insistently erect penis. She loved the way his pubic hair melted into blond down on his legs.

He came to her, finally, and began undoing her blouse. Moments later she was nude to the waist, and Mitchell, kneeling, was kissing her on the nipples. Then the doorbell rang.

"The champagne," Mitchell said hoarsely. "I'd forgotten."

"I wonder why," Laura said. "Do get rid of the man as soon as possible and hurry back."

"You might use the time to finish taking off your clothes," Mitchell said lasciviously as he moved away. He took a towel from the bathroom and wrapped himself in it.

As soon as Mitchell had left Laura tore the bedclothes back and was nude in seconds, lying back on the bed in lustful anticipation. She waited eagerly for the sight of Mitchell's body in the doorway, and the delight of his touch. Faint light was coming in through the sheer inner curtains, falling on the television, the damask-upholstered chairs, the phone, the VCR, the pay TV console . . .

Then, like a movie slipping its sprockets in midframe, the whole room looked wrong. Laura's stomach was suddenly churning, and without understanding why she pulled the blankets up to cover her, drawing her legs up against her abdomen.

Mitchell found her that way when he returned, carrying an ice bucket and glasses. He put them on the night table, threw his towel into the corner, and climbed into bed. He slipped a hand under the covers and felt her bare thigh, and smiled. But Laura shivered involuntarily. She looked at the phone . . . at the TV . . . the whole room was filled with ways They could come in. She could hear them giggling, poking each other in the ribs, enjoying her nakedness and thrusting themselves into her intimacy with Mitchell.

She fought down the feeling and met Mitchell's lips with her own. Slowly he drew the covers away, and Laura sat up to embrace him, feeling for him, touching him and sensing his excitement. She rose to her knees and Mitchell's arms encircled her. He kissed her earlobes, then her neck, and over his shoulder she saw them reflected in the television screen: Two lovers, nude, entwined, captured in glass. Completely alone except for Them. A jolt of fear shot through her body and she pulled away from Mitchell, leaving him perplexed. He reached to touch her cheek.

"Laura, what is it?"

She shook her head, running a hand through her hair. "I don't know, love, I don't know." She felt tears coming, suddenly irresistible. "I don't know," she repeated. "I'm losing my mind." She pulled the covers up over her body again, covering herself, almost cowering, and hating herself for her irrationality.

"Laura, you can tell me," Mitchell said. "You can tell me anything. Look at me."

She turned to him, resting on his knees, innocent and ardent, and suddenly pulled him to her, crying uncontrollably.

"Mitchell, it's mad, it's crazy, I'm losing my mind," she said. "But I'm afraid."

"It's all right," Mitchell said, patting her shoulder. "It's natural to be afraid after what we've been through."

"No, not that," Laura said. "It's them. I feel them watching me. Watching us."

"There's no way they can see," Mitchell said.

"I know it's crazy, but I feel them watching all the same. I haven't been able to move without them knowing. Now I can't make love to the man I want more than I've ever wanted anyone, because they're here, next to us, watching . . ."

Mitchell held her silently for several moments until her tears subsided. Then he looked her in the eye.

"Get dressed," he said quietly. "We don't have to go any further if you're that uncomfortable."

She wiped her eyes. "Poor man," she said. "First I get you all hot and bothered, then I back out and break into tears besides. You don't deserve that."

"It's okay," Mitchell said. He got out of bed and walked over to the chair where his clothes lay in a heap. His erection was gone and without it he looked once again like a little boy. Laura watched him dress, then dressed herself, and they met in the living room. Mitchell had brought the champagne.

"No reason to waste it," he said. He poured two glasses and handed one to Laura.

"Believe it or not," he said, "I *do* understand how you feel."

"Imagine," Laura replied. "I used to think the right to privacy was an abstraction."

She looked at the golden liquid in her glass, then at Mitchell, and she held the glass up inviting him to toast.

"What are we drinking to?" Mitchell said.

"To a simple fact, recently discovered," Laura said. She fixed him with a steady gaze and added: "I love you, Mitchell. More than I ever thought I could."

They were asleep on the sofa when the phone rang. They had drifted off in midcuddle, Mitchell's hand resting idly on Laura's breast and her head lying against his chest. The phone's ring was strange, quiet, electronic, and the little red message light on the handset flickered with each new signal.

Wrong number? she thought. Would They call us, even if They knew we were here?

Mitchell stirred and came awake as Laura sat up to answer the phone.

A thin, reedy voice came over the wire. It sounded like old Sewer-Mouth from the night of the cable broadcast.

"We got your message," the voice said.

"Who is this?"

"Doesn't matter," the voice said flatly. "Are you Laura Madison?"

"Yes."

"The one that's dead?"

"That's right."

"Wanna be dead again? For real?"

Laura took a deep breath. "I'm going to hang up in three seconds if you don't come to the point. One, two—"

"*You're* the one who wanted a meeting, right? A negotiation, you said, although you're in no position to bargain for anything."

"You owe it to me, you sneaky bastard," Laura said. Mitchell was motioning for her to calm down. "I've got evidence. Proof."

"Proof? Of what, I wonder?"

"A meeting," Laura said. "It's got to be face to face, and it's got to be in a crowded public place."

"The lobby bar in the Plaza," the voice said. "Right now." And the line clicked.

She looked at Mitchell. "He says to meet downstairs in the lobby bar. Now."

Mitchell thought a moment. "No way we'll be able to tail him. He's bound to be too smart for that, and he might not lead us anywhere anyway."

"So what do we do?"

"You go meet him," Mitchell said. He picked up Marin's revolver and reloaded it, then shoved it into his waistband.

"Please be careful," she said.

"You, too," Mitchell replied. "I'm taking the stairs, so give me a head start."

She waited an extra minute at the elevator, then rode down to the lobby. Glancing around nervously, she made her way to the bar. She saw nobody that seemed likely to be Him, and when the maître d' approached she took a corner table and ordered a white wine.

The man arrived before her drink and sat down without being asked. He was about forty, Laura guessed, thin and pale and dressed in an unremarkable gray suit.

"Madison?"

"Yes."

"Your man going to do what he has to do, or not?"

"You have a name?" she asked.

"How about Smith?"

"Very original." Smith lit a cigarette, shook the match out and tapped the tabletop.

"Well?"

"The Senator isn't going to admit to knowing Jonathan Marin," Laura said. "And we've got proof the two never met."

"As you know, there's proof they did," Smith said. "And there could easily be more. There could be some nice tidbits about you, too."

"You can't scare me," Laura said. Smith chuckled.

"Oh, no? You don't know the half of it. You can't begin to imagine."

"Is Erhardt behind this?" Laura said, feeling her skin tighten.

"Give me a break, lady, I've got things to do."

"Where did that photo come from? When and where was it created? Give me some reason to believe it's real," Laura said.

"It doesn't matter what *you* believe," Smith said. "Sixty million other people will take it at exactly face value."

Laura saw Mitchell leaning against the wall far across the lobby, pretending to read a newspaper. She forced her eyes back to the man at the table, but he had noticed her glance.

"Ah," he said, "tricks. I might have known." He stood up and stubbed his cigarette out on the tabletop. "Well," he said, "the whole world is going to see that photo of Gillian and Marin Monday night. We might make it a double feature. We've got a nice one of you, you know, in your birthday suit, having fun with a dog." Smith sneered. "I must say," he added, "we improved on your body considerably."

[147]

"Bastard," Laura muttered. The man turned to leave, and she saw Mitchell stand up and start moving casually across the lobby. Smith was five paces away when she jumped up and raced after him.

"You son of a bitch!" she called. "Who do you think you are?" She grabbed him by the shoulder and spun him around, then surprised him with a hard slap across the face. Mitchell was at her side in moments. She'd gotten the attention of everyone in the bar.

"This little creep just shoved his hand between my legs," Laura said loudly, and Smith colored deeply, then tried to push by her. Mitchell grabbed him and punched him in the stomach, doubling him over.

Suddenly they were surrounded by men in hotel blazers and quickly, almost in a blur, spirited through the lobby and into the security office. After a few minutes of tense silence the head of security came in, a bundle of papers in his hand. A tired-looking man in his fifties, he sat down behind his desk and motioned for everyone else to take seats.

"He was molesting my wife," Mitchell kept repeating. "What the hell do you expect me to do?"

"Your wife," the house detective said, and shook his head. "You checked in earlier today, didn't you, with a gym bag for luggage, and paid cash? Then ordered champagne from room service?"

"She was waiting for me in the bar," Mitchell said loudly. "Just having a drink, minding her own business, when this misfit comes up and starts groping her. Why the inquisition on us?"

Smith was sitting silently, sneering at Laura. Now he began making obscene noises at her, and Mitchell jumped across at him in a rage. One of the security men got between them, and suddenly they froze. The security man patted Mitchell on the hip, then reached under his jacket and brought out Marin's gun.

"Jesus H. Sebastian God," the house detective said. "Why'd you pick my hotel, anyway?"

Mitchell took a deep breath, let it out, and stayed quiet.

"Don't turn this around," Laura said. "This man assaulted

[148]

me. My husband was just coming to my aid. What are you going to do about it?"

"What I'm going to do," the detective said with a sigh, "is let the NYPD sort it out." He picked up the phone, dialed, then turned to Laura.

"For the record," he said over the mouthpiece, "you folks are all under arrest."

"Close the door, Carlo."

Maddalena shut the glass-paneled door and leaned against Captain Turley's filing cabinet.

"Carlo," Turley said. "I asked you to have somebody follow this Rydell guy, you didn't have to make a crusade out of it. What the hell was Hanna doing on Sapphire Island, for Christ's sake?"

"There's a lot more here than meets the eye, Captain," Carlo said.

"What? You all but disappear from the precinct for days at a time, nothing else gets done, papers piling up on your desk till you can't even see over them—"

"Captain—"

"And Rydell ends up dead anyway!" Turley exploded. "Hardly a smart application of manpower, Carlo."

"The whole case is fishy, sir," Maddalena said.

"Bullshit," the Captain interrupted. "And as far as you're concerned it's over. I want you to take a couple of days off."

"But you just said the work was piling up on my desk."

"Don't wiseass me. Whatever interest City Hall had in Rydell is over. He's dead."

"He was murdered."

"Carlo, he died in a fire. The propane tank exploded. These things happen. And this one happened on Sapphire Island, not in the City."

"There were two earlier attempts on his life," Maddalena said. "It's all linked to his asking questions about the McCarthy accident, if it was an accident."

"*If* it was . . ." Turley slapped his desk blotter hard enough to knock over his pencil jar, then came around to the front of the desk, chest to chest with Maddalena.

[149]

"You losing it, Carlo? Seeing murders and conspiracies? Whatever happened to being a cop, to doing your job?"

"This is my job, Captain," Carlo said. "It's called investigation. Why is it so important to you that I back off? What's going on here?"

"Lieutenant, I resent the innuendo you're making."

"I'm not making any innuendo," Carlo said. "I'm saying I have prime cause to suspect homicide in the Rydell case and you're not letting me pursue it."

"For the record," Turley said slowly through his teeth, "I am the captain here. Even if this alleged crime had occurred in our jurisdiction, which it didn't, it would be my right to pull you off it and assign anyone I wanted. And any officer under my command would have the right to seek other work if they don't like it. Now about those few days off, I strongly suggest it."

"That an order?"

"Call it advice from your CO."

Maddalena stepped back and looked at Turley. The captain's nostrils were flaring and his eyes quivered with rage. Maddalena felt his stomach fluttering as he walked slowly across the office to look out the window at the street, then through the glass panels into the busy station. He reached into his pocket, pulled out his badge wallet, and tossed it on Turley's desk.

"Carlo, you out of your mind?"

"No, sir," said Maddalena. "Just feeling a little sick."

"You're a good cop, Carlo. Don't do anything stupid."

"Sorry." Maddalena reached under his jacket and took his service revolver from its holster, then dropped that on the captain's desk, too.

Turley watched him in silence as he let himself out of the office. Officer Hanna was standing in a corner of the precinct lobby, leaning on a desk, and when he saw Carlo he turned his back. Carlo was crossing the squad room heading for his locker when a commotion coming in the double doors got his attention. Then he looked up and came face to face with Mitchell Rydell. There was a young woman with him, and a skinny, foul-looking man who had apparently been giving the arresting officers a hard time. They had tight grips on his upper arms and were handling him rather firmly, Maddalena thought.

"What the hell are you doing here?" Carlo asked Rydell in a low voice.

"Good question, Lieutenant," Rydell replied. One of the officers spoke to Carlo.

"They caused a little disturbance at the Plaza," he said. "The hotel don't care about pressing charges, they just wanted to be rid of the lot. The lady here has an assault charge against the skinny guy, who by the way is a pain in the ass."

"No reason it can't all get settled very simply," Maddalena said. "Let him go."

The officers let go of Smith, and he straightened out his lapels very officiously.

"What's the story?" Maddalena said to him.

"I don't have to talk to you," Smith said. Maddalena shrugged.

"That's true, you're entitled to wait for your lawyer."

"What am I charged with?"

"I'll think of something," Carlo said.

"Stuff it, Lieutenant," Smith said. "My lawyer will be along any minute and explain the facts of life to you."

"Charming," Maddalena said as he turned to Rydell.

"Come with me," he said. "Bring the lady." Over his shoulder, he told the desk sergeant, "Interrogation One."

In the interrogation room Maddalena took a chair and gestured for Laura and Mitchell to do the same, but they stood silently.

"What's going on, friends?" Maddalena said.

"What are we charged with?" Mitchell replied. Maddalena stared at the ceiling.

"Geez, all these lawyers," he said. "You ain't charged with nothing, and you're not going to be charged. Unless the lady really wants to press that assault charge, there's no reason you can't just walk right out of here."

Laura headed for the door and grabbed the knob, but stopped when she heard Maddalena's voice behind her.

"Then maybe next time they *will* get you. Maybe next time you *will* burn up. Or get shoved off the highway. Or get struck by lightning."

[151]

Laura turned to him. "You know what's been happening?"

Carlo nodded. "A little."

"You followed me out to Sapphire Island?" Mitchell said.

"I had a man follow you. He saw what happened on the highway. And I talked to Dominick D'Anselmo this morning. I don't know as much about what's happening as you do, but I know enough to know it stinks."

"That man out there," Laura said. "Smith. He works for them."

"Who's them?" Maddalena said.

Mitchell and Laura exchanged glances. "Erhardt, or at least his people," Mitchell said. "Emile Loubert. Some pretty heavy company."

Maddalena frowned. "You hit me at a bad time," he said. "It seems I just turned in my badge." He stood up. "Well, let's get out of here and get somewhere we can talk serious. First, let me see if I can arrange for your friend to spend some time downstairs."

Laura and Mitchell followed Carlo back to the front desk. Hanna was standing off to the side, avoiding Carlo's glance.

"You had a talk with the captain, huh?" Carlo said.

"Just answered his questions," Hanna said, shrugging. "What else could I do?" His hands were shaking, and he rubbed them together nervously.

"Nothing else," Carlo said. "I don't expect you to put your own career on the line for my little passions." Carlo put an arm on the younger man's shoulder, trying to soothe him. Hanna was glancing around the room dartingly and breathing in short gasps. "Don't worry about it," Carlo said.

Hanna nodded, smiled, and backed off a step or two. Carlo turned to the desk sergeant.

"I think there's a warrant out for this guy," he said.

"Horseshit," Smith said.

"I'd hold him while I checked," Carlo said. "Maybe even talk to him a little, in private."

The desk sergeant chuckled and nodded.

Laura began backing away from Smith before anything had happened, she didn't know why. She saw everything that happened over Maddalena's shoulder. Hanna, twitching, hyperventilating, murmuring "Jesus, dear God," again and again, then the pistol in his hand, the tiny flowers of flame at its mouth. Turley and Maddalena moving toward him. Blood covering the front of Smith's suit as he started to fall forward. The crashing reports of shots in the tiny room. A bullet shattered a ceiling lamp and glass fell on them. Maddalena reached for Hanna, but the young cop, eyes bulging, shoved him back, then turned the pistol toward his own face. The black barrel going into his mouth. Another terrible crash, a fountain spray of blood and bone, shouts of horror from toughened men. Smith on his hands and knees, crawling toward Laura. She backed away, shaking her head, mouthing soundlessly, no, no. Mitchell held her and she dug her fingernails into his arms.

"Madison," Smith gasped. There were policemen all around now, pulling his clothes apart, straightening him, seeking his wounds.

"Ambulance on the way!" someone shouted.

"Madison," said Smith, in barely a croak. He held out his hand.

Slowly Laura crouched by him, and he grabbed her shirt-front with his bloody fingers. Blood was seeping from his nostrils.

"Loubert . . ." he said.

Smith fell away from her and she pried his hand from her blouse. She heard a cop say, "Tell the ambulance no hurry."

"Are you all right?" Maddalena said, offering her tea. They were at his apartment in the Bronx. His wife was away, he said. Dominick and Mitchell shared the sofa, whispering. Laura had said nothing since they came up here at dusk. Now she ignored the lieutenant's offer of tea and he walked away, shaking his head, taking her silence for shock. She saw Mitchell's glance of concern.

She had no words to explain that the shock of what had happened at the station was giving way not to fear or grief but to a cold, growing rage.

Again and again she saw Smith falling toward her, and Hanna's brains spraying on the station-house wall. Foot soldiers, she thought, doing what they thought was their job. What had they found on Officer Hanna? she wondered. How had they induced him to silence Smith and himself at the same

[153]

time, and stamp "Dead End" on that avenue of investigation? Perhaps a terrible secret kept that way forever, she thought, and cash to the family for future security. A quick job, and a painless exit, kid. Do the right thing. For God and Country.

And they'd kill anyone who got in their way. No trials, no discussions, no appeals. Just kill and kill.

Again and again she heard Smith's last words, driven from his throat by his last choking breath. Loubert. The right-hand man to the President of the United States.

So it was Erhardt. The President of the United States. Bastard—sleazy, cheating, murderous bastard.

Mitchell came over to sit by her.

"Laura?" he said softly. She looked at him and thought of making love and thought of Mitchell dead in a wreck by the side of the road, the man she loved gone because he was honest and unafraid and in the way.

Bastard. Despicable son of a bitch.

"Dom and I think we ought to run through it all," Mitchell said. "With everybody here. Everything each of us knows, things we may have overlooked or not told anyone else. You don't have to talk, just listen, okay?"

She nodded.

"Well," Dom said, sitting forward. "We have a link here between President Erhardt and Loubex, the company Emile Loubert founded, that Erhardt's company bought out. They're friends, and Loubert is the President's advisor. And he's a genius, one of the real certifiable wizards of the computer age. He doesn't just wire components together or write programs for somebody else's machines. He creates new concepts."

Dom got up and paced a little, arms folded, thinking out loud.

"There have been three attempts on Mitchell's life—on the road, at the hospital, and at my beach house. Mitch's old friend Dennis McCarthy is dead, under suspicious circumstances. With"—Dom glanced at Maddalena—"some very iffy police paperwork. The Gillian campaign has been scuttled by allegations that he's a Nazi, backed up by what might be manufactured proof, transmitted over a cable television hookup in the middle of the night.

"There's a common thread in all of this. The cable transmission, the photo, the phone taps, the Life Card. None of these technologies is all that remarkable in and of itself. In fact, they're all pretty commonplace. But the pattern seems to lead to some conclusions."

Mitchell nodded vigorously. "First conclusion. Erhardt is trying to sabotage Gillian and guarantee the outcome of the election."

"More than that," Dom said. "He's using Loubert as his point man in a systematic attempt to screw his enemies, political, journalistic, whatever. And somewhere in this country there's a computer system helping him to do it. And it's got to be a big one."

"They tapped our phones," Mitchell said. "They accessed my line and took your number from my phone's memory."

"Phone taps are no great challenge, given the technology at their disposal," Dom said. "In fact, the combination of Loubert's brains, the $300 or $500 million Erhardt's company paid for Loubex, plenty of time, nothing else to do, and all the resources of the U.S. government to back them up . . . hell, it would be a surprise if they couldn't reach into every house in America."

"Isn't that a little paranoid, even for these circumstances?" Maddalena put in. "We know somebody tried to kill Rydell, but there's no evidence of any more than that."

"Let's consider," Dom said. He sat back down and pointed to Mitchell. "They went after Mitch with a phony Life Card. What does that take?

"First of all," he continued, "it has to be plausible. You want to plant the fatal little piece of false information, in this case Rydell's supposed diabetes, among as much real stuff as possible. Ideally it's the only untrue thing on the card. That way, even if it's detected, it could be passed off as a mistake, not deliberate. And you need a large volume of data, not just a little skeleton. It has to look like a card you've been adding to for years."

Laura was watching Dominick's face, then Mitchell's. Your life changes so completely, so fast, she thought. A short time ago I was on top of the world. I had an exciting job on a presidential campaign. My life was finally starting to get back together. Now I have to fight to stay alive.

"Now," Dominick said, "what do you need to build a Life Card?"

"A medical history," Mitchell answered. Laura stared at him, thinking, nobody's taking you away. Not without a fight.

"And how tough is that?" Dom said.

"It's confidential," Mitchell said. "It would be a huge job to compile even a little bit, and there's no guarantee even that would be available."

"Oh no? You got health insurance?"

"Of course, through the *Times*."

I'm alive, Laura thought, and she played the idea over in her mind. She felt her eyebrows furrow closer together, and noticed that Mitchell shot her an inquisitive look. *And the people trying to kill me are the only ones, outside of this room, that know it.*

"Then every medical bill you've had since you've been in the plan is on a computer somewhere," Dom said. "With identifying code numbers for every procedure a doctor's done on you, every lab test you've had, every prescription. Plus all your doctors' names, labs, hospitals. Somewhere in there is your pediatrician's name, your parents' names and address, and the big prize, your Social Security number. With a little study and imagination, a very plausible medical history for you, or for anybody, could be invented and recorded digitally. Once it's in the computer, of course, it becomes the truth whether it's real or not. The hospital isn't about to run a blood test to see if you really *have* diabetes. The card says so, and it provides your dosage, so here comes the needle."

"And with my Social Security number—"

"They can access tax returns. They know what banks are holding your money and how much it is. From the bank computers they can find out what kind of car you drive and access your credit card records. Which tells them where you go, where you eat, what hotels you stay in. It reveals married guys on business trips ordering room service for two when their wives are at home with the kiddies. You name it. How often have you presented a credit card and driver's license as ID for a check?"

"A million times."

"A few extra steps, they find out what you buy, what you earn, your whole driving record. You got cable TV?"

"Two-way," Mitchell said. "Like everybody else on the East Side."

Maddalena grunted.

"You love it, right?" Dominick said. "You order your groceries through the cable and it debits your checking account. You dial up a friend and you can see him while you talk. You take part in instant public opinion polls using your cable TV keypad. Hell, I read last week there are even a hundred communities in America that intend to conduct their elections through their cable systems. But has it occurred to you that somebody's keeping track of what movies you watch, and that there's a little video camera built into your set that can see you, and that's turned on and off from somewhere else, without you knowing?"

"I never thought about it," Mitchell said. "I guess I try not to."

"You're too busy living your life to worry about these things," Dominick said. "They're so damned convenient you figure the downside is mostly paranoia."

"But nobody can compromise all these systems," Mitchell said. "You'd have to get into every computer in the country."

"No," Dom replied. "All you need is a telephone, and an understanding of the wonderful world of computer matching. Social Security, IRS, the FBI data bank, maybe a bank check clearinghouse—get into those four computers and you've got America by the balls."

"But wouldn't that take a lot of resources?" Maddalena interrupted. "A huge computer, maybe several . . ."

"They've *got* huge resources," Dominick said, sawing the air with his palm. "They've got the United States of America, maybe the biggest computerized operation in the world. Hell, nobody even knows what half the computers in the government are doing, and most of them are only using a fraction of their capacity. You could hide in the IRS computer system alone for a thousand years and nobody would know. Especially now. Erhardt's so proud of how he simplified the tax code and eliminated so many forms. But did he lay anybody off at IRS?

What are those huge computers doing now that they've got half the work they used to have?

"And besides, the trend has been away from giant computers and toward smaller computers linked in networks. Which, in the process, makes it easier to spread the dirty little secrets around and reduce the chances of discovery even further. Use your imagination. Put a billion dollars in their hands and see what they could do.

"They've got another advantage," Dom said, crossing the small living room to look out the window. "The climate is right for it. Computers are so firmly entrenched now that nothing can dislodge them. And as Mitchie here pointed out, they're making things so convenient and easy for so many people that nobody even wants to ask the questions. The Selective Service System buys mailing lists from Baskin Robbins Ice Cream, for Christ's sake, because the little kiddies come in for free birthday sundaes and have to prove their age. So they go on file.

"You try to rent an apartment, and your landlord can call a computer database that lists 'troublesome' tenants nationwide. You ever had a fight with your landlord? You're blacklisted. Or you go to a new doctor, with one call he can find out if you've ever sued anyone for malpractice. The IRS checks local real estate records by computer to catch tax evaders. Payroll records are matched against student loan delinquents, welfare records cross-matched to bank accounts, Social Security against death records. In some states you can't get a marriage license if you have outstanding parking tickets. All done by computers, all nice and quiet. Completely unrelated information linked into a bigger and bigger network. It's here to stay, and hardly anyone realizes it."

"But most of what you're talking about," Mitchell said, "the doctors, the landlords, that's not the government. That's all private."

"Exactly," Dom said. "Nobody's a bigger fan of this stuff than business. Your employer ain't in business to protect the Constitution. If you've tested positive for AIDS he wants to know. If you're using drugs he wants to know. If you've ever missed a day of work to go get a shot for syphilis, he thinks he's got a right to know that, too.

"Look at that cockamamy war on drugs Bush got so hot about a few years ago," Dom went on. "He never could have gotten away with the government mandating drug tests for every citizen, even though the public was ready to give him carte blanche. Instead, he tells the business world, assure us you're maintaining a drug-free workplace. And good old business, they're up there on the ramparts waving urine jars, ready to trash the Bill of Rights in the name of productivity.

"The drug scare was the pretext. The camel's nose under the tent flap. Except that right now, the camel's ass may still be outside, but that's about all."

All at once Laura stood and crossed the room. The men's faces followed her, startled by her sudden activity.

"Laura?" Mitchell said. "You okay?"

She turned to him.

"I'm alive!" she said. His face was perplexed and concerned, so she shouted it: "I'm alive! And the people trying to kill me are the only ones that know it!"

She grabbed the phone from its cradle and began dialing. Mitchell came over behind her and put a hand on her shoulder.

"Laura, take it easy," he said. "The phones aren't safe."

"So what?" she replied. "I'm through hiding."

There was an answer on the line and she spoke into the mouthpiece. "Western Union, I want to send a telegram. To Marty Madison, aboard the *Hotspur* . . . it's a boat . . . Slip Fifty-one, Doubloon Marina, Key West, Florida. Message. Dear Dad . . ."

"Laura!" Mitchell snapped. "You can't . . ."

"Horseshit," Laura replied above the mouthpiece of the phone. "Yes," she said into it, "excuse me. Dear Dad. Alive and well. Coming to see you and will try to call. Much to explain. Be extra extra careful. Love you a lot, signed Laura."

She gave the operator her home number for the charges, then hung up. Mitchell was watching her with his arms folded.

"You trying to get your father killed, too?" he said quietly. Laura looked over at Maddalena, but the lieutenant only shrugged.

"In an odd way," he said, "you guys may all be safer today than you were yesterday."

"How so?" Mitchell asked.

"You're dead. You have death certificates now, all official. They do away with you now and they have to explain the previous time. Especially since you've been seen around, by people like police officers. So if they get you, it has to be absolutely private. Stay in public, in crowds, and you might be okay."

He turned to Laura. "When are you going?"

"Tonight," she said.

"Laura," Mitchell interrupted. "We should discuss this a little more carefully."

"No, Mitch," she replied. "No more sitting around waiting for them to try again. This time *you* have to trust *me*."

Maddalena was riffling through his phone book, then picked up the phone and dialed.

"Information, Key West, please, or anywhere on the Keys," he said. "I want the number for the Florida State Police substation nearest Key West." He waited, scribbled, hung up and dialed again.

"I'd like to speak to the commanding officer, please," he said. Another wait. "Lieutenant? This is Lieutenant Carlo Maddalena, New York City Police, and I need a favor, one cop to another. I'd like to ask you to keep a sort of protective eye on a citizen whom I think may be in danger from some mob types there. I wouldn't ask you for around-the-clock. Just a little extra look-in now and then. The guy could turn out to be an important witness, if he lives. Anything you can do. Of course. Appreciate it. Name is Madison, Marty, lives on a boat called the *Hotspur*, in a marina . . ." He looked at Laura.

"Doubloon," Laura said.

"Doubloon Marina," Maddalena said. "In Key West. Slip Fifty-one. Many thanks. You ever need anything in New York, you call me."

He recited his phone number into the line. Laura pulled on her coat, avoiding Mitchell's eyes.

"When will you be back, can you at least tell me that?" Mitchell said.

"No later than tomorrow night, I promise," she replied, and they shared a small kiss. Laura hesitated, then went back to the phone and dialed again.

"I want to get a message to Marty Madison, at Slip Fifty-one," she said. "Tell him his daughter called. She's fine and coming down. He should be careful and if *anything*, I repeat, *anything* unusual should happen before I get there, he's to call Lieutenant Carlo Maddalena."

She read the number off Carlo's phone.

"It's super-urgent, please get it to him as soon as possible," she said. She hung up and faced the men.

"What now?" Maddalena said.

"The key to the whole thing is Loubert," Dominick said. "I think we should split up, and spend tomorrow finding out everything we can about him."

Maddalena smiled weakly. "I gotta go to my captain, eat some crow and get my badge and gun back. And tell him I need some personal leave to sort out my life. I think *this* is going to be my job for a while. Listen, tell me something," he said, and squeezed his lower lip with his fingers.

"You folks are in politics, some of you. Would anyone really kill over an election? I mean multiple killings, killing people they don't even know, just for an election?"

"Who knows?" Mitchell responded. "Your values get twisted around once you're in office. A sort of us-against-them mentality takes hold. You start thinking you're on a mission from God and nothing can be allowed to stop you."

Laura zipped up her parka. "I'll call," she said. "Here or wherever I can. Mitch, do me a favor?"

"Anything."

"Call Cavanagh. Don't explain, just say I'm okay for now. And have him tell the Senator to give 'em hell tonight."

The planes to Florida were full. Laura bought a ticket and listed herself on stand-by for three flights, two to Miami and one to Orlando, then watched one of the Miami flights and the Orlando plane take off full. It was nearly nine o'clock. She couldn't stand to sit idle another moment, and finally she gave $500 of Marin's money to a woman for her boarding pass. She was among the last to get a seat on the second Miami flight, boarding just before the doors were clamped shut. She sat back, tired, and watched first the runway, then the city lights, slip out of sight.

It was after midnight when they arrived in Miami, and she

passed through the deserted terminal quickly, paying cash for a rental car and finding her way out to the Florida Turnpike easily in the light traffic.

Just after crossing onto Key Largo, she passed a trailer park with a gravel parking lot out front, pulled into a far corner where she hoped she'd be unobtrusive, and napped awkwardly for another couple of hours. Then she drove the lonely black two-lane highway with the radio on. Route 1 is Route 1, she thought, no matter where you are. Fast food joints, some open all night. Used car lots up north, used boat lots here. Restaurants, motels. And long stretches of emptiness, the mangrove swamps and islands to either side invisible in the night.

She crossed the Seven-Mile Bridge and felt the expanse of ocean to her left, Florida Gulf to her right. Straight right, she thought, it's a thousand miles to the first landfall. Where would that be, New Orleans? Straight left, the ocean went on and on. She felt its presence as a void, enveloping her as she followed the skinny asphalt path.

She saw the light rising as she neared the end of the highway, and the sun was above the horizon when she crossed onto Key West and took A-1-A along the south shoreline. The waves pressed in on the beach. There was a man jogging in the dawn, with his dog.

She winced at an overwhelming, keening noise above her, and peered up through her windshield in time to see the underside of a jet fighter streaking toward the Naval Air Station, its gear down for landing.

Sunday, November 3

Let Dominick go to the library, Maddalena thought as he walked through the doors of 125 Worth Street in lower Manhattan. Libraries are his thing. Me, I'm a cop.

In the lobby, near a sign directing him to the Bureau of Vital Statistics, City of New York, Carlo waited for the man from Police Liaison to arrive. The inner doors were open and some people were at work, even though it was Sunday. They never stop filing the stuff, Maddalena thought. Because the public never stops creating it. Births, deaths, marriages, divorces, home sales . . .

The police liaison was an overweight man in drooping jeans and an Aran cable-knit sweater, who barely acknowledged the lieutenant before leading him through the hall to a cluttered office behind a frosted glass door.

"Technically," the liaison man said, "corporate records reside with the Secretary of State. But we have a workstation here that can access them. The city needs the data all the time, to cross-check on sales taxes, safety code violations, all sorts of stuff."

He sat down at a computer console and turned the machine on. It went through a quick initialization procedure and was soon ready for work.

"Name?"

"Love Bytes, Inc.," Carlo said, giving him the name of the registered owner of the white car.

"And what do you want to know?"

"Incorporating attorney, corporate secretary, principals, whatever."

The man hummed tunelessly while jabbing at the computer keys. In a few moments the laser printer on the next table began to hum and printed out a precis of the corporate record. The incorporating attorney and corporate secretary were names that meant nothing to Carlo, but on the list of principal officers and stockholders, three names down, he found Sam Peterson Mochrie. Good old "S," Carlo thought, is part owner of the company that owns the car that drove Mitchell Rydell into the bridge support. Mochrie's listed address was an APO, overseas military posting.

The report included basic data from the previous year's corporate annual report. The balance sheet showed a small amount of cash on hand, no assets in the form of furniture or equipment, a couple of other cars (Carlo jotted down the license numbers), and no debts. Under assets, more than twenty patent numbers were listed, but no details.

"Tra la," the liaison man said. "Anything else?"

Carlo was thinking. "Not right now," he said. "Okay if I come back?"

"You let me go now, you can't get me back until tomorrow," the man replied. Carlo paused a moment, then folded the papers up and put them in his jacket pocket.

"Good enough," he said.

Next, he walked a block across the park to the New York State Department of Motor Vehicles. On Worth Street he was accosted by a woman handing out Erhardt flyers and pushed by her with a grunt. Nearly every street lamp had a campaign poster or two attached to it. At the DMV he found another police liaison officer waiting for him, smiling ear to ear.

"Great day, eh, Lieutenant?" he called. "Great day for a little time-and-a-half. And home in time for the football game."

He continued to prattle as he unlocked the main door and led Maddalena to his own office. Inside, they sat down on either side of an incredibly cluttered desk. The bureaucrat leaned forward and folded his hands like a priest.

"What can I do for you?"

Carlo handed him his handwritten list of tag numbers. "I know the current owners of these vehicles, and I'd like to know the previous ones. And I'd like to know anything else about them, like unpaid parking tickets, other vehicles registered to the same people, something . . ."

"Gonna take a little while," the liaison man said. The all-purpose excuse, Carlo thought.

"I got time."

"Give me, oh, say, an hour?"

Carlo extended his hand. "Good deal," he said. "Listen, you ever need a favor from a cop—and who doesn't, now and then?—you call me, okay? I'll be back."

A public record is a wonderful thing, he thought as he stepped back into the midmorning sunshine. He walked a few minutes enjoying the weather, then bought a hot dog from a vendor and sat down on the front steps of City Hall.

Mitchell Rydell sat on a bench at a bus stop and stared across the street at the Great Neck Medical Center. He had walked entirely around the building, trying to reconstruct where he'd been Thursday night, but everything looked different. A boy stood on the corner with a boom box stuck to his ear, and Mitchell heard the beat of the music give way to an announcer's frantic voice, giving the headlines as though the Russians were landing in Montauk. Senator Amos V. Gillian was resuming his campaign today, after his startling television broadcast last night . . .

The boy cut the announcer off in midword, switching to another station for music. Mitchell saw Gillian's name again, on a billboard overlooking the avenue half a block away, next to the Senator's serious face.

A bus came and went, leaving behind a clattering echo and a gray cloud of exhaust. Mitchell watched a steady stream of people go through the hospital entrance. Finally he stood up, stretched, and crossed the street as casually as he could.

He passed through the lobby unchallenged. Five, he thought, I think I was on five. He took the elevator and paused a moment as he got off, looking around. The nurses' station was ten yards to his left, and a dayroom to his right was filled with patients and their families, enjoying the sun that streamed in through the large plate windows.

Mitchell was sure the nurse at the station was not the one

he'd knocked out making his escape. He approached her slowly, eyes scanning the corridors for trouble.

"May I help you?" The nurse was twenty. Maybe twenty-two. She had dark hair and eyes and a perfectly white smile. Mitchell smiled back at her a little sheepishly.

"I was a patient here the other day . . ."

"I thought so," the girl said. "Weren't you in an accident or something?"

"Something," Mitchell replied. "I left in sort of a hurry."

"So I hear," the girl said. "I came on duty just afterwards and heard all about it. Should I call security right now?"

"Please don't," Mitchell said. "I just want to get my Life Card back, that's all. I've already squared things about the other night. I was confused and panicked, that's all. Could you dig up my card, possibly? I'd hate to be without it."

The young nurse turned her back to Mitchell, rummaged in a file drawer, then returned with a folder.

"It says here the card was turned over to your doctor," she said. "He signed for it yesterday, saying he would return it to you. He said it needed updating."

"My doctor?" Mitchell replied. "My GP or a specialist?"

The nurse shrugged. "Doctor Fontana, whoever that is." She showed him a paper with a signature on it—Peter J. Fontana, M.D. "Actually, I think he came out here expecting to find you still here. But you had already, like you say, left in a hurry."

Mitchell smiled, shrugged, and left the nurses' station. He returned to the hospital lobby and found the administrative office. A middle-aged woman sat at a computer terminal just inside the door.

"Can you tell me if you have a Dr. Fontana on staff?" Mitchell asked her.

"Doesn't ring a bell," she said. Touching the keyboard she called up a scrolling list on the screen.

"No, sir," she said after a moment. "No Fontana, either on staff or attending."

"You allow doctors from other areas to use the hospital, if they have patients here?"

"In an emergency, of course," the woman said. "Any licensed practitioner."

[166]

"Any way you can check and see if there's been a Dr. Fontana in the facility in the last few days?"

"Why?"

"He mistakenly took my Life Card," Mitchell said. "Thought it belonged to one of his patients. I need to contact him and get it back."

The clerk cleared her screen and with a few keystrokes called up more records. "We have no insurance billing or other paperwork for any procedures ordered by a Dr. Fontana," she said. "That would indicate he didn't actually use any hospital services, even if he were here." She continued to tap the keyboard. A long, scrolling series of names ran over the screen.

"The New York State Medical Society has twenty-one entries for Fontana," she said. "None in our immediate area."

"Where's the nearest one?"

"Manhattan," she said. She isolated the entry and Mitchell, peering over her desk, made a note of the address, on First Avenue.

"You got an instinct, Lieutenant," the police liaison man said when Carlo returned to the DMV. He was behind his buried desk, looking up with a delighted grin. "I guess that's how come you're a detective."

"What are you talking about?"

"I traced those tag numbers," the man responded. "And one of them has a list of parking fines as long as your arm, all unpaid. Your uniformed brothers ever find that car, they're gonna put it away in the farthest impound lot they got." He held a sheaf of papers out to Maddalena.

The lieutenant glanced down the list, noting first of all that none of the cars turned out to be a white Chevy. The tags from the white car—which he had noted in the alley the night Marin disappeared—ought to be on a dark blue Volvo. Just as Hanna had reported.

It was the Volvo that had the outstanding tickets. There was nothing on any of the other cars.

"Do me a favor," Carlo said.

"Anything. I ain't had this much fun in years."

"The registration on this Volvo with all the tickets, it's got the vehicle identification number on it, right?"

"Right."

"Can you find out the first time Love Bytes registered the car, whether it was new, or were there any previous owners? And I'd like the locations of the parking tickets."

"Ten minutes," the liaison man said. Maddalena made himself at home in the office while the man busied himself with key tapping and humming. The lieutenant took the *Sports Illustrated* swimsuit calendar down off the wall and checked each month for typographical errors. August required particularly close scrutiny. That occupied him until he heard the liaison man say "voila!"

"Here you go," the man added, as paper began to emerge from his laser printer. The first sheet was a list of dates and locations of twenty-two parking violations, going back about a year. The second sheet was a registration history of the car that should have had the white Chevy's license plates.

Love Bytes registered the car for the first time in 1989, it said. Private sale, appropriate taxes paid, inspection completed, all nice and legal. Previous owner, Emile Loubert, 185 Grand View Avenue, Cornwall-on-Hudson, New York.

"Wow," the liaison man said, looking over Carlo's shoulder. "A celebrity."

Bingo, Maddalena thought.

He bought a cup of coffee and a jelly donut in a Chock Full O'Nuts across the street from the city clerk's office, which he took to a table in the back. Setting the coffee aside to cool, he pulled the list of unpaid parking tickets out of his jacket pocket, along with his street map of Manhattan, well worn and tearing at the creases.

Patterns, he thought. Right from the start they tell you to look for patterns, as though there always *were* a pattern and as though you could always detect it by looking. It was like the story about Michelangelo he'd heard in high school, how he carved a statue of a horse by taking a big hunk of stone and chipping away everything that wasn't part of the horse. A cinch.

Still, it was something to do, and every now and then being conscientious paid off.

Everybody, no matter how smart or thorough, has a little failing hidden somewhere, just big enough to unravel the most perfect operation. Now these guys, he thought, they just don't like to pay parking tickets.

He went down the list of unpaid tickets and noted the addresses, marking each location on his map with a black dot. Long before he finished with the list he knew the pattern had emerged. Of the twenty-two violations, nineteen had occurred in a single two-block section of First Avenue. Carlo knew the place well. Every cop in Manhattan knew it: The New York University Medical Center complex, adjoining Bellevue Hospital, the city's great dumping ground for Saturday night gunshots and ODs.

What did it mean? Carlo thought most likely a single user was parking at the hospital regularly. Then ignoring his tickets. Since the main benefit of transferring the car to a corporation was anonymity, Carlo was willing to jump to the conclusion the user was Emile Loubert. Mochrie and the others were just about unknown to begin with, and anonymity wouldn't mean much to them. So that meant old Emile was stiffing the city for a couple of grand in parking fines. A nice embarrassment for the National Security Advisor.

Next step, he took out his pocket calendar and checked the dates of the infractions. All weekdays, and all during business hours.

So he's seeing a doctor? Why wouldn't the National Security Advisor just go to Bethesda Naval Hospital or something—get a doctor to come see him at the White House? Carlo thought it over as he took a bite of his donut and let the jelly squirt out over his lips. Maybe he's visiting a sick friend, he thought, or copping drugs. Or maybe it's something else entirely.

The drive up to NYU Hospital took about a half hour. He found the blocks where the tickets had been issued. There were enough on the east side of the street to suggest visits to the medical complex rather than to one of the bars or pawn shops across the street. And they all fell within two blocks, even though the medical center stretched for more than ten, a mingling of pre-1900s red brick buildings and drab modern shells.

Getting out of his car and leaning on the front fender, Carlo found himself looking at a huge residence hall for the med school, and an equally huge medical office building. He pondered the residence a moment, thinking, maybe the old man has a young honey in the dorm.

But interns and residents don't have time for flings, at least not in the middle of the day. So odds are he's seeing a doc in the big building. That narrows it down to two or three hundred.

The building was open, and he entered the lobby. He scanned the directory, but none of the names rang any bells, and none of the offices would be open today, anyway. In the lobby were a pharmacy and a clinical testing laboratory, both of which undoubtedly did a bustling business with three hundred doctors just upstairs. Enough to be open Sundays, at least.

Carlo took the lab first, and showed his badge to the receptionist.

"I'd be interested in any medical tests you've run recently on a patient named either Loubert or Mochrie," he said.

"I wish I could help you, Lieutenant," the receptionist said. "But our records are confidential. I'm afraid I couldn't disclose any test results without the patient's authority."

"I don't want the results, just what tests you've run."

"Can't do that, either," she replied. "You see, you could deduce from what tests a doctor orders what kind of medical problems the patient might have. So we keep that confidential, too."

Carlo let a sigh pass between tightly pressed lips. "Look," he said, "I can't find a judge and get a subpoena on a Sunday. I'm on a legitimate investigation, and I'll keep it quiet. There won't be any trouble."

The receptionist smiled and shrugged. Nothing I can do, her eyes said.

"Can you tell me *whether* you've done any tests for Loubert or Mochrie, and the name of the doctor?" Carlo said. "I can take it up with the doctor from there."

The receptionist thought a moment, then relented. Carlo paced in the anteroom awaiting her return.

"Sorry," she said when she came back. "Nothing. But he could have gone to any of a number of other labs."

"Near here?"

She nodded. "There are a bunch. Sometimes the doctor

[170]

recommends a particular lab, and sometimes the patient goes elsewhere because they're cheaper. Some of them are cheaper for very good reasons."

"I can imagine," Carlo said. "Can you direct me?"

The receptionist handed him a printed sheet. "We get enough inquiries that we've printed up a list. These six are all within a block or two."

Carlo thanked her and headed back out into the sunlight. It was still early in the afternoon. He inspected the list, found the nearest address, and crossed the street. The first lab he visited was upstairs from a bakery. No result. The second was around the corner, in the basement of a brownstone that had seen better days. He showed his badge, repeated his request, and in a few minutes was handed a printout under the name of Loubert, E.

"All quite unpaid for, you can be sure," the male receptionist said irritably. "Lots of expensive work, and no insurance." He rolled his eyes. "Why we keep doing it, I don't know, but it's not my decision, or so they keep telling me."

"Isn't it unusual to order such a comprehensive group of blood and urine tests so frequently?" Carlo said. The clerk shrugged.

"Tell me there aren't wasteful doctors in the world," he said. "Go ahead, tell me."

"I guess so."

The man smiled smugly. "There, you see."

Carlo was still studying the list. All the tests had been ordered by the same doctor, a Dr. Fontana, with an office in the NYU building. He put the list in his pocket and climbed the outside steps to the street.

You order a million tests when you don't want anyone to figure out which one you're interested in, he thought. And if you're not going to pay the bill anyway, who cares?

He stood at the corner of 28th Street and First Avenue a long time, diagnosing a feeling in his stomach. Then he knew what he was going to do. He crossed the avenue quickly, reentered the medical building, and found Fontana's name on the directory. He took the one working elevator up to the fifth floor. The corridors were empty and his footsteps echoed. That's good, he thought. Unless there's an alarm. He stood outside the doctor's door looking up and down the hall and listening to the silence.

Moments later he was inside. Five years on the street teaches you some useful things, he thought, shutting the door behind him and marveling at the ineffectiveness of expensive locks. A cinch, he thought, looking around the darkened room.

The waiting room was small and plain, and Carlo passed quickly through into an interior corridor. There was an examining room, with a battery of sophisticated looking equipment. Then another room, then the doctor's office. On his wall was a large collection of diplomas and certificates. Harvard undergrad, Johns Hopkins for his M.D., and a master's degree in chemistry. A fellow of the American College of Surgeons and a full professor at the New York University School of Medicine.

All the file cabinets were locked. Carlo sat down behind the desk and idly riffled through the Rolodex next to the phone, finding nothing but unfamiliar names. Then he stopped: Emile Loubert was in the Rolodex, with the White House phone number. So, he's a patient, maybe even a friend, Carlo thought. Big shots sometimes have big-shot friends. He pushed all the buttons with labels on them next to the memory phone and found nothing interesting. Then he began pushing the unlabeled ones. They accessed one blank, unused memory cell after another, but he kept pushing. Then he tried the second-level memory, pushing each button in combination with the key labeled 2nd.

The next to last one, out of an array of sixty memory buttons, each commanding two cells, showed Carlo the now memorized number assigned to "S" on Dennis McCarthy's phone. He checked the number in his notebook, and pushed the button again. They matched. And it was arranged so nobody was going to dial it, or even find it, by accident. The doctor talked to "S," and it was very private.

Well now, Carlo thought, sitting back. He pulled on the desk drawers and to his surprise they slid open. The center drawer contained only an appointment book. He quickly checked the dates of the parking tickets and noted penciled-in appointments with EL on each day, at an appropriate time.

In the right-hand drawer he found the keys to the doctor's file cabinets.

The files were alphabetical and well kept. Carlo found a file on Emile Loubert, bulging with papers. In the half-light he browsed through long enough to satisfy himself that it was a legitimate medical file. There were copies of blood test results, reports from consulting specialists, copies of prescription records, and the minutiae accumulated by a patient in a long-term relationship with his doctor. On one of the topmost sheets Carlo saw neat handwriting, and although he didn't understand most of the notes, he could easily read a line midway down: "Pancreatic cancer."

Emile is a very sick man, Carlo thought. He put the Loubert file back and slowly slid the file drawer shut. That explains the many visits, and even the secrecy.

Carlo froze. His hand was still on the edge of the file drawer. It had still been moving when his eye fell on another file, closer to the front of the drawer.

King, William.

The mostly dead elected president of the United States.

The memories flooded back to Carlo. The distinguished but fatigued medical man who had been on all the nation's television sets for three days in February, almost four years ago. He explained over and over again, with chalk drawings and models, just what had gone wrong inside the labyrinthine cerebral capillaries of the new president, and exactly how unlikely it was that President King would ever open his eyes again.

The King file was slender. There were no medical records, only a few sheets. On official stationery of the New York County District Attorney, an announcement that a grand jury had found no grounds for criminal proceedings. A letter from the FBI thanking Dr. Fontana for his cooperation in their investigation. A few news clippings with his picture in them. And a note on White House stationery, thanking Dr. Fontana for his extraordinary services and efforts. Signed by Erhardt, who called himself vice president because he was still in the process of implementing the Twenty-fifth Amendment to take over the top job.

And Dr. Fontana has "S's" phone number programmed in his machine, but not labeled.

Carlo was back out in the corridor an instant later. He

took the stairs to the lobby, then another flight to the basement. He walked quickly through a parking garage until he found the street entrance. There he paused against a pillar in the darkness, heart pounding, looking up the ramp at the brightly lit street.

Calm down, he told himself. A grand jury found no cause for proceedings. The FBI investigated and found nothing. No evidence of anything other than a medical accident, the kind of thing that happens to lesser-known people a thousand times a year. Ten thousand.

But . . .

But Laura is in deep, deep trouble, he thought. If this is where the trail leads, there's nobody they won't kill to keep it cold.

He told himself to be disciplined and face reality. There was no way he was going to nail anyone for trying to kill President King. That was a closed case. Forever.

And who could he nail for killing Dennis McCarthy? Probably nobody. There was a lot of circumstantial evidence, but no real link, nor was there likely to be. Dennis was the one who could connect the Nazi story to the Erhardt campaign. Now he's gone, and his killer's unfindable. Another cold trail.

But somebody *had* killed McCarthy, and tried several times to kill Laura and Rydell. There'd been a murder and a suicide right at the sergeant's desk in his own precinct house. They had that kind of grip on the people they wanted to squeeze.

Laura's tough, he thought, and cool. She'll know how to handle the political end of this.

The political end, he repeated to himself, in disgust and rage. What else is there? Just the fact that somebody has committed murder in my city. On my turf. Under my fucking nose. And is going to get away with it.

He tapped his fist against the concrete pillar.

He thought: You're a good cop, or were. You've never been a Boy Scout. You remember how to break and enter. What else do you remember? Do you remember what to do when you've got eighty percent of a case and you want nothing to do with a grand jury or a judge?

You find the weakest individual in the chain and push him, hard. The one with the most to lose.

The doctor, Carlo thought.

Fontana lived on First Avenue, but a far cry from the NYU area. Instead, his apartment was on the fortieth floor of a brand-new building at the corner of 75th Street. Carlo could tell just by looking that the building had a health club, a private restaurant, and a concierge or two to look after the residents' little whims.

He presented himself, badge and all, at the lobby desk. There was a long delay while the clerk phoned upstairs and repeated a half-dozen times that a city police lieutenant was here to see the doctor. Finally, the clerk turned to Carlo and indicated the elevators.

"He'll be waiting for you," the clerk said.

Carlo's heart was still racing, partly with anger and partly in anticipation of the shot he was about to take.

Dr. Fontana proved to be a tall, thin man with silvery hair and a fine mustache. The model of a respected medical veteran, Carlo thought. He greeted Carlo at the door of his apartment, which took up half the fortieth floor. He wore gray pants, a red sweater, and tasseled loafers.

"Come in," he said curtly, holding the door open.

In the living room to his right Carlo could see a woman he took to be Mrs. Fontana, working on a jigsaw puzzle with the TV on.

Fontana led the way to his study and shut the door behind them.

"This is a little odd, Lieutenant," the doctor said. "To what do I owe the honor?"

"I'm on an investigation, and thought you could help me," Carlo said. He looked around the study. Shelves full of books, a small TV, a couple of tasteful and probably expensive watercolors. Under the TV was a VCR, and a video camera stood on a tripod in the corner.

The doctor was standing in the center of the room, and Carlo pointed to the chair behind the desk.

"Why don't you sit down, doc?" he said.

"Are we going to be that long?" the doctor said. In reply,

Carlo sat down in the armchair facing the desk. Fontana, obviously annoyed, made his way around the desk and took his seat.

"Can we come to the point?" he said. "We're expecting company."

"The point," Carlo repeated. "Okay. Doctor, what are your thoughts on the possibility of doing some serious time in a serious prison?"

Carlo thought he detected a momentary flush in the doctor's face, quickly mastered. In a low, even tone, Fontana replied, "I don't know what you mean."

"Sure you do," Carlo said. He kept his voice dark and barely audible, and began to lean forward as he spoke. "It has to do with Emile Loubert, and a fellow named Mochrie who's chatting with the DA at this very moment. And a dead man by the name of Dennis McCarthy and a half-dead man named William King. And a well-respected medical man who's being set up as the fall guy. That's you, doc. There's a pile of evidence leading right to your door. It led *me* to your door, after all, and I'm no rocket scientist. You're going away, doc. And I do mean to a serious place, not one of those country-club penitentiaries you hear about. You ever been butt-fucked, doc?"

Fontana's lips were moving involuntarily as he stared across at the lieutenant. Deciding, Carlo knew. Gauging how bad it is, and how bad it could get.

"The butt-fuck, it's practically part of the orientation," Carlo said. "An elegant older gentlemen like yourself, you wouldn't have to wait more than an hour or two. Picture something, doc," Carlo went on, whispering urgently. "Picture your wife coming to Ossining to see you. Picture her in the waiting room with all those niggers—"

"You're crazy," Fontana said.

"Oh? There's a mountain of evidence, doc. We've got it all. Even the plates from the car they drove when they went to firebomb the house on Sapphire Island. The same car they drove McCarthy off the road in, and tried to do the same to Mitchell Rydell. Who by the way is a reporter for the *New York Times*, in case you're wondering if all this will see the light of day.

"Think about it, doctor. We found the fucking *tags*. Just

[176]

thrown away in the most casual way. You fell in with some careless people, doc. We know about Mochrie, we know about Emile Loubert's high-tech blackmail, about Life Cards and computerized medical records . . . about all the killing."

Carlo thought he could see Fontana shivering inside, but there was no outer sign of disturbance. The doctor's face was still calm and his eyes still stared straight ahead.

"You're part of it, doctor," he said. "Part of a conspiracy to commit murder and to obstruct justice. We've got you seven ways from Sunday. As it stands now, you're the only one with dirty hands. Loubert, Mochrie, everybody else goes to Switzerland or something, and you go to jail. Can you see yourself in jail, doc? I doubt it. I doubt if anything at Harvard or Johns Hopkins prepared you for it."

"Stop it," Fontana said, but quietly. Carlo sat back in silence, resting his hands on his knees. Now, he thought. Now you break or you strengthen, and if you strengthen I'm through.

There was a knock on the door. "Peter?"

Fontana's wife. The doctor looked at Carlo and Carlo nodded. A glimpse of the wife would be a helpful thing right now, he thought.

"Come in," the doctor called, his voice catching.

The door opened a crack. "The desk called. They said there's a Mr. Rydell downstairs asking to see you. He's from the *Times*."

Carlo practically shouted. There *is* a God, he thought as he jumped up and put his hands on the front of Fontana's desk.

"Send him away," he said loudly. "Tell him to go to hell. You don't have to talk to him." Fontana hesitated, then nodded to his wife, and the door closed.

"They're coming, doc," Carlo said. "Now is when we determine whether we keep this quiet or let it all blow up. We don't want you, we want Loubert, and whoever is behind him. *Now*, doc—"

"All right, dammit," Fontana snapped, on the verge of either fury or tears. He subsided.

"We must keep my family out of this," the doctor said a moment later, more composed. "I have a son and a daughter, both at good colleges. They think the world of me. And my wife, . . ." He glanced around the study as if to indicate the whole apartment.

"It's a long fall to prison from a million-dollar apartment on the East Side," Carlo said.

"What do I have to do?" Fontana asked. Cool customer again, Carlo thought, and imagined the doctor saying the same thing to Loubert, or Erhardt, four years ago.

"I want nothing to do with a grand jury on this," Carlo said. "For all the obvious political reasons. It would be more . . . more patriotic to handle it as quietly as possible."

"I agree," the doctor said. "God, do I ever."

"So what you need to do, doctor, is tell me all about it." Carlo looked over at the video camera in the corner. "And while you tell me the story, I think you're going to be looking into that lens over there."

A half hour later, a knock came on the door.

"Everything all right, dear?" the doctor's wife said from outside. Fontana was sitting behind his desk, head down, depleted and silent.

"Answer your wife," Carlo said. He stared at Fontana in disgust, repelled by all he'd heard in the past thirty minutes.

"Just fine, dear," Fontana said weakly. "We won't be much longer." To Carlo he added: "Will we?"

Carlo shook his head.

"That reporter is still downstairs," Fontana's wife said.

Carlo held up a hand to soothe the doctor.

"Tell him Lieutenant Carlo Maddalena of the city police will be coming down shortly, and if he's still there I'll run him in for trespassing," Carlo said.

He leaned over and pushed the Play button on the VCR. "One run-through," he said. "Just to be sure. Not that I want to hear it all again."

He fast-forwarded through the preliminaries—Fontana holding up a copy of the day's newspaper, identifying himself, showing his driver's license to the camera. Carlo stopped the fast-forward and touched Play again.

". . . the secret, of course, was in the reliance on computers," the videotaped Fontana said. "The medical profession, the insurance industry, even the patient advocate groups have all made a priority of minimizing human error in medical procedures. And cost. If a doctor stitches you up, he charges per stitch. If he administers a drug, he charges for that, too. But a machine can do that cheaper *and* more reliably. So today so much is done by computer you'd hardly believe it."

"So it counts up the sponges before you close?" Carlo heard himself say.

"Much more," Fontana replied on tape. "Not only did the computer keep the inventory of oxygen canisters for this procedure, but each canister was delivered robotically, removed from storage, conveyed to the O.R., and connected to the system. The log of the operation—the master document everyone would rely on in reconstructing what happened—listed three canisters of oxygen consumed by the anesthesia. And three canisters were indeed consumed."

"Three canisters of what?"

"Two of oxygen, one of carbon monoxide," Fontana said. His face on the TV screen was lizardly pale, his eye sockets deep and dark.

"And what did that do?"

"Killed his cerebral functions," Fontana said. "His thinking, senses, and so on. His involuntary functions, like heartbeat, went on."

"What about after, during the investigations?"

Fontana shrugged on the TV, and the real doctor Fontana, a few feet away, put his face into his hands.

"Of course there was an investigation, the most extensive ever," he said. "Every single line of the computer record was reviewed in detail. But as to a physical reenactment, or any effort to verify what happened in objective reality, by the time they got around to that the canisters in question were gone. Everything they wanted to know was in the computer record anyway, every drug administered, every sponge, every stitch, his vital signs minute to minute, all there, permanently recorded."

"It wasn't true, but it was on the computer," Maddalena said.

The doctor was silent.

"Why?" Maddalena heard his own voice ask. The doctor hesitated.

"Why did you do it?"

"Lieutenant, I got ten million dollars in cash, deposited in a Swiss bank account. I needed the money. And I was afraid."

"Of them?"

Fontana nodded.

"Of Loubert, or Mochrie?"

"Of Mochrie, mostly. Emile and I were old friends. He was the one who broached the subject to me, but it was Mochrie who found things to threaten me with, who went to Dartmouth to see my daughter . . ."

Both Fontanas now sat with their faces buried in their palms. Then the doctor on TV looked up again.

"That's it," he said. "We thought King would die. We never expected him to linger."

"And you could hardly go back and try again," Carlo said. He punched the VCR off. There it all was, he thought. Worth every drop of blood they had to shed to keep it quiet. And he thought of Laura, alone in Key West, drawing attention, possibly about to go one-on-one with this Mochrie character.

"Doctor, there's still one thing I don't understand," Carlo said. "Why are you still alive? Why haven't you fallen from a high window or something?"

"Emile needs me," Fontana said quietly.

"He's dying, isn't he?"

Fontana nodded. "I'm the only doctor he trusts," he said.

"When?" Carlo asked. Fontana shrugged.

"Any time," he said. "He's in a bad way."

"Have you given any thought to what Mochrie and the others will do to you as soon as Loubert is dead?"

The doctor nodded. "Yes," he said. "That's part of why I talked to you instead of throwing you out."

"That," Carlo said, "and the fact that the news media are onto it now. Your friends got cute with this Nazi story. Maybe they wanted to see just how far they really could go. But they fed it to a reporter who wouldn't bite, and rather than just shrug and say the hell with it, they tried again. And soon the reporters will be beating down the doors. Not just the guy downstairs."

"I always knew you'd come some day," Fontana said. "I never expected the FBI, the Secret Service, but I always thought a plain city police detective would ring the bell some day and the jig would be up. You know, it's true what they say, it *is* a relief."

Carlo shoved the cassette tightly into his inside jacket pocket.

"Listen," he said. "Keep this visit just between us."

"No problem," Fontana replied.

"And don't be surprised by anything that happens from now on," Carlo said. He let himself out of the study, and smiled reassuringly at Mrs. Fontana before leaving the apartment.

He found Rydell in the lobby.

"We both have the same question," Mitchell said. "What are you doing here?"

"Well?" Carlo said, pulling Mitchell through the glass doors onto the sidewalk.

"A Dr. Fontana picked up my Life Card at the hospital yesterday," Mitchell said. "This is the only one it could have been."

"You don't know the half of it," Carlo said. "First thing, somehow, we have *got* to get hold of Laura."

Laura took a roundabout route to the marina although she knew the direct way by heart. Her father had lived here eight years now, since her mother's death. It had been his escape: Something to dive into instead of diving off a high building. He'd always loved to sail, and as Laura drove through the silent, palm-lined back streets of Key West, the memories of her childhood and youth flooded back to her. She could remember being on a boat at an age when her tiny body was engulfed by a life jacket and held to the main mast by a tether. That was a small boat, and they kept it in a cheap yard off the West River, about a mile from its opening to the Chesapeake Bay. There was a bigger boat, and then a bigger one still. She saw her father clearly in her mind, as he was then: young, with full hair and broad shoulders, mastering the tiller, scanning the horizon. To the child Laura he had seemed completely in control, so much the captain.

Her mother, too, had loved the bay, and loved to be on it. She had brown ankles that showed between her nylon pants and her deck shoes, and she raised and struck the sails eagerly, pumping her arms as she pulled the lines. Dad trusted her with the tiller, too, Laura thought. She knew the winds and the water as well as he did, and she had the muscle to fight the currents.

"If you can't pull your weight, you don't belong on a boat," her mother had told her a thousand times. Then she'd nudge Laura and whisper, "Besides, muscles come in handy when you have to beat up men."

Laura backtracked and circled through the streets, letting the sun get higher in the sky and watching for bad omens. She'd decided to park in town and walk to the marina because she felt more maneuverable on foot. And it was better to wait until there were more people on the street. The old part of Key West, away from the shell shops, T-shirt boutiques and pricey restaurants, was a community of Victorian houses in varying repair. The better of them nestled behind rows of coconut trees, back from the sidewalk. It was a charming little town, Laura thought, a favorite of such different men as Harry Truman and Ernest Hemingway. But on Duval Street it was just another beach resort.

She parked and walked, her parents' long faded images for company.

Had she led her enemies to her father? She tried not to dwell on the thought. She had to see him, she knew that. She couldn't let him go on thinking his daughter was dead, and just by sending her telegram she'd exposed him. He was one more person who knew she hadn't burned up on Sapphire Island. Once warned, Dad was a formidable adversary, fully capable of taking care of himself. And she had to talk to him. Just being with him would make her feel safer. God knows, she thought, being with Mitchell doesn't make me feel safe. Sexy maybe, but not safe.

And it was just possible she could flush them out, get them onto unfamiliar turf, and get them to make a mistake.

Soon she was within sight of the marina. Next to the Doubloon, and sharing with it a tiny inlet behind a stone breakwater, was a fish-processing company. Its boats were gone, its long wharf open. Laura stood a moment at the limit of the land, then stepped onto the pier. There were a handful of others there, walking, or simply standing in the brilliant morning sunshine. New lovers, Laura thought, trying to puzzle out what the previous night might have meant. Or good-timers slowly recovering their wits after a drunk. In any case, either early risers or people who'd been up all night, like me.

She knew the farthest end of the wharf would give her an overview of the Doubloon Marina. She could watch her father's boat for signs of activity, and keep an eye on the approaches as well. She made her way, as casually as possible, along the pier. But when she was halfway out, she stopped.

He was there. Standing at the very end, staring across the water. Even from the rear, she felt viscerally this was not just another black-haired man in a windbreaker. She'd seen this man at the ferry slip on Sapphire Island, looking out over water just the way he was looking now. Staring across the narrow, sheltered yacht basin at her father's sailboat. An assassin.

She fought the impulse to run. It's broad daylight, she thought, and there are people around. And it may not even be him. After a long moment of cold indecision, she took a step further, then another. She paused, looked down into the oil-slicked water of the boat yard, and listened to the squawking of the gulls. She heard a voice, and spun around nervously. A young couple was coming along the wharf, arms around each other's waists, extending a night of love into the morning.

Laura turned back and the man was coming toward her. His hair was very black and he had a small beard and mustache, which she had not seen before. He seemed about forty but his face had a tan leanness that disguises age. He carried a nylon sports bag that seemed half empty, and as he strode toward her he shifted it from one hand to the other. She forced herself not to run, thinking: There's nothing he can do here. Not with witnesses. She met his gaze directly, and with each step felt her heart pounding harder and her breath catching in her throat. God, she thought, *he's coming right at me.*

Two steps away from her he broke into a grin and chirped, "Good morning!"

Then he was past. The lovers passed Laura in the opposite direction, and she stood still, confused. She watched the assassin climb the steps at the end of the pier and walk casually across the twenty yards to the marina entrance. He stopped at

[183]

the service counter outside the harbormaster's office and got a Styrofoam cup of steaming coffee. Then he sipped at it, leaning on the fence rail and looking around like any marina regular.

Laura walked the length of the wharf briskly, then crossed to the marina. She slipped through the parking lot and around the pool, down onto the main dock, thinking she'd come around without his seeing her. She glanced up and saw him peering through the eyepiece of a camera, attached to a huge telephoto lens. The thick lens barrel rested in his palm and he slowly swept the area with it, as though waiting for an appealing image to pop into the viewfinder. As Laura watched, he panned the camera across the horizon, pointed it at her, paused a moment, then moved on.

She walked down the main dock and onto one of the intersecting piers, then out to its end—past her father's boat, which lay silent and apparently empty, swaying lightly on the rolling water. At the pier's end she stopped and watched two men polishing the bright brass fittings on a handsome houseboat. She stole a look toward the harbormaster's office, and the assassin was gone. She picked him up again in moments, walking along the terrace above the seawall. The camera hung by a strap from his shoulder, the sports bag in his left hand. They were serving morning juice and coffee at the veranda bar, and Laura saw the black-haired man shake his head at the girl behind the bar.

She walked back the way she'd come, more slowly this time, letting her eyes examine the *Hotspur* more closely. As usual, every line was perfectly coiled and the teak deck boards gleamed. But the ports were all shut, and there was no sign of life. He must be around the marina somewhere, she thought.

Alongside the marina a six-story condo building rose, with balconies looking out over the yacht basin toward the deep water. At its base was a swimming pool the marina slip holders could use, although the condo owners disliked them. Plus the bar, where crowds gathered almost every night to watch the sunset and drink margaritas. Laura slowly climbed the gangway and walked out to the end of the terrace. The assassin was nowhere in sight. The sun, now above her shoulder, was beating down. It would be a hot, shiningly bright day.

Suddenly her stomach churned: What if he had already gotten to Dad? What if the silence on his boat meant . . .

But he must have gotten her message and been on his guard, she thought. She circled the terrace and pool area, but except for two mothers with a small brood of children, nobody was around.

He might be in the health club, Laura thought. On the ground floor was a small gym with Nautilus machines, a sauna, and showers, where her father liked to work out two or three times a week.

She found it empty. The ceiling lights were bright, the indoor/outdoor carpet more worn than she remembered. Two basketballs lay forlornly against the wall of mirrors, and looking at the glass she saw herself with a start: An oddly tattered woman of uncertain age, looking tired. She wandered through the tiny gym, resting her hands on the equipment. In the mirror there were bags under her eyes, and her sweater—God, it was warm in here!—drooped from her shoulders. She bent and picked up one of the balls. She saw herself three feet away in the mirror, and then she saw the assassin three feet behind her. The door was closing behind him. His bag was slung over his left shoulder and there was a gun in his hand, a thick silencer at its end. She spun.

"Miss Madison," he said. His voice was quiet and his lips turned upward in an almost comforting way. "At last . . ."

She threw the basketball at him, hard, ducked low and followed it, driving her shoulder into his midriff. The gun went off with a tiny thud and behind her the wall of mirrors erupted into shards, cascading noisily to the floor. The assassin stumbled backwards and Laura got to the door before he could fire again. She raced down the corridor and out to the pool deck. People, she thought, people mean safety. Be seen.

Heart thumping frantically, she paced back and forth the length of the deck, panting, feeling sweat trickle down between her breasts. She pulled off her sweater and threw it over the deck railing, down onto the rocks where the incoming tide was breaking. She turned back, leaned on the railing and thought she might vomit. The young mothers were looking at her suspiciously. The assassin was strolling nonchalantly across the opposite end of the pool, not even glancing in her direction.

He looked up at the sun, put his bag down, took off his windbreaker and stretched comfortably.

Laura took off, striding across the parking lot and off the marina grounds. The sun bounced off a wall of white stucco and blinded her, and she almost walked into a parked car. She staggered up the street toward Duval, thinking, Dad, where are you, what have I done?

At the corner was the Conch Train tour terminal, and a train was loading, three open-sided passenger wagons pulled by a redecorated jeep. She circled it, stopped behind the ticket shack, and from its shelter peered down Front Street.

He was coming along the street at a steady and unhurried pace. She waited a moment, and the train half-filled with colorfully dressed tourists. A slight blond girl climbed into the driver's seat, started the engine, and pulled the train out into Duval Street. Laura walked along beside it, letting the jumble of shirts and hats mask her retreat.

Soon she had to trot, and when they reached the first corner she ducked down a side street, flattened herself against the side of a building and surveyed Duval.

The assassin was walking once more as though in no particular hurry. He paused to look in a store window, then pulled out his camera and took a few perfunctory shots of the street scene.

Laura ran down the side street and quickly circled the block, hoping to come out behind him, but when she got to the corner she saw him only a few yards away, across the street, pacing, waiting for her. She shrank back, she hoped, before he had seen her.

Then a new strategy struck her, and she stepped out onto Duval and made straight for him. Turnabout, she thought, is fair play. And in fact his face did seem puzzled when he saw her coming, and he busied himself examining the brightly colored beachwear on the sidewalk racks. She walked right up to him, and past, and on down the sidewalk as though she owned the town. From time to time she glanced in a shop window and caught a reflection that told her he was following.

Buried in a dresser drawer at home in Manhattan was a tiny bikini—very tiny, she thought ruefully—that she had bought here years ago, and she thought the shop was in the next block. Once upon a time she'd had the body for that suit, she thought. The image brought back a memory of sand, boys, and Frisbees flying into the surf at sunset.

She found the shop and stepped inside. At the back was a rack full of terry beach robes, and she began sifting through them idly, like a woman trying to fill up a morning until it got hot enough to hit the beach. The assassin appeared in the entrance. Laura studiously ignored him, moving on to the swimsuit rack. She selected a suit and held it up for examination, letting her eyes wander over the form in the doorway. He was leaning on a concrete column, arms folded, watching. Just a cool guy, she thought, checking out the chicks. The sports bag lay on the sidewalk at his feet.

Laura took two suits, gestured to the sales girl, and started to the dressing room to try them on. But once past the curtain she merely hung them on the hook in one of the cubicles and headed for the back door she'd known would be there.

In back was a concrete paved alley with huge clumps of wild grass poking through the surface. A dumpster sat alongside the building. If she'd lost him, she thought, she'd go straight back to the marina.

But when she started up the alley, there he was. He stepped into the alley, silhouetted by the bright sunlight. For a second they were alone in the alley, surrounded by silence. Then Laura turned and went back quickly through the store, out onto Duval, and down the street toward the water.

In moments she became aware of him following again, this time more purposefully. She quickened her stride; so did he. They came to a small shopping mall that served as a town center, a triangular plaza with storefronts and restaurants on all sides. On Duval as it passed the plaza, Laura saw a young woman with a clipboard. Laura knew her game: Free fishing trips, restaurant meals, whatever, and all you had to do was visit the latest time-sharing condo. The young woman approached and Laura began to shake her head, but the woman came closer. Laura put her hand up to fend off the imminent sales pitch, but when they were only a foot or two apart, the young woman whispered to her.

"Next left."

Laura went to the corner, glanced back over her shoulder

and saw the salesgirl approaching the assassin. She was looking back at them as she turned the corner.

"So who is he?" a voice said, and she whirled.

"Dad!"

Their embrace was strong and he cut it off before she wanted to.

"Let's move," he said. "Moira's even money to sell him a condo."

"I'm no genius," Marty Madison said a few moments later, "but I can add two and two. I got your telegram yesterday, and minutes later the harbormaster came by to relay your phone message. All my life, nobody ever had to tell me twice to be careful. So I packed a few things and stayed the night on a friend's boat, a few slips down. And I sat up and watched."

They were hurrying along Front Street toward the Doubloon, and although Laura looked back frequently she never saw her pursuer.

"Unless he wants to slug her in broad daylight," her father said, "he's not going to get away from Moira in less than five minutes. We have to move fast."

They reached the Doubloon and Laura saw the *Hotspur* at the fuel dock, with a small tail of exhaust coming from the diesel. Two men held the mooring lines.

"All ready for you, Marty," one of them said as Laura and her father reached them.

"Thanks a million." They jumped aboard and in moments were headed away from the dock, through the marina, toward the stone breakwater. The signs posted on pilings said 5 MPH—No Wake, but Marty had the *Hotspur* wide open and was churning for the sea.

Laura crouched in the cockpit, almost at his feet, and surveyed the shoreline. No sign.

"So," her father continued, "what do you suppose happens around midnight, but two uniformed members of Florida's finest, the State Police, happen by for a stroll. I guess they were just in the neighborhood. They found the *Hotspur* and looked her over good, then headed into the harbormaster's office and stayed a long time.

"At that point I decided I didn't need any sleep last night.

Around six this morning this fellow turns up, the one that's after you. And damned if *he* doesn't come out and inspect my boat like he wants to buy it or something. Then I saw you, and I saw everything that happened from then on. I've been following him, assuming he had you in sight."

"He gave me a scare when he went into the health club," Marty said. "I was about to come to your rescue when you came out. How did you manage it?"

Laura told him, and he chuckled and said, "I always told you it was important to know sports. You know you shouldn't have gone in there, not knowing for sure there was another way out."

"I know," Laura said.

"Next time be more careful," Marty said, and Laura smiled weakly. "Where are we going?" she asked. They were perhaps a mile offshore now, and the contours of Key West were low against the horizon.

"Anywhere you want," Marty said. "We could sail around and talk, if you want to tell me what the hell is going on. Or we could head for the Dry Tortugas. We've got lots of food and water. We could sail north, along the coast. We don't ever have to come back."

"Yes, we do," Laura said. "The election is Tuesday."

Marty idled the engine and unfurled the jib sail. Together they raised the main, standing on top of the cabin and pulling the halyard alternately. Marty trimmed it just so, and it filled with wind. In moments they were sliding along the surface of the water, and Marty turned off the engine.

"All this has to do with the election, hey?" he said. "Who is this guy, one of Gillian's Nazi friends?"

"Senator Gillian has no Nazi friends," Laura said.

"Sorry."

"How much do you really want to know?" Laura said. "It's dangerous."

"Tell," Marty said. "I've been in danger before."

Laura talked for more than an hour, interrupted only occasionally by a question or a grunt of surprise from her father. She told it all, talking faster and faster, glad to have it all out at last, and glad to have someone she knew would be on her side.

"So," Marty said when she was finished, nearly breathless. "The upshot is, Erhardt is trying to guarantee the election by sabotaging Gillian, and along the way he and his buddy Loubert put together this big computerized system for spying on people, blackmailing them, and killing them if they have to. That about it?"

Laura nodded.

"And how do you propose to defeat them?"

"Damned if I know."

"You get enough evidence, and this Rydell fellow can probably get it into the papers," Marty said. "Not that that would help Gillian on Tuesday. You could give the evidence to David—"

"Please, Dad—"

"I know, he's a jerk," Marty chuckled. "I seem to remember telling you that myself some time ago. But he's also an FBI agent, and I have to believe he takes that seriously."

"But the FBI may be in on it," Laura said.

"So you don't know who you can trust," Marty said, nodding. "One of your prime needs right now is to find out just how far it all reaches."

He fell silent, staring off over the gray ocean. "You stumbled onto their little plot," he said at last. "It's hard to believe they would have killed anyone to keep quiet the fact that they fabricated a little photo here and there to embarrass Gillian. Granted, it would have been a scandal, but they'd just have indicted some sacrificial lamb and moved on. But the deeper you looked, and the more you looked, the more you scared them. Now, for some reason, they're willing to kill. There are implications for them that go beyond the election. There's a much broader operation, and more offensive. Presidents can get impeached for less than this."

"But killing people . . . so many people?" Laura said. Her father's gaze had turned from an idle stare to a more specific attention.

"You're right," he said. "It still doesn't make sense. It still seems like such an overreaction."

He was peering intently over the water now, and Laura followed his gaze. Near the horizon, back toward the land that

[190]

was now out of sight, was a tiny plume of water. A powerboat's wake.

"Is that . . ."

"Could be," her father said. "Maybe not. Maybe just a joyrider."

"What can we do?"

"Go on sailing," Marty replied. "If it's an honest boat it will give us a wide berth."

He pulled on the main sheet to let out a little more sail, and gave the wheel a half-spin. The boat heeled a little more and turned its nose away from the track of the powerboat. They sailed for five minutes while the white wake of the speedboat came closer.

"You're in a spot," Marty said. "But it sounds like you're not alone. What's the story with this guy Rydell?"

Laura felt herself blush, and her father must have noticed it.

"I thought so," he said. "Congratulations. I'm happy for you. He must be quite a guy."

"He is, I think," Laura said.

"Don't sound so unsure," her father replied. "He must be a heck of a guy or you wouldn't have let him anywhere near you. I always knew it was going to be a big job satisfying you. You didn't exactly get the standard little girl's upbringing."

"I wouldn't trade it," Laura said, and her father smiled a little bit and nodded, then looked back across the sea to the pursuing powerboat.

"It's him," Laura said. "Has to be."

"Fast work," Marty said. "Hiring a boat like that so quickly."

He stood up, looked out at their pursuer, and back at Laura.

"Ready about," he said.

Laura quickly uncleated the line that anchored the jib on the starboard side and held it tightly. Leaning across the cockpit she grabbed the loose port line, wrapped it around the winch, and inserted the winch handle.

"Ready," she said.

"Hard a-lee," her father said, and spun the wheel. At once the main sail deflated. Laura let out the starboard line. The jib, up ahead, began to flap and Laura worked the port winch as fast and hard as she could. The untied starboard line ran out and the port line came taut. She cranked hard, pulling the jib into a tight new position to port. Then she ducked instinctively to let the mainsail boom sweep over her head. The boat had changed direction by almost ninety degrees and was now headed across the line of the powerboat, closing the distance between them.

Moments passed, and then she could make out the man in the speedboat. It was the assassin, standing at the wheel, head above the windshield, heading right for them.

They waited until he was bearing down on them, then came about again and headed away. Now he had to change direction, too, and as soon as he did, Marty jerked the wheel around and the mainsail, boom, and jib danced back to port. The *Hotspur* crossed the speedboat's wake with a series of dull, hard thuds that sent showers of spray into the cockpit.

"Laura," Marty said, "raise the Coast Guard on the radio."

Laura climbed down two steps into the cabin and turned on the ship-to-shore, dialing to the emergency frequency. Then she heard the sails flap above her and knew her father had turned into the wind. He was suddenly at her elbow, taking the microphone from her.

"This is the sailing vessel *Hotspur* calling the United States Coast Guard."

He waited, then repeated his message and heard a voice acknowledge.

"We wish to report an act of piracy," Marty said. "We are approximately five miles from Key West, bearing one-eighty. A speedboat has accosted us and fired a rifle shot across our bow. We are now being boarded. Request assistance."

"Please repeat."

Marty repeated the entire message with great patience, while Laura heard the low rumble of the powerboat coming alongside. There was a thump.

"Away from the radio, old man," the assassin called.

"Help is being dispatched," the Coast Guard operator said. "Unable to project an ETA."

Marty stood in the cockpit. Laura saw that the black-haired killer had his rifle pressed into her father's ribs.

"Up," the killer said to her. She climbed the steps and stood in the cockpit next to her father.

"Sailing vessel *Hotspur*, please acknowledge," the radio said. The killer leaned into the cabin and fired a shot that silenced the electronic voice. His speedboat, now shut down, floated idly a few yards away.

"It'll take them all day, Dad," the killer said. "Distress calls from sailboats aren't a super-high priority. Believe me, I'm not worried about the Coast Guard."

He retrieved his mooring line from the siderail cleat and tossed it to Marty. "Tie her off," he said, and Marty obeyed quietly, making the powerboat fast to the back of the *Hotspur*.

"Okay, Dad," the man said, "here's the way this is gonna go. You're gonna fire up the diesel, and we'll put my little boat in tow. Then you're gonna steer just where I tell you, and I'm gonna keep this rifle pointed at your head to make sure you do."

Marty was staring levelly at the younger man. Now he shrugged.

"What choice do I have?" he said.

The killer nodded and said, "That's right. The fun's over."

"Laura," Marty said, "strike the mainsail." Their captor jerked his glance to Laura, who was still in the cockpit. She could see the distrust in his eyes. She held out her hands, palms up.

"I have to strike the sail, don't I?" She glanced at her father and saw his eyes wandering off to starboard. The black-haired man climbed up on the siderail, one foot on the deck above the cabin, the other on the rail. The rifle was pointed between them now, the better to cover them both.

"Quickly," he said. Laura climbed onto the deck and crawled on her hands and knees beneath the boom to the big belaying cleat on which the main halyard was wound. She saw her father at the wheel, again stealing a glance to starboard. Was there another boat? The Coast Guard? Her father was inching the wheel around, one spoke at a time, unnoticed. *He was turning the boat to starboard!* She looked out to starboard and saw nothing . . . then she saw it.

Or rather, them: The tiny ripples scurrying across the surface of the rolling water. The mainsail above her slapped listlessly in the weak breeze, but she had sailed with her father often enough to know what the little ripples meant.

She turned her left shoulder to hide her hands from the killer's sight, and quickly tied a double knot in the halyard. Then she occupied herself with busy work.

"Come on," the killer said after a few seconds. "Let's move it."

She held up the knot. "It's snagged," she said. "It'll never go through the davit."

Gust, dammit, gust!

"Screw it, then," the gunman said. "The engine will govern the sail anyway."

Laura turned and crouched on her knees. The man was gesturing with the rifle. "Get your ass back here."

Where was the damned gust?

She took a crawling step, then felt it on her cheek. It freshened quickly. The assassin seemed to feel it, too, and he looked up at the sail above him, now flapping madly and loudly in the changing breeze.

At that instant her father jerked the wheel hard, and the gust hit the sail in earnest. The boom moved almost imperceptibly, an inch at first, then in a sudden rush, sweeping across the cockpit as the sail filled with air.

The rifleman saw it coming and anger flooded into his face. But his rage overcame his reason, and as he turned to train his rifle on Laura's father at the helm, the boom struck him flush in the face.

Laura leaped into action, crab-walking across the deck. She grabbed the boom with both hands, curled her legs up into her chest, then uncoiled explosively, kicking the teetering killer in the stomach. The rifle, angled up, went off with a report that vanished instantly in the wind and the sound of the filling sail. She heard the pop and tear above her that meant the bullet had torn through the sailcloth. Then the rifle was flying through the air and its owner, arms wheeling, was hitting the water.

She dropped safely onto the siderail and looked back at her father in triumph, but he was bent over, switching the diesel on.

"Now," he said loudly, pointing, "strike the goddam sail!"

He was turning the boat under power into the wind, and the sail was slackening. Their would-be murderer flailed in the water, already ten yards behind them.

She leaped to the mast, undid her puny knot in an instant, whirled the halyard off the cleat and looped it once around the winch above. Then she stood and began letting out some of the line. As the sail pillowed along the boom she fastened it down as best she could, tying it to the boom in bundles with an unused length of nylon line. She let out the halyard slowly, tying down the sail as she went along. The work took her three or four minutes, and she looked repeatedly out beneath the boom. The man was now swimming in earnest behind them, as though he had a chance of catching up with his boat as it trailed behind the *Hotspur*. Marty pulled the speedboat closer and re-tied the mooring line. Then, with the diesel running, he turned away from the swimmer and circled, until he had the man off the bow.

The swimmer stopped, treading water, and looked up at them.

"All right," he called. "You win. You can't just leave me here."

"The hell I can't," Marty said.

"I'll die out here."

"That would be a shame."

"I think I know you," the swimmer called, his voice now quivering in anger and fear. "I don't think you're a killer."

"I am when I have to be," Marty said. "I killed a man with my bare hands in 1952, and it got me out of a Korean POW camp. If I let you live, you'll only try to kill me again, or Laura. I think I know you, too, and you *are* a killer. I'm just protecting myself."

Marty turned his back on the man in the water and pulled the powerboat alongside the *Hotspur*.

"Laura," he said, "get down there and fix his engine. There's tools under the chart table."

Laura climbed down into the powerboat and in a few moments had removed the spark plugs from its outboard motor. She tossed them into the sea. Then she leaned far over and found the oil drain plug. She struggled with it a few moments, then black, dirty motor oil spilled out onto the ocean surface.

Climbing back onto the sailboat she took her father's hand. When their hands touched, and she was back on board, she suddenly had the feeling everything would turn out all right after all. All these years, she thought, and Daddy can still do that.

"Dammit," the assassin called from the water. "What do you want? What do I have to say or do?"

"Don't beg," Marty called back. "It ain't becoming for a tough guy like you."

"I *am* begging," the killer replied. "Listen, I don't come empty-handed. I have information to trade for my life."

Laura's father glanced at her.

"He's right," she said quietly. Her father climbed two steps down into the cabin and pulled out a bulky, big-barreled gun. He checked its load and handed it to Laura.

"It's a magnesium flare," he explained. "He tries anything funny, you fire it right into his face. You think you can do that?"

"Yes," Laura said.

Her father pulled a spare coil of half-inch line out of the locker and rapidly tied a small noose in one end.

"What do you say?" the man in the water called.

"Swim over here," Marty replied. He and Laura watched in silence for the two minutes it took him to get alongside the boat. He began to reach up for a hand, but Marty waved him away and tossed the noose to him.

"You put that around your neck first," he said, "and tighten it up nice and snug."

The man found the noose in the water, looked at it, and at them, then slipped it over his head.

"All right," Marty said, "climb into your boat." As he was doing that, Marty made the noose line fast to the second stern cleat. The killer crawled into the speedboat, shirt and hair slicked down to his skin. Marty tightened the noose line a little until it hung almost taut between the *Hotspur*'s stern and the killer's neck.

"Simple proposition," Marty said. He dug in his pocket for a knife. "We cut both the lines, and you float on your own until somebody picks you up. Like the Coast Guard, maybe. We just cut the one tied to the boat, and it floats away without you. What happens to you then is anybody's guess."

Laura wondered if her father would really do that. She had never heard about the Korean POW camp before. She sat in the corner of the cockpit and kept the flare gun trained on the assassin. This could be the man who drove Mitchell off the road on Long Island, or the one who had killed Dennis McCarthy the same way. At the very least, he had given the orders for those actions. Had he been the one who had shot Mitchell on the golf course in Great Neck? She searched her memory and replayed events that seemed so long ago. He had gotten out of a white car at the Sapphire Island ferry slip and stood looking over the water. The same man? She looked at him. His hair was slicked down and his face white from the cold ocean water, but it was him. She felt the weight of the flare gun in her forearms and rested her elbow against her leg, keeping the gun level. You tried to kill me, she thought, and you tried to kill the man I love. She glanced at her father, standing opposite her and steering from the side of the wheel. *Both the men I love,* she thought.

"Good job, Laura," her father said, interrupting her reverie. "I'm proud of you. Erhardt hasn't got a chance."

"Dad," Laura said quietly. "Was what you said about the POW camp, about killing a man, was that true or were you just trying to scare him?"

Marty put his hands on his hips and nodded slowly. "It's true," he said. "I got a medal for it, and I put it in the bottom drawer of my dresser."

Laura turned to face their prisoner.

"Well?" she said.

"Well?" he echoed.

"Talk," she ordered.

From a pay phone booth on a subway platform Mitchell dialed Melissa Lyons at ABC, thinking about Laura the whole time. Lyons answered the phone herself, on the second ring.

"Melissa, Mitch Rydell here," he said, trying to sound jovial. There was a brief pause before Lyons replied, "Mitchell? Really?" Her voice sounded wary.

"Really."

"What about that story that said you burned up out on Long Island?" Lyons said.

"It's a story, all right," Mitchell said. "That's why I called you."

"Come to think of it," Lyons said, "what were you doing out there with Laura Madison? No, let me guess."

"Melissa," Mitchell said, "this is a little delicate, I know, but what can you tell me about the source of that Gillian story?"

"Nothing."

"It wouldn't happen to have been Dennis McCarthy, would it? A sort of portly guy, my age but not as good looking?"

"No, it wasn't," Lyons said. "It was someone I didn't know, and didn't care to know. He provided ample supporting material, proof enough for anyone. Even you."

"Evidently," Mitchell said. "Since you chose to open the story for the first time on a nationally televised presidential debate. Hardly fair to Gillian, I'd say."

"He had the chance to deny it with fifty million people watching," Lyons said. "And what did he do? Blow his stack. People are always complaining about how denials never catch up with stories. Well, the story and the Senator got an equal start on this one, and the public is making up its own mind."

"Melissa, can we get together? I want to speak to you about this, privately. We can't trust the phone."

"I can't see why. I certainly have nothing to say to you, and I'm not about to reveal my source."

"What if I told you that story was part of a broader effort to blackmail Gillian, an effort that has already led to at least one murder and several attempts on innocent people's lives?"

There was a pause. Then: "That would be a story, if you could prove it."

"I can't," Mitchell conceded. "Not yet. I have to trace the original story first, as far back as I can. There's some connection in there somewhere that will lead to the proof I need."

"You're fishing," Lyons said.

"I'm asking you for help," Mitchell countered.

"And why would I help you?"

"Because you're a journalist," Mitchell said. "The truth is supposed to matter to you"

"Good-bye, Mitchell," Lyons said.

"Hold on a second," Mitchell said. The line stayed open.

"I'm not listening to any fucking lectures on my journalistic responsibilities, Mitch," Lyons said.

"Somebody is trying to kill me," Mitchell said. To his astonishment, Lyons laughed.

"Does Madison have a mean boyfriend?" she said.

"Melissa, if you don't want lectures on your responsibilities, you might try taking them seriously," Mitchell said.

"Right, Mitchie," she replied. "Bye-bye now."

She hung up. Well I'll be damned, he thought. *She* wanted you all along. The things you learn. He couldn't help but chuckle, as a subway train clattered into the station a few yards away. There was a time, not even so long ago, he thought, when an "arrangement" with someone like Melissa Lyons, for the duration of a long campaign, would have struck him as seventh heaven. Not anymore. Laura's face flashed through his mind again, and he thought: My tomming-around days are over. It's women like Laura who cause monogamy. He was smiling when he stepped away from the phone, then he noticed the graysuits.

One was leaning on the wall just around the corner, pretending to read the *New York Post*. The other was on the subway platform, on the far side of the turnstiles, staying behind as the train pulled out. He'd been there before, Mitchell thought. Both of them had. They're conspicuous, he thought, and they don't care. My safety in crowds is starting to wear thin.

It was early afternoon when he arrived at the building near Rockefeller Center that housed the Gillian campaign headquarters. He had spent an hour trying unsuccessfully to lose the Graysuit Brothers. He boarded the elevator and rode up twenty floors. At twenty-one he got off, along with a young woman in a business suit and track shoes, who strode off purposefully down the corridor. The brothers lingered with Mitchell in the elevator lobby. Mitch snapped his fingers and pushed the "up" button. The two men stood there trying to look nonchalant.

"You guys get off at the wrong floor, too?" Mitchell said.

They didn't answer, and almost immediately another elevator arrived. He got on with his little escort, then shook his head a little sheepishly and got off again. The two men leaped out, and as the doors began to close Mitchell reached back through the electric eye, stopped them, and reboarded.

"Sorry," he said to the other passengers. The two Graysuits, faces filled with rage, got in and stood on either side of him as the doors closed again. Mitchell glanced from one to the other.

"You guys don't look like murderers," he said. He turned to another passenger. "You think either of these guys is a killer?" The woman averted her eyes.

"Nah," Mitchell said. "CPAs maybe, but not murderers. You're misassigned."

They arrived at Gillian's floor and Mitchell got out. The two men stayed on the elevator, but Mitchell assumed that wasn't for long. He walked to the office door and let himself in.

"Cavanagh in?" he said breezily to the receptionist as he swept past.

"You can't—"

"He's expecting me," Mitchell said. He knew the way from past visits, and walked through the big room full of desks to the offices in the rear. The campaign manager was on the phone, back to the door. He cupped a hand over the mouthpiece and called, "Just a sec."

"I can wait," Mitchell said, sitting down. Cavanagh started at the sound of his voice, turned around, and blanched when he saw Mitchell sitting opposite the desk. Into the receiver he said, "I'll call you back."

"You look like you'd seen a ghost," Mitchell said.

"What the hell is going on here?" Cavanagh demanded. Mitchell held up his hand.

"I'll tell you everything," he said. "First of all, Laura wants you to know she's okay. She can't make contact herself, for reasons I'll explain."

"What happened in that house on Sapphire Island?" Cavanagh said. "If you two weren't killed, why the hell didn't you let people know it?"

"We *are* letting people know it," Mitchell said. "Selected people. It's the only thing keeping us alive."

"The Senator's got to know."

"Exactly," Mitchell said. "Is he here?"

Cavanagh nodded. "It's a bad day," he said. "They've all been, lately."

"I'd appreciate your calling him in," Mitchell said. "I've got a story to tell you, and it's long and complicated, and I only want to tell it once."

Mitchell waited nervously while Cavanagh left the room, his eyes scanning the mountains of papers and books piled around the tiny office. Outside, he could hear the steady ringing of telephones and an indistinct hum of earnest voices.

The door reopened and Amos Gillian preceded Cavanagh into the room.

"Laura," he said immediately. "She's all right?"

Mitchell nodded.

"Thank God," the Senator said. He looked awful, Mitchell thought, huge bags under his eyes and a pastiness to his skin as though he'd been living underground for weeks. "Needless to say, I'm rather curious to hear your explanation for all this."

"I don't have an explanation, yet," Mitchell said. "Just a hell of a story."

He told it all, from the beginning. It took quite a while, and he wondered how his buddies out in the hall were handling the wait.

When he was finished, Cavanagh said, "How'd you like to tell that story on national TV?"

Mitchell shook his head. "The big missing element is proof," he said. "It's a crackpot story, let's face it. It's full of wild accusations and stuff nobody in his right mind would believe."

"What about the doctor?" Gillian said. "What about that horrible story about President King?"

Mitchell shrugged. "The doc makes his accusations, and the whole machinery of government, from the president through the FBI to the Secret Service and the management at Bethesda Naval Hospital, all close ranks to declare him loony tunes."

"He's right," Cavanagh said. "I'd love to give it to them

right between the eyes, but as it stands the most likely result would be to make us look desperate and foolish."

Mitchell nodded. "I wanted somebody in authority to hear the story, even without proof. There's no telling what might happen, to any of us. We're all still trying to find the bottom of the whole mess, but time is getting short."

Gillian surprised Mitchell with a big, long yawn.

"Do you want to hear a remarkable thing?" he said to nobody in particular.

"What's that?" Cavanagh replied.

"I've spent the last two years running for president, and I spent two years before that getting ready to run," Gillian said quietly, eyes focused on a vague spot across the room. "And today, on the eve of the conclusion of that process, I can't really think of anything else I've done in my life that I've regretted so much."

Gillian put his hand up to his chin and rubbed it thoughtfully for a moment. Mitchell suddenly wanted to leave, but the Senator held him in a trance of silence.

"It's really a hell of a thing," Gillian said. "I've all but become a stranger to my family. I've lived out of suitcases and gotten to know the details of hundreds of hotel rooms. I've had to deal with obnoxious, nosy reporters who confuse their salacious curiosity with investigative instinct. I haven't had a happy or satisfying day in more than a year. And now it turns out I've greatly endangered the life of a young woman who means a lot to me. My name is being dragged through the mud, and to cap it all off I'm going to lose, and lose big."

"You're tired," Cavanagh said. "It's the darkest time, right now. Everybody gets discouraged."

"I'm more than discouraged," Gillian said. "You know, some people thrive on this. Those are the guys that get elected. Some qualifications for president, huh? An iron stomach, endless energy and no conscience. There's an old saying that anyone who *can* get elected president shouldn't be."

Cavanagh stood up and gestured for Mitchell to leave the room with him.

"You'd better shake him out of that," Mitchell said.

"It'll pass," Cavanagh replied. "Listen, what made you come to us with all this?"

"Laura asked me to let you know she was okay," Mitchell said. "You and the Senator are very important to her."

"I can't say you were ever my favorite reporter."

"I know."

Cavanagh chuckled. "Well, things change, I guess. Listen, we're gonna raise all the hell we can, right?"

"Damn right," Mitchell said.

"We'll beat them," Cavanagh said. "We'll find a way. You can't get away with shit like this in America."

"I used to believe that, too," Mitchell said.

He found the elevator lobby empty, and decided to take the stairs down the twenty-one flights. He had reached the fifth floor when he found Graysuit #1 waiting for him. He turned and started back up the stairs, but heard a door open and close somewhere above him and knew it was Graysuit #2. He looked up, shrugged, smiled, and punched as hard as he could toward Graysuit's groin. His fist was intercepted in midair and he was flipped backwards into waiting arms. A pinch in the small of his back, and the world disappeared.

Laura said good-bye to her father at Key West Airport. She'd fly to Miami, and had reservations on six different flights, all leaving Miami within an hour. She'd wait until the last moment to check in on a flight. Perhaps that would confuse them enough to gain her time.

She had no baggage, so she had killed the ten minutes before her Miami flight by making several phone calls and walking with her father. A Florida State Police officer stood just out of earshot. He'd been with them since they returned to the marina.

"So," she said after a short silence. "Take care."

"You take care," Marty replied. "I'll manage."

"What are you going to do?"

"Go with the officer to the state police, talk to this Sergeant Novak, press charges on our friend. Boarding a boat by armed force is fairly illegal. When he's arrested we'll try to intimidate him into repeating his story on videotape, like you said."

"He's probably got the connections to get out of it," Laura said.

"Maybe, if he wants to," Marty replied. "But he may not want to. If I can convince him the whole house of cards is falling down, he might want to cover his ass."

"Do you think he was telling the truth?" Laura said.

"Most of it. He was good and scared, but still cool. I think he was figuring angles the whole time. If I get what you want on tape, I'll call your machine and wish you good luck."

They were calling for passengers, and a few people began straggling out to the plane.

"Remember what that New York cop told you," Marty said. "You're in danger. Don't be foolish and go it alone when you don't have to."

"I'll meet Maddalena in Washington," Laura said. "He's obnoxious but tough."

"One thing I did believe," her father said as they started for the gate. "When Erhardt's guy said he hadn't told anyone he was coming down here after you. I think he wanted to slip down and get you before anyone caught wise that you'd given them the slip in New York. He was covering his ass."

"I wonder who'll meet me in Miami," Laura said.

"My guess is, nobody. But watch out when you hit D.C."

Laura smiled, and her father chuckled.

"Those sorry SOBs don't know what they're in for," he said. They hugged a long moment, then Laura got on the end of the line and boarded the plane.

A few minutes later she was watching the keys flip by far below. She felt tired and closed her eyes, but sleep was out of the question. Against the black insides of her eyelids she saw the scene on the ocean, her would-be assassin tied up at the neck, talking in a low, casual tone as he told her a story that made her stomach flutter.

It was simple, and beautiful. A state-of-the-art application of state-of-the-art technology.

And how could she begin to prove it, any of it? Where could she look for evidence that had long ago been destroyed? Where would she find witnesses still living, bold enough or stupid enough to cross them?

They were on the cutting edge, she thought bitterly, and that's all that mattered to them. The very latest, most advanced and most powerful forms of everything were at their command. They were far ahead of ordinary people, way beyond our comprehension, certainly beyond accountability.

The whole beauty of it was it encouraged people to believe what they wanted to believe anyway.

The sun outside the jet was dazzling, and the fine necklace of islands that made up the keys—many too small even to have names—was far off on the horizon.

The future is for those who take the risks, after all. The world belongs to those who understand its resources and use them in maximally effective ways.

Maximally effective, Laura thought. She could think about all this forever and not get closer to understanding any of it. A small group of men with virtually unlimited talent and energy, headed by one of the great technical geniuses of the age, backed by a half billion dollars and the president of the United States.

Backed by him? No, she thought, Erhardt was the puppet. It wasn't a matter of him directing the conspiracy . . . the conspiracy was to ensure their pliable man stayed in power as long as possible.

It's for the good of the people, after all. Erhardt has achieved so many great things . . .

He's on the right side of everything, Laura thought. He's got every modern virtue. He's for peace, prosperity, disarmament, productivity, teaching the Japs a lesson, equality, fair taxes. He's tough on drugs and drunks, a friend of the working man and a tireless worker himself. Being a crook and a murderer didn't count.

As soon as Laura stepped into the terminal at Washington National Airport, she knew she was in trouble. A man in a dark suit watched her walk down the concourse, then fell into step behind her. Laura immediately saw two more men ahead, on either side of the passageway. They're not even bothering to be discreet, she thought. I must be the only one left. She walked resolutely forward and felt them fall in next to her as she passed. Then she sensed the two men drifting steadily closer until they had her hemmed in. She came to the junction of the American Airlines concourse and the main terminal waiting room. To her right was the New York shuttle boarding area, packed with business travelers. Beyond that, she recalled, was a narrow corridor leading to the baggage claim.

She paused a moment, pretending to be looking for someone, and out of the corner of her eye she saw her escorts pause, too. There was no time to lose. She clenched her fist and swung it, hard, in a wide arc away from her body. The blow caught the man on the right squarely in the jaw, and while it didn't hurt him much, it startled him and gave Laura an opening. She bolted away and began dodging through the air shuttle boarding lines.

At the entry to the narrow corridor she paused and looked back, and could see the commotion her pursuers were causing as they struggled through the crowd. She dashed into the baggage claim area and jumped over the low barrier separating it from the corridor. She heard voices behind her and, spinning around, saw the three men getting closer.

Laura ran across the room, vaulting over bags stacked on the floor. As she neared the exit, another dark-suited enemy appeared. She stopped abruptly. They had her boxed in. She turned back. The three men were coming at her slowly now, the one in the middle smiling and shaking his head slowly. Then a skycap cut him off with a push cart, and the man shoved him aside. The skycap, indignant, shoved back, went chest to chest, and Laura seized the moment.

She jumped onto the carousel. Her pursuers were almost on top of her as she crossed the moving metal surface and mounted the conveyor housing in the center. Then she pulled herself up over the top of the conveyor and dropped down onto it. Suitcases were riding the belt upward and she fought through them, sliding down roughly a few feet at a time. A large bag hit her from below and pinned her to the wall of the conveyor tube. She wrestled it away, pressing herself flat against the sheet metal wall, then used her feet to kick clear of the next several bags rising on the conveyor. Finally she reached the bottom and was almost hit in the face by a garment bag, pulled back at the last instant by an astonished baggage handler.

"Lady," the man said. "What the . . ."

She dashed past him, and started to run down the length of the loading area. It was a sheltered tunnel with a steady traffic of three- and four-car baggage trains, pulled by tractors that filled the confined area with diesel fumes. At the end Laura saw a corrugated metal door, and rushed through it out into the night.

The keening whine of jet engines overpowered all other sounds, and she could feel the waves of hot exhaust sweeping through her body. Ahead of her, five jets sat at their gates in varying states of readiness, service crews loading meals, beverages, fuel, and baggage. The evening was chilly, bound to get colder, and Laura felt her lungs fill up with a sickening mixture of cold, damp air and jet exhaust.

She fell into a steady run, thankful for her years of jogging through the city streets. Risking a glance back over her shoulder, she detected no pursuit, and she cut across the tarmac to run along the line of jet tails. If she could make it to the end of the runway, there was a chain-link fence she could climb. She slowed down beneath the tail section of a 727, surveying the dark area behind her. Where would they come from, if they were pursuing her? The dim glow of the baggage tunnel showed nothing, and the headlights of criss-crossing service vehicles intermittently lit up the recesses along the terminal wall. All empty.

"Who the hell are you?" a voice called to her, barely audible above the jet noise. She turned. A ground crewman was approaching, in white jumpsuit and huge orange earmuffs. Laura turned and dashed away, crouching low to pass under the belly of the jet and crossing on her hands and knees behind the giant main landing gear, the wheels towering above her . . .

Towering and turning. Laura froze in horror as the huge black forms bore down on her. Out of the corner of her eye she saw a pair of bright orange batons, handled by a crewman in white, steadily directing the pilot backwards out of the gate. She could smell rubber and grit and feel the power of the huge engines driving her into the ground, motionless.

Then she threw herself backwards, rolling over and over on the hard asphalt, coming up into a rapid crawl. She saw the ground traffic director frantically signaling a stop to the pilot, and crewmen converging on her from both sides. She straightened up and ran again, as hard as she could. Leave them in the dust, she told herself. Now is when it really counts.

[207]

She rounded the end of the jetway and moments later, breathing heavily, found herself in the general aviation area. There was virtually no foot traffic here, and she slowed down, gasping for breath. The jet noise and stench receded behind her. She walked with forced casualness across the tie-down, through the gate, and out toward the parking lot. She crossed the short-term lot, crouching behind cars every few minutes to survey the scene behind her. There was still no sign of pursuit. On the far side of the lot she found a grassy embankment alongside a road overpass, and slid gratefully down against the stone abutments, slowly catching her breath and letting the damp sweat evaporate from her face and neck.

She remembered what the assassin had told her in Key West. She knew where the center of the operation was now, where they did their dirty work. She thought of Erhardt: You bastard, I'm going to bring you down.

She slowly forced herself upright, her legs quivering from the exertion. She'd overreached her own strength and stamina. She touched the stone wall for support, and was resting there when a bit of stone flicked off the wall in front of her eyes and hit her in the face. She heard a tiny ping and smelled something burning.

A bullet! It had missed her head by inches. She ducked to her hands and knees and crawled desperately along the base of the wall toward the road. There was steady traffic coming from the main terminal, and at first she didn't notice that a car was crossing three lanes of traffic, horn blasting, lights flashing. In terror she looked back, trying to find the rifleman stalking her. She pressed herself down against the grass. The car skidded to a halt in front of her. It's over, she thought, I've failed . . .

"Get in," a voice called to her urgently. The back passenger door of the sedan flew open. "Move it!"

She looked up. Carlo Maddalena was leaning out the driver's window. She lunged through the open door onto the backseat and in moments they were accelerating into the traffic flow and leaving the airport behind.

"Jesus," she gasped.

"Yeah," said the lieutenant from the front seat. He tossed something over the seat that hit her in the thigh.

"Here," he said. She retrieved the bundle. It was wrapped

in heavy cloth, and when she undid the wrapping she found a small automatic pistol.

"Don't let that out of your sight from now on," Carlo said. "In fact, don't let it out of your hand."

It began to rain on them as they turned north onto Route One. Laura had consulted the road map and located their destination just above the Washington Beltway. Traffic was heavy, and an unbroken stream of red taillights receded in front of them, rushing into the damp grayness. Soon they had slowed to a steady twenty miles per hour.

"They snatched D'Anselmo from my place," Maddalena said. "Just barged in and took him, the bastards."

"Who?" Laura said.

"The feds . . ."

"They work for Erhardt. I couldn't get hold of Mitchell either. Cavanagh said he was going to your place . . ."

"So what's your thought?" Maddalena said. "Just ring the bell and tell them they're under arrest?"

Laura fell silent. She watched the lieutenant drive through the rain, with the oncoming headlights flaring on his face and crystallizing the drops of water on the side windows. She fingered the pistol in her lap and looked over her shoulder out the back window.

"No tail," Maddalena said. "At least none I can see."

"Let's take a drive around the place," Laura said. "Check it out."

"According to the map, it's enormous," Maddalena said. "Plenty big enough to hide on."

The Beltsville Agricultural Research Station appeared on their right as a sign on a fence, and the fence continued into the distance. They drove on for a long time, with empty fenced fields on both sides, and occasionally a squat, dark little building. But nothing matching the description she'd gotten from the man in Key West. Then again, she thought, she had no reason to expect a word the man had said to be true.

They found the north entry just as described, however, with a single guard in the shelter and a blacktop road leading into the wet void.

"I think I get the picture," Maddalena said. "This is more in the nature of a rescue mission than a bust, right?"

Laura nodded.

"You don't care about shutting them down, just getting Mitchell out?"

Laura nodded again.

"And the facility is supposed to be where?"

"Three quarters of a mile beyond the north gate, with its own perimeter fence," Laura said. That's where they've got Dom and Mitchell, she thought, in the nerve center of Loubert's dirty little operation. And on federal land? Could such an operation go on here for long without not only the knowledge but the active cooperation of the highest levels of government?

In Laura's mind the link between Erhardt and Loubert was firmly established, and all that the lieutenant had told her on their drive—about McCarthy, his overseas duty, his superior officer named Mochrie, Loubert's unpaid parking tickets, the phony auto registrations, the medical center, his illness, all of it—only strengthened her conviction that the President of the United States was behind everything that had happened. And now it was Erhardt, or Erhardt's men, holding Mitchell, threatening him, possibly torturing or killing him.

"A second perimeter fence?" Maddalena said. "Probably with barbed wire or electricity to boot. I'd feel better going in with an army."

"An army couldn't get in," Laura said. "But two people could. They don't know we're coming, and don't realize anyone even knows where they are. We'll have surprise on our side."

"A grossly overestimated advantage," Maddalena said.

"Then let me out," Laura snapped. The lieutenant looked at her. "Really," she said. "Pull the hell over and let me out. You're free. Go on home."

Maddalena began to chuckle and shake his head.

"What's funny?" Laura demanded.

"Nothing. Funny is not the word. I like it, in fact."

They were silent a moment, then Maddalena looked over at her. They were driving through a lonely stretch of forest with high fences and government Keep Out signs on both sides.

[210]

"You mind a little advice from a cop?" he said. Laura didn't answer.

"There's things that don't belong in court, you know what I mean?"

"No."

Maddalena was staring out through the rain-spangled windshield, and he spoke very slowly and carefully.

"Sometimes, you know what a guy did but you can't prove it," he said. "And if you observe all the . . . niceties, he's gonna get away. But maybe you can arrange to send him up for something else. Or you can bring him in and explain things to him with a little added persuasion and he'll cop a plea to something. In any case, you put him away. There's things you don't want to talk about in front of a judge and a jury and a bunch of reporters."

"If you mean we can't prove anything against Erhardt and Loubert, that's already occurred to me," Laura said. "And I don't even care that much. As long as Mitchell's okay."

Maddalena glanced at her.

"No," he said. "I mean there are solutions other than legal ones." He took a deep breath and let it out slowly in a sigh. "Laura, look under the seat."

She reached down and felt around under her seat until she found a small plastic box, which she pulled out. It was a videocassette.

"That's a tape of an interrogation I conducted this afternoon," Maddalena said. "With one Dr. Peter Fontana."

Laura said nothing. Maddalena's obvious unease had given her a sense of dread.

"That's the guy that operated on King, remember?" Carlo said. Laura felt her stomach flutter.

"And?"

"And it's the bottom of the barrel," Carlo said. "They did it to him. Just the way they tried to kill Rydell in the hospital. They turned King into a vegetable to make Erhardt president, so they'd have free rein."

"The doctor confessed that?" Laura said incredulously.

"He's scared shitless," Carlo replied. "He was scared of me, scared I'd expose him. Scared this Mochrie fellow is going to kill him. His confession is his life insurance policy, the way he sees it."

"And you believe he's telling the truth?"

"Yes, I do."

Laura turned the box over in her hand. "I see what you mean about not going to court."

"You can't," Carlo said. "Not ever, with that. Any good defense lawyer would get it barred, and then where would you be? Besides, it would be better for everyone, better for the country . . ."

"To handle it quietly," Laura said. "Yes, it would."

They'd gotten back to Route One and Maddalena drove a long way north while they both sat in silence. It was about nine o'clock and the rain was letting up, leaving great black lakes standing across the road, stirred up by passing cars. Carlo turned the car around in Laurel and headed back south.

Laura looked out the window at the passing body shops, car dealers, and bars. What Maddalena said explained their willingness to kill almost casually. They'd do anything to protect themselves now.

That, in turn, meant Mitchell Rydell was dead.

There, she thought. That's the little nub you've been afraid to touch.

Mitchell is dead. That they'd keep him alive one moment longer than necessary was just too much to hope for.

Maddalena pulled the car off the road below a sign that said U-Lok-It—U-Keep-Key—24 Hrs. He went into a small office without a word and emerged a few moments later to drive them through the lot until they found their assigned garage. He pulled in, opened the door, took the cassette from Laura and simply put it on the floor next to the car, then shut his door again.

"One more time," he said, "describe to me that guy who attacked you in Key West."

Laura repeated her description of the black-haired assassin.

"Now," Carlo said, gesturing at the gun in Laura's lap. "Do you think you can fire that thing?"

"At someone? I don't know," Laura said. "If I have to, I guess I'll find out."

"That's the only right answer," Carlo said.

"You have a plan?"

Carlo nodded. "Not much of one, but better than nothing. We have to wait a few hours."

MONDAY, NOVEMBER 4

Mitchell awoke groggy and lay still for a long time trying to sort out where he was. Finally he sat up, his back and neck aching, and stared into the darkness as the past returned to his mind.

To his left, above eye level, was a small window through which moonlight illuminated a simple cot and a folding chair. The room was perhaps six by ten feet: A cell.

He walked unsteadily to the window. Outside it was dark, and the view from the window told him nothing. There was an empty yard overgrown with weeds and wild grass, and perhaps a hundred feet away was a hulking shape of some kind, maybe a barn.

He yawned and stretched, and felt a small ache in his right arm. In the moonlight he examined it: A tiny red dot, a little bruise around it, and the remains of adhesive on both sides. An IV needle, he thought. He'd been given something, and it was a safe bet he'd told them everything he knew.

He crossed to the door and tried the knob even though he knew it would be locked. Alongside it he found a light switch, flipped it on, and heard, a split second later, a tiny click within the switch plate. A second switch inside, he thought, sending a signal. Turning on the light let them know he was awake.

The window was not quite shoulder width. The wall around it had the uneven look of plaster, and Mitchell guessed it was old and substantial.

Seconds later he heard footsteps outside his door, seeming to come down a long corridor, from the left. He pressed his ear to the door as they approached, and wondered if there were other rooms like his to either side. Had they gotten Laura, too?

The footsteps stopped and a voice addressed him.

"Rydell?"

He didn't answer.

"If you're awake, my orders are to offer you something to eat."

Mitchell's mind raced: They'd have to open the door.

"I'd like a glass of orange juice," he said, surprised at the croak that came out of his throat.

"Anything else? A sandwich?"

"Sure," Mitchell replied. "But mostly something to drink. My throat's dry."

"The drugs do that, they say," the voice answered. "I'll be back in about ten minutes."

Mitchell listened to the footsteps receding, then spun around. The window offered no escape, unless he could smash out some of the wall around it, and without tools there was little chance of that. But the guard, when he returned, not only had to open the door, he had to come into the room. Somehow, Mitchell thought, I've got to get him in here, and he's got to be alone.

He stripped the sheets off the cot and began methodically tearing them into long strips, working quickly and as quietly as he could. Then he knotted the strips together and tied one end to the leg of the cot. He pulled the cot over by the window and climbed up on it.

Now he could see better, and a few yards off, he saw a man approach the building with a flashlight. The man was walking carefully, and the ground seemed thoroughly drenched and muddy. He had a small bag in his hand that Mitchell guessed could contain his meal. Wait, now, he told himself, don't give it away.

When the man was out of sight, Mitchell threw the sheet chain out the window and pulled the cot over on its side. The window's absurdly small, he thought, slipping quickly back to the door. Then, as he heard the footsteps coming, he slipped off his right shoe.

"Here we are," the guard's voice said. "Some nice, homey hospitality."

Mitchell held his breath and waited for the guard to respond to his silence.

"They told me not to let you go back to sleep, either," the guard said. Mitchell heard a jingle outside, then a key in the lock, then the door opened and he saw a hand toss in a brown paper bag. "Holy shit," the guard muttered. "How'd he get through there?"

Come in, come in, Mitchell pleaded silently, his lungs bursting. And the guard obliged, rushing to the window to investigate the miraculous escape. Mitchell was behind him in a second, still silent, and bludgeoned him hard with his shoe heel, then hit him a second time as he was already falling, face first, onto the cot.

Mitchell slipped his shoe back on and quickly frisked the guard's body, retrieving the keys and taking his pistol from its holster. He jumped out the open door, pulled it closed behind him, and tested it. Locked.

He was in a corridor now, with an exit door to his left and two other doors between him and a corner off to his right. Laura . . . Laura could be in one of those rooms. Had they drugged her, too, or worse?

He rushed to the first door and tried a key. No luck. He tried another, then another, then stopped because he heard another door open far off—probably around the corner. No time, he thought. He slipped back down the hall, away from the door that might be Laura's cell. The footsteps came closer. They'd round the corner at any moment.

Mitchell bolted for the exit door, opened it as quietly as he could, and stepped out into the cold November night. The open yard meant exposure, and he ran across it quickly, to the side of the barn where shadows and high grass seemed to promise safety. It must have rained hard, he thought, for the ground was nearly ankle deep in mud in some places and even the grass was slippery. There was a thick, lung-chilling mist in the air. He crept around the barn until he was away from the prison building, then crouched down and looked back.

The building he'd escaped from was a one-story wing attached to a three-story brick building in which only a few lights were burning. Through the windows he could see some of the office walls, but they were undecorated and told him nothing. In the distance, beyond the three-story building, he could make out the shape of a high hurricane fence with a gate in it, on which there appeared to be several signs.

He moved stealthily along the barn wall and wished he knew what time it was. When dawn came, he'd need to be off the property somehow or the game was over. Was the fence topped with barbed wire? Electrified? Were there guard stations around the perimeter? And once outside, where the hell was he? He listened intently for a moment, praying for a highway sound, but heard not even a rustle. And for as far as he could see, the lights in the brick building were the only signs of habitation. There was a stand of forest a short jog away, and that would offer some cover, but not much.

He continued his investigation of the barn. It was dilapidated, with peeling paint and rotten wallboards, and from time to time Mitchell could peer inside through gaps in the wall, but it was too dark within for him to see anything. He heard movement inside that he attributed to mice. Finally, he came to the front of the barn, and pulled himself back out of sight quickly. A guard was sitting in a beach chair with a shotgun across his knees. The barn doors appeared to be closed and padlocked.

Mitchell crept back along the wall to the gap he'd looked through before. It was, barely, wide enough for him to slip through sideways, but he did. Inside he found himself knee-deep in wet hay and nearly blind in the darkness.

He sat that way for a long time, thinking and trying to get his eyes accustomed to the dark. His neck and back still hurt in a dull, chronic way. Finally he thrust himself forward onto his hands and knees and began to traverse, a few inches at a time, the floor of the barn toward the front door.

He hadn't gone far when he realized he was approaching a series of large objects, and reaching forward tentatively he felt his hand rest on a rubber tire. Groping, he made out the shape of an automobile's front fender. He guided himself along the bumper, then found another car, and another.

The keys? he thought.

Then he heard voices outside. Someone had approached the guard, and Mitchell strained to hear what they were saying. A moment later, he heard a key in the padlock and saw the

[218]

barn door begin to open. He scurried back the length of the car, then fell to his stomach and crept back into the darkest recesses of the barn.

The newcomer entered and reached for a shelf by the door. Then he climbed into the nearest car—Mitchell recognized a fairly new Volvo—and cranked the engine to life. The Volvo's parking lights came on, and in their glow Mitchell saw the shape of the car next to it.

It was a white Oldsmobile. Mitchell felt his stomach tighten as he realized it was the car that had driven him off the Long Island Expressway. A conclusive link, he thought, *if* I can get the others out and reach neutral authorities with the evidence.

Which was a lot to hope for. Mitchell pressed himself into the damp hay on the barn floor and watched the newcomer drive out into the night. The door closed and Mitchell sat up, thinking. He crawled through the darkness by memory, until he reached the back end of the white car.

He ran his fingers over the entire surface until he found the big dents on the right front and in the passenger door. He crept around to the driver's door, opened it silently and climbed in. Inside, he felt a jab of regret for Dennis, for how he'd treated his old friend that day in Brooklyn. That was your holier-than-thou phase, he thought, before you realized how fine a thread you hung by.

He opened the glove compartment and felt inside with his hands, wishing for a light. Then, on a hunch, he poked and probed along the dash until he found the cigarette lighter, and pushed it in.

When it popped out he took it and held it into the glove compartment. It bathed the tiny cubicle in a fast-fading orange glow, and did not die until Mitchell had found a registration card.

He recharged the cigarette lighter and checked the rest of the front seat, then the back. Nothing useful. Get the keys, he thought. Get over to that shelf and get the keys, then back here and wait. For what? he thought. There was still a locked gate between him and freedom, even if he got out of the barn. At least, he decided, with the keys in my pocket nobody will be using these cars to chase me. Except for the Volvo, which might be back at any moment.

He dropped to his knees outside the car and let the door close gently. He could see the faint outline of the barn doors against the lighter world outside, and began to move toward them slowly and silently, keeping well to the side. He brushed against a vertical beam and, feeling it out, found a ladder leading upwards. He tested the rungs and found them firm but mossy. Above was a hayloft, he thought, probably long unused and none too safe.

Mitchell inched his way over to the barn doors, then crept across the doorway and began to slide his hand up the wall, searching for the shelf where the keys were. He could look through a crack between wallboards and see the guard outside, facing away, smoking. Groping, he found a little pile of metal, clutched it tightly, and brought it down. It was two sets of car keys on plain steel rings, and he slipped them into his pocket. He saw two more men approach the guard, and began to make his silent way back into the barn. The voices came to him clearly.

"Shit's hitting the fan, I guess."

"How?" the guard replied.

"I don't know, exactly. Just orders to shut down and move out. Bundle up our guests."

"Has to do with Gillian's speech?"

"Maybe."

"I heard the old man died. There's a million reporters outside his place that don't know it yet."

The guard chuckled.

"What's so funny?"

"Nothing. Nothing at all. It's just like the army. Build it up, use it a while, tear it down, throw it away, then build it again."

Mitchell heard the guard standing up. He was caught near the front of the barn, and instantaneously chose the ladder, pulling himself up hand over hand as quietly as he could. The padlock on the barn door was being opened.

"They in shape to move?" the guard's voice said.

"Rydell is up, but the other guy is still out cold."

Is that all? Mitchell thought. Just two men? Dominick and himself? Or Maddalena? Where was Laura?

As the barn doors creaked open, Mitchell pulled himself up the last step and stretched out full length in the loft, his face against the clammy, mildewy wood. He watched the scene below through the trapdoor. He pressed his stolen pistol against his shoulder, feeling the barrel just inches from his face. He realized he didn't even know if it was loaded.

The newcomer was a tall, thin man and he reached onto the key shelf.

"Where the fuck's the keys?"

"They ain't there?" the guard said, coming over to check.

"Maybe in the ignition," the newcomer said, and he crossed to the Olds and opened the door.

"Shit," he said.

Mitchell shifted his weight and pulled himself over for a better view. The newcomer was trying the door of the second car and finding it locked.

"I'll be damned."

Mitchell propped himself up on one hand and craned his neck to see better. Then his hand vanished through the wood with a loud crack, and he fell heavily against the loft floor. The pistol discharged thunderously in the tiny, confined space.

"What the . . ." said a voice from below. Suddenly, the universe filled with shrill shrieks and a mad fluttering of dark forms. Bats! The air was full of wings and cries, and Mitchell, in terror, covered his head and neck with his arms as they beat around him, by him, through the trapdoor and down into the barn.

He lay still until they were gone, then ventured a look. The men below were gone, frightened into flight. They'd left a car door and the barn door open. Mitchell slowly pulled himself together and inched down the ladder. His hands, arms and the front of his clothing were covered with filth, and he shook it off as best he could. He wasn't bitten, he thought, only shaken up and dirty. Through the open door he surveyed the yard. The guard had had the presence of mind to grab his shotgun as he left, Mitchell noticed.

Quickly, he took the car keys from his pocket and opened the Oldsmobile's trunk. It was empty, so he unfastened the tire iron and shoved it into a belt loop. He checked the other car's trunk and found nothing. He slipped out of the barn and crouched in the foliage on the far side as the guards returned.

They went inside, and while they were occupied Mitchell slid back through the mucky darkness to the one-story prison wing. He pressed himself against the wall and moved along the brick surface until he guessed he was beneath Dominick's window.

The other guy is still out.

"Dom?" he whispered. He turned, reached for a handhold, and pulled himself up until his chin was above the window ledge. Dominick was inside, sitting on his cot, with the lights out.

"Mitchie?"

"Here," Mitchell said, dropping back to the ground and holding the tire iron in through the bars. "For what it's worth. Is Laura here?"

"I don't know," Dominick said quietly.

Mitchell dropped to the ground. He was alarmed, then, to see a sliver of light on the horizon, faintly visible through the trees. Dawn, he thought. Oh, hell, at least we're armed. And I've got the car keys.

He made his way back to the exit door he'd used before and let himself in. Now all was quiet as he went to Dominick's door and unlocked it.

"How many against us?" Dominick said in a whisper.

Mitchell shook his head. "Two out in the barn, maybe one or two more on the grounds."

"They've been moving stuff," Dominick said. "I've been awake for hours, listening. Trucks coming and going. Lots of voices, then it got pretty quiet."

"I never killed anyone before," Mitchell said, holding his pistol away from his body.

"What do you take *me* for, the Sundance Kid?" Dominick replied.

Mitchell took a deep breath, checked the safety on the pistol, then gestured for Dominick to follow him. They went to the opposite end of the corridor and inched the door open.

On the other side was an area that looked like an elementary school office, with waist-high metal partitions topped by

[222]

frosted glass reaching to just above head height. There was a radio playing easy-listening music a long way off. Mitchell opened the door wider and the two men slipped through, weapons ready.

There seemed to be nobody there. At the end of the row of cubicles they found an office with a bank of television monitors, each giving a view of the outdoor areas. On one screen two men were slowly patrolling alongside the hurricane fence. Mitchell looked around, shrugged.

"There's got to be people here," he said. Then they froze at the sound of footsteps approaching. Dominick inched over to the edge of the partition and stole a glance around the corner. Someone was coming fast. He got a grip on his tire iron and waited until the footsteps were on top of them, then leaped up and around the corner, swinging the iron.

He hit the security guard in the stomach and made him double over. Instantly, Mitchell was on top of him, pressing the pistol barrel into the man's temple. They fell together onto the floor. Mitchell pulled the guard's pistol from his belt and tossed it up to Dom.

"Quiet," Mitchell hissed. "Quiet as can be, to save your ass."

All three men were silent for a second. Nothing moved, nothing was heard.

"Okay," Mitchell said. "First thing you're going to do is call your buddies back from the barn. How many others are there?"

"Three," the guard said.

"The two in the barn and you?"

"One more."

"Where?"

"I don't know." Mitchell pressed the gun barrel into the man's flesh. "Honest to God, I don't," the guard said.

"Get on the phone and get the two from the barn. Tell them to stand outside in the field, midway between this building and the gate, where we can see them easily."

The guard did as instructed, and as soon as he was off the phone Mitchell nodded at Dominick, then went down the hallway toward the prison wing and the rear exits.

He was outside in the growing light, behind the prison

building, when he saw the other two guards walking hesitantly across the open field to stand where they'd been told. He stepped out of the shadow.

"Hey," he called, and trained his pistol on them. "I can get you both from here real quick. Toss your weapons over the perimeter fence."

He watched them undo their gunbelts and throw their pistols away.

"Now, you on the right, come toward me, real slow."

He directed the guard through the back door. Keeping several feet between them, Mitchell led the guard to the prison wing and locked him into the cell he had himself occupied a short time ago. Then he returned to the yard and repeated the procedure with the second guard. Dominick was still holding the security man at gunpoint in the control post.

Mitchell returned to the barn and started the Olds, driving slowly out onto the muddy grass, feeling the tires fight for traction. Get the gate open, he thought, and bring our prisoners to the State Police. Get a few troopers in here to check the place out.

But something was wrong. Dominick was coming out the front door of the guard house, but without his gun . . . in fact, with his hands behind him. Then three more bodies materialized behind Dom, and the rising sunlight glinted off the barrels of two shotguns.

And behind Dominick, walking slowly and looking straight at Mitchell, was the black-haired man he'd seen on Sapphire Island.

Mitchell slammed the gas pedal to the floor and the wheels below him spun wildly. He aimed straight at the small group, but the car fishtailed out of control. As he drew closer, he saw Dominick crouch and kick at the legs of his captors, then make a quick dash across the field. Mitchell leaned over and opened the passenger door, then spun the car madly toward the guardhouse. The headlights caught Dominick first, then three men lowering shotguns, then the air filled with gunshot reports and Mitchell recoiled.

The windshield shattered loudly into a rain of fragments. He risked a glance above it and saw the men preparing another round. Dom was alongside, fighting to climb into the front seat. Mitchell aimed the car's big, heavy nose at the hurricane gate and floored the accelerator again. And again came the thunder of guns, this time a fusillade that smashed against the metal side panels of the car and blew out both left tires. At maximum speed and with minimum steering, the car careened drunkenly across the compound, and Mitchell had just enough time to let up on the gas before a massive tree trunk appeared before him, and he was smashed against the steering wheel and blacked out.

Moments later hands pulled him from the car. He was roughly thrown against the back fender and his arms pulled behind him. His captors tied indestructible plastic cords around his wrists and upper arms. He looked around groggily and saw Dominick, already tied the same way. They shared a look that said nice try, buddy, then Mitchell was spun around and was looking into the double barrels of a shotgun.

The black-haired man looked at him levelly and said, "Now, just what are you doing here?"

Mitchell stared back silently.

"Very brave," the man said. "In two more minutes you will be a dead man. Whatever crazy crusade you were on won't matter anymore to anyone."

Mitchell felt his heart pounding in his chest and thought of it stopping.

"Move it," the man said, and the whole small group started toward the woods. Mitchell fought with himself to keep his gait steady and his eyes ahead, and tried his best to think despite the terror that was rampaging through him. His throat was dry and he tried to force himself to swallow, but couldn't. He could taste death, closer every inexorable second.

As they reached the first few scraggly trees, the black-haired man muttered something to the other guards, and the group stopped. Mitchell heard footsteps retreating, then the black-haired man spoke.

"Let me know when you're finished."

They stood in the edge of the woods a long time, long enough for Mitchell's feet to get numb and his legs to begin quivering. He could feel the plastic wires cutting into his flesh, and tried not to struggle against them. But even when he relaxed completely, he couldn't get enough slack to do anything.

"What are you going to do with us?" Dominick's voice asked.

The man behind them snorted. "Ask me a question you don't already know the answer to." It was the leader's voice.

"All right," Mitchell said, surprised by his own sound. "Who's in charge of this operation, Erhardt or Loubert?"

"Now that's a question," the black-haired man said. "I'll say this for you, you've got balls."

They fell silent again, and another few minutes passed in fear and agony. All around Mitchell it was still dark, but with signs of approaching dawn. He heard the footsteps of others coming back.

"All set," one voice said. "Truck's loaded."

"All right," the leader replied. Mitchell looked over at Dominick, and saw his old friend's eyes wide with terror. The black-haired man stood directly behind Dominick, put a hand on his shoulder, then struck him hard in the lower back. Dom let out a little gasp, then started to speak, then with a quizzical look fell forward onto the ground. His executioner leaned forward as he fell, crouching with him, and when he was prone pulled the small injector out of Dominick's back. He felt in Dom's neck for a pulse, then looked up at Mitchell.

Seconds left, Mitchell thought. What happens? Does your life flash before you? Do you feel your regrets, resent the years taken away? A bright, all embracing light, he thought, then thought of his mother, then Laura. Then, instead of philosophy or faith that could answer his last cry of need, Mitchell's only thought was the dispassionate realization that he was thinking his last thoughts.

"Get him out of here," the black-haired man said. The guard pulled Dominick's body up onto his shoulder and left them. The silence lengthened until Mitchell wanted to scream. Then he felt the black-haired man's presence at his shoulder, and braced for the jolt in the back and the last, delirious fading fall.

Nothing.

"For God's sake," Mitchell said.

"Nervous?" the killer replied. "Don't be. It doesn't hurt. Or so they tell me. It's quick. Most of all, it's clean."

"Do it," Mitchell said.

"Not now," the man said. "Oh, you're going to die. Make no mistake. But right now I need you for bait."

Just before dawn Laura crept through wet brush and looked out across a narrow clearing. A brick building sat there, three stories tall, with a long, low wing attached to its rear. Beyond it stood the black shape of an old barn. A high steel hurricane fence encircled it, with strands of barbed wire on top. It was all just as Mochrie had described it to her in Key West. Too much like it, in fact. It made her nervous.

Laura made her way through the thin foliage parallel to the fence, thinking that the rain had made the ground soggy and helped her move more quietly.

In the building there were several lights on but no sign of activity. She tried to visualize the interior. Where was the elevator? How deep could the shaft be? How many guards and others would be on duty at this hour of night? Did they use the barn? If so, what for?

There was no sound of traffic behind her on the blacktop country road where she and Maddalena had left his car. She knew the lieutenant was across the clearing somewhere, slowly completing his circle around the facility. She saw a tiny glimmer of light, then another little flash, and responded with the pocket flashlight she'd bought in an open-late hardware store on Route One. Then she sat down in the wet grass and waited. Maddalena arrived a few minutes later.

"Ready for a surprise?" he said.

"What?"

"The front gate's open." Laura looked over her shoulder, then crawled twenty yards through the brush to get a view of the front gate. Sure enough, it hung open, a heavy-duty chain dangling through the lock fittings. She returned to the lieutenant.

"It's a trap," she said.

"I think so, too."

"Or they may have broken it all down and moved out," she

[227]

added. "They don't need much of a facility anymore. The election is tomorrow."

"What do you want to do?"

"Go in," Laura said. "Me through the front, you the other way. They don't know about you, I don't think."

"I'll be there," Carlo said. "You have your gun?"

Laura nodded, and put her hand on the stock of the pistol.

"Any sign of life at all?" she asked, and Maddalena shook his head.

"Place looks deserted."

Laura stepped out of the brush and walked slowly, evenly. In two minutes she had reached the gate, passed through it, and was approaching the building. The front door was also open, with light from within pooling on the concrete terrace outside.

Mitchell's not here, she thought. I'm too late. They're gone without a trace. Mochrie knew they would be, and that's why he didn't mind telling me all about this place. I've been on a wild goose chase all night, while they were escaping.

While they were killing Mitchell.

She stepped up onto the concrete patio. The door lay open within her reach. She stepped over the threshold and into the lobby.

Inside was a guard station with several television monitors, a radio transmitter, and assorted other security paraphernalia . . . all turned off. A corridor led off behind the checkpoint, silent, eerily lit by ceiling fixtures every thirty feet or so, with no doors on either side. Laura entered it warily. After a few tentative steps, she walked briskly to the other end. A steel door hung open a few inches, and she pulled the knob back slowly, hiding behind the steel.

Another corridor, at right angles to the first. She glanced both ways at rows of doors into unseen rooms, all silent, all empty, all beckoning and threatening at once.

The signs of a hasty departure were everywhere. But so were signs that until recently the facility had been very busy, indeed. Desks were shoved together against walls, chairs overturned in the middle of floors. On one desktop there was a small bowl of empty peanut shells.

She moved quietly, peering in each door where a light was

on, but leaving the dark ones alone. Her ears searched for sounds of movement, for any indication that someone was still there.

She was convinced everything Skip Mochrie had told her in Key West was true . . . or had been true until tonight. This was Loubert's center of operations, the place from which he managed his whole network. There was computer detritus in many rooms: Piles of snapped-off tractor-feed paper, half-inch strips with holes every inch or so; in one room, a six-foot cable, in others, disconnected telephone lines. But they had gone, and gone so quickly they'd pulled the lines apart. Why?

Had Mochrie sent them an alarm from Florida? Had they shut down, or merely moved elsewhere?

Or was it a trap?

Had the assassin had time to get back here from Florida? Certainly, Laura thought, considering how quickly he'd gotten *down* there.

Most of all, where was Mitchell? He could be imprisoned here, or they could have taken him with them, she thought, perhaps in a plastic bag.

She stood in the middle of the corridor collecting her strength, then shouted.

"Mitchell!"

Her voice echoed, and that was the only sound. She called again, and thought she heard a thump far off, like a heavy footstep. It might be Maddalena, she thought. She stepped to the end of the hall, to the corner, and slowly turned it.

Mochrie was in the corridor, leaning against a door frame, smiling.

"Hello, Laura," he said. Laura slid back out of sight, pulled the gun from her waistband, then stepped out into the middle of the corridor and leveled it at him. His smile didn't waver.

"Sure you can fire that thing?"

Laura did not respond.

"It's not likely to be very accurate from that distance," Mochrie said. "Especially if you've never fired a thirty-eight before, and I doubt you have."

He was silent for a moment. Laura aimed the gun carefully at the center of his chest, just as Maddalena had told her.

That way, if you miss by a few inches in any direction, you still hit something important.

The gun was heavy, and she felt her forearm tightening. The assassin stood up straight, and she followed him with her aim.

None of that kneecap bullshit, either. Forget about shooting to wound.

"Besides," Mochrie said, "you don't want to kill me until you know about Rydell, right?"

"Is he alive?" Laura said, her voice barely more than a croak through her nerve-tightened throat.

Mochrie nodded. "For the moment," he said. "He's in there," he added, nodding back toward the door he had been leaning on. He started to walk toward her. As he stepped under a ceiling light Laura realized his face and hands were sunburned raw. And he was carrying something, a long steel rod, in his right hand.

"He brought you to me," Mochrie said. "Like my tan?"

"Stand still," Laura said.

"Seems I spent too much time out in the sun recently, without the right protection." He kept walking.

"Stop right there, goddammit," Laura said. She fought to maintain her aim, thinking: How much closer will I let him get?

"I owe that to you, don't I? And that's just the beginning," Mochrie said, taking another deliberate step.

"What went on here?" Laura demanded. "Where are they all now? Where is Emile Loubert?"

Mochrie smiled and took another step. "Dead," he said. "Emile passed away at nine o'clock. Which meant he didn't make his midnight call-in. You see, Emile needed to call the mainframe computer every six hours and enter a special code that proved he was still alive. When the time passed without his code, the whole thing went poof! He'd planned it that way."

He stepped closer, again. "A software bomb, he called it. Every little scrap of memory, programs, data, everything, in every memory medium in the joint, all erased in about six minutes, and there was nothing anyone could do to stop it."

Another step toward her. He was about fifteen feet away

now, and in two or three more steps she'd be within striking range of that steel rod.

"Where are the computers?" she said.

"Carted off," he answered. "The order came, we closed down. It's all over. Except, of course, for us."

She felt the gun, felt her need of Mitchell burning inside and out, felt the focused hatred of Mochrie's grin just a few feet away. The moment of decision is here, she thought. And still she hesitated. Then he stepped closer again, and she stepped involuntarily back.

The killer noticed her retreat and moved toward her quickly, raising the steel rod. She focused her whole consciousness on the center of his torso and pulled the trigger.

Nothing.

Oh, Jesus, Laura, the safety! The fucking safety!

The gun flew from her hand against the wall and her whole body contorted in pain. The weapon in his hand was an electric cattle prod, and he delivered another jolt, this time to her abdomen, as she fell forward toward him.

"In case you're wondering," he said, "I'm going to kill you with my bare hands. This is just for preparation." He waved the cattle prod at her. "Sort of like the picadors at a bullfight."

Laura pulled herself to her knees. The pain still rang throughout her body. Nothing she had ever felt was remotely like it. Mochrie came closer, held the rod out to her, and jabbed her on the point of her chin. It was like a major toothache in every part of her head, and she coiled, then sprang backward, sprawling on the floor. She pulled herself over to the wall and started to try to climb up. She heard him laugh.

"You know, this thing has several settings on it, and I'm still on the lowest."

Laura pulled off her sweater and wrapped it into a big, bulky ball around her left fist. Then she stood up.

"I'm impressed," Mochrie said. "You're a strong little lady. Tough." He came toward her, shoving the prod forward. She dodged it, and fell a little off balance, the tip of the rod hitting the wall and clinking noisily. He spun to pursue her and for a split second the cattle prod was above Laura's head. She brushed it away with the sweater ball and as he drew it back to strike again she lunged below it toward his midsection, driving her right fist as hard as possible into his groin.

She hopped back, against the wall, facing her attacker.

"Bitch," he said, grimacing. He hurled the prod at her like a spear, and it caught her in the chest. The shock and pain threw her against the wall, where she hit her head and fell sideways. Mochrie was on her in an instant, jabbing her again and again, sending wave after wave of unendurable pain through her bones and joints.

Enough, God, enough, oh Jesus, oh sweet Jesus . . .

"Freeze! Police!"

Maddalena's voice came to her through her mist of pain as she fell into a hump on the floor, the tile cold against her cheek. She was dimly aware of Mochrie turning away from her, saw a flash of black steel at his belt, then heard the echoing thunder of both guns. Mochrie fell against the wall, his legs covered with blood. Maddalena was next to her in a second, gun trained on the black-haired killer.

"Sorry," he said. "I had a little more trouble getting in than I thought I would." He helped Laura lift herself from the floor and cradled her in his arms as she rocked the pain away. He kept his gun trained on Mochrie.

"That's superficial," he said, gesturing to the leg wound.

"I know," the other man replied. He started to rise, then grimaced and fell back.

"Where's Rydell?" Carlo demanded.

No answer. Laura stood up and slowly, achingly, made her way along the corridor. She found the doorway Mochrie had indicated and opened it. Mitchell was inside, bound to a straight-backed chair by dozens of fine white plastic strips, a thick gag in his mouth and his eyes bulging from the effort of trying to breathe. Laura pulled the gag out and Mitchell gasped in several deep, fast breaths.

"He told me if I made a sound he'd kill you," he said hoarsely. "And I had every reason to believe him."

From the door Carlo slid a pocket knife across the floor to Laura, and she quickly cut the strips binding Mitchell to the chair. He leaned forward, massaging his thighs and calves, and Laura pulled him into her arms.

"Mitchell," she said softly. "Mitchell."

[242]

"You saved my life," he said. But there was an odd overtone to the way he said it, Laura thought.

"Maddalena saved us both," she said.

"And a lot of good *I* was," Mitchell said.

"You're alive, I'm alive, and we're going to be all right," Laura said, hugging him close again. But he stood up, almost rough in shoving her aside, and went to the door.

"Dominick is dead," he said. "He killed him. I watched."

"Mitchell, I'm sorry," Laura said.

"If I hadn't gotten him involved in all of this, he'd still be alive and happy in Brooklyn." Mitchell stepped out into the corridor and Laura followed. Maddalena was tying up Mochrie's wound with paper towels, tightened with his belt.

"We've worked out a story for the hospital," he said. "We'll brazen it through. I don't think he wants to explain all this any more than I do."

Suddenly Laura's breath was coming in tiny gasps and she felt a shiver run through her body, felt her legs about to give. Maddalena was looking at her sadly.

"Shit," she said, putting a hand to her eyes.

"I know," the lieutenant said. "You pulled the trigger tonight. That changes everything."

"But the safety . . ."

"Doesn't matter," Carlo said. "You aimed at another person and pulled the trigger. You learned something about yourself tonight."

Mitchell crouched next to Skip Mochrie, staring at him.

"You blew it," Mitchell said.

"It's all gone, Mitch," Laura said. "Every scrap of evidence, all destroyed."

"No," Mitchell replied. "We've still got him." He turned back to Mochrie. "You committed a murder tonight. I saw you. And you're going to pay for it."

Laura saw Mochrie's eyes dart from Mitchell to Maddalena to her, then back to the lieutenant.

"I'm sure you've got a lot of testimony to trade for the murder rap," Carlo said. "Want to think it over?"

"No!" Mitchell shouted. "He killed Dom and he has to pay for it."

"There's more going on than you realize, Mitchell," Laura said.

"I don't give a rat's ass," Mitchell replied. "Not for all your politics, your Senator, your fucking election. I want justice."

"You want vengeance," Laura said quietly. "And you're not thinking. We haven't lost yet. We can still put the big things right."

"You go to hell, then," Mitchell said.

"I know what it is," Laura said. "You're frosted by the thought that *I* saved your life, while you just sat there all tied up—"

"He killed Dom and he would have killed me in a second," Mitchell shouted at her. "You have no right to say that to me."

"But you're saying it to yourself. And it's got you so mad you're not thinking straight."

Mitchell spun away from her, stared at the lieutenant, then spun again and stomped off down the corridor. At the end of the corridor he kicked the door and turned back to her.

"Go to hell!"

"Laura," Maddalena said, handing her a set of keys. "You know what you have to do now. I can handle things here."

Laura took the keys and looked at Mitchell, who averted his face. So be it, she thought, and with tears welling up in her eyes made her way back through the corridors, out of the building, and through the woods to where Maddalena had left the car.

"The President will be glad to see you," Steve Shaw said. "If only for a few minutes."

They were in the anteroom of the Oval Office. While Laura had been very busy in the hours since the confrontation in the woods, her day had not included a change of clothing or a shower. She itched, and was sure she smelled.

"The news conference starts in ten minutes, you know," Shaw said. "Responding to all your boss's allegations. Pretty wild stuff, though I suppose Loubert's death makes it all more or less moot."

Shaw shook his head in wonderment. "Imagine getting away with all that, all this while!"

Yeah, Laura thought. Imagine.

[234]

The door of the Oval Office opened and President Erhardt stepped out, hand on the knob.

"Hello, Miss Madison," he said genially. "It's a pleasant surprise to hear you didn't burn up in that fire after all."

"No, Mr. President, I didn't," Laura said.

"What can I do for you?"

"I need to talk to you."

"About the election?"

"Partly."

"Well?"

"It has to be private." The President glanced at his watch, then at Shaw.

"Buzz us when it's time," he said.

The Oval Office door closed behind them. The President walked slowly across the room, into the pool of bright sunlight that flowed in through the tall windows behind his desk. The Washington Monument rose against a light blue sky in the distance. The President sat down between two flag staves and folded his arms. Then he smiled.

"I was a little surprised to hear you'd been holed up in that beach house with Rydell," he said. "A little romance budding by any chance? Or were you just consoling Rydell for losing that story to ABC?"

"Neither, sir," Laura said. She breathed deeply, then felt her heart flutter. "Mr. President, I'm sure you realize by now that Senator Gillian has been blackmailed, that the whole Marin story was made up, and supported by an electronically created photo."

"So your boss says," the President replied, suddenly serious. "I must say I'm not impressed by his evidence. Emile Loubert was a good friend of mine. I hate to see his name smeared in this way."

"Not smeared, Mr. President," Laura said. "It was the truth."

Erhardt slapped his desk top. "It was *not* the truth!" he shouted. "It was Senator Gillian's paranoid fantasy. A last-minute ploy to affect the election, which by the way he's going to lose and lose big."

"I'm afraid I disagree with you, Mr. President," Laura said. She was struck, suddenly, by how distant and unreal the whole experience seemed to her, sitting in the Oval Office with the President of the United States, on a bright, sunny day. Focus, she told herself. Get on with it. Face him down. Her chest burned and she found herself fighting for breath, and then there it was, in her mind: The image of Mochrie coming toward her, and the feel of the trigger in her finger.

Erhardt was leaning back in his chair, turning to face the window. "Not that there couldn't have been some dirty work," he said, using his fatherly, reassuring tone. "There's always some, but the Republic survives. The Republic endures." The speech-making voice.

"Jefferson knew all that," Erhardt said, gesturing out across the Ellipse at the far-off dome of the Jefferson Memorial. "He said, 'Indeed, I tremble for my country.' I know what that feels like."

His pose echoed in her mind. He looked so . . . presidential, sitting there, fingers thoughtfully placed on chin. She had seen pictures of John Kennedy sitting that way, in a rocking chair because of his bad back. And Lyndon Johnson, hair vanishing and face aging month by month as Vietnam undid the Great Society. All her life she'd trusted the man behind that desk, whatever his party, whatever his policies. He was a symbol. And now Erhardt sat there, letting his impressive moment draw out.

"Mr. President, I know that quote," Laura said. "The whole statement goes, 'I tremble for my country when I reflect that God is just, and His justice cannot sleep forever.' "

Erhardt turned to face her. "Very good," he said. "What do you think it means?"

"It means you can't be president anymore," Laura said. Erhardt raised his eyebrows and snorted.

"What?"

"Mr. President, tell me something," Laura said. "How did you know Mitchell Rydell had lost the Nazi story to ABC? How did you know he'd had it first?"

"You told me, if I'm not mistaken, or you told Steve Shaw, that time—

"No, sir," Laura said. "You knew because you were in on it, from the start."

A knock came on the door. "Time, Mr. President," Shaw's voice said from outside.

"It will have to wait," Erhardt shouted. Turning back to Laura, he added: "What the hell are you talking about?"

"You set Loubert up in business to create a computer network that could threaten and blackmail anyone you chose—"

"Lie," Erhardt said.

"That network created the story about Marin and my boss, then killed Dennis McCarthy, their messenger. Then they tried three times to kill Mitchell Rydell because he was investigating it, and they tried to kill me, on Sapphire Island and again in Key West. For the longest time I just didn't understand why they would shed so much blood to cover up a simple campaign prank. Then we learned what had happened to President King."

Erhardt crossed the room toward the door. "You're raving," he said. "I should have you thrown right out of here. I can't think of a reason not to have some serious charges pressed against you."

"I hate it too, Mr. President, but it happened. It's all true. Dr. Fontana will testify, and so will Skip Mochrie."

"I think I *will* have you arrested," the President said.

"I'll get my day in court, then," Laura said.

"There's not a shred of evidence, and you know it," Erhardt said. "Face it, Laura, it's all gone. Vanished without a trace. Emile Loubert did it, he was out of control, beyond my authority, and I'm certainly going to repudiate it. And that's the way it will stay. An underling out of control. And now that Emile is dead, there's nothing else you can prove."

"Maybe not," Laura said. "But I'll tell you what I can do, what I *have* done. I have Jonathan Marin, Dr. Fontana, and Skip Mochrie on digital video, safely stored in the memory of the Gillian campaign mainframe computer. We have our final download to the media scheduled for four o'clock today. That download will consist of all that video, in full, together with my own written statement of everything that's happened. Names, dates, and what I think it all means. By five the networks will have reviewed it, and the shit will hit the fan. Pardon my French."

"And to stop this reckless assault, all I have to do—"

"Is tell the truth."

"As *you* see it, of course."

Laura was silent. Erhardt still stood by the door, staring at her.

"And you're willing to see the country torn apart just to protect your boss's reputation?" he said finally.

"There's more to it than that, and you know it," Laura said. "What you did to the Senator is just the beginning of what you did, and what you could do, to all of us."

Erhardt seemed to turn reflective for a moment. "I'll be vindicated in the end," he said. "I'm confident of that."

"Mr. President," Laura said, the title tasting rancid. "I can cancel the download and erase all that memory with a single coded command. I will keep my mouth shut forever about this. Forever. And so will Mitchell, and so will Lieutenant Maddalena. The whole network Loubert created is gone. But the technology was never the problem. The technology will do its little dance for anyone who knows how to call the tune.

"As long as you're in this office, I'll never be sure," she went on. "If, God forbid, I ever need surgery, I'd like to think I have a fair chance of waking up. I'd like to be able to drive a car without flinching every time another car pulls up alongside me. I'd like the chance to work out my relationships without feeling there's a gun to my head. I'm not going to live through another four years not knowing. It has to end, and now."

Laura stood up. Erhardt was staring at her with venom in his eyes.

"Like they say," he snapped, "never get in a pissing match with a skunk. Gillian must be glad he's got you to crawl around in the slime for him, to steal an election he's got no chance of winning fair and square.

"Let me tell you something," he continued heatedly. "I had nothing to do with President King's mishap in surgery. But believe me, it's the best thing that ever happened to this country. Look at all that's been accomplished in four years. Look at the healthy, safe, prosperous society we have now. Do you know how many kids were killed by drunk drivers last year, and how many died the year before I took office? How about the figures on drug overdoses, do you have those at your fingertips? Or are you just another one of those carping negativists? How about tax cheats, abused children—"

Laura crossed to the door. Erhardt stood between her and her escape, and she was afraid he wouldn't let her go.

"I want to leave, Mr. President," she said. "Please."

Erhardt's lip was quivering. "I'm going to make a strong statement condemning everything that's happened," he said.

"It won't do," Laura said.

"I'll lay it all out, vindicate your boss, maybe save the election for him."

"No," Laura said, shaking her head. "You can't. Dennis McCarthy and Dominick D'Anselmo are dead, along with who knows how many others. Take a look at me, Mr. President," she said, swallowing. "If you keep this quiet and get reelected, Mitchell Rydell, Carlo Maddalena and Laura Madison will *be* your second term."

Erhardt began to shake his head, slowly. "I won't have the country torn apart," he said quietly. "Not just to prove my innocence. Nixon did that, and it was hell. I've sacrificed for my country before, I can do it again. I know the truth . . ." He trailed off.

"Yes," Laura echoed. "You know."

She passed around Erhardt and out the door. Shaw was pacing in the anteroom. "Christ," he said, "I've got an unruly mob in the East Room."

"Sorry for the delay," she heard Erhardt say behind her, back in his good-old-boy voice. "Had to make a few last-minute changes."

"Ready now?" Shaw said.

"Ready," the President replied, and Laura watched them walk off down the thickly carpeted corridor to the East Room of the White House.

Election Day
Tuesday, November 5

Erhardt's announcement stunned even the TV commentators. But by the next morning—when Laura awoke in her old familiar bed, brewed herself a pot of old familiar coffee, and commenced staring out the window—they'd gotten their tongues back. Their consensus was that it was the most amazing, astonishing, and utterly unexpected thing that had ever happened on the eve of a presidential election.

Erhardt's vice presidential candidate, campaigning in Chicago, had been caught by surprise and had made a rambling, almost incoherent statement. But Gillian had been fine. Going through the motions in Southern California, he'd simply said he hoped the President's health improved, he sympathized with the man and his family, and was content to leave the future of the Republic in the hands of the electorate.

And Laura? Yes, she thought as she sipped and stared, what about Laura Madison. Laura the Dragon-Killer. Face it, girl, you did it to Erhardt just like he tried to do it to you. You knew the buttons to push. Technology *will* do its dance for anyone who knows how to call the tune. You knew how to use that video data to hold a gun to *his* head for a change. You undid him with circumstantial evidence, innuendo, threat, and bluster. But he could have fought you, he could have called your bluff. He didn't because you were right. There was a moment in his office when that became perfectly clear. And what was the result? Can you believe that for *some* people, *some* times, *some* ends justify *some* means? Is that maturity, or just lack of principle?

She spun out of her chair and hurled her full coffee cup across the living room. It shattered on the wall and left a spreading, dripping brown stain. Then she stalked to the door and down into the street.

She went to the South Street Seaport to lose herself in crowds. She crossed town to Madison Square Garden and bowled three games, giving herself a huge thumb blister. She rode the subways uptown and down, wandered through Macy's, and had two lingering bottles of Anchor Steam beer in a small tavern on Ninth Avenue. From the tavern's pay phone, finally, she dialed Gillian headquarters and soon reached Felix Cavanagh.

"Laura, old girl," Felix said, "I don't know what you did, and I don't want to know."

There was a sticky, buzzing silence on the line.

"Is there a plan for tonight?" Laura said. "I don't want to be alone."

"Why in God's name should you be alone?" Felix replied. "We'll be expecting you. Dinner in the Senator's suite at seven-thirty, TV until the results are clear, then downstairs."

"Good," Laura said emptily. "I'll see you there."

It was late afternoon when she returned to her apartment, and found a small white envelope leaning on the door. The coffee stain had dried and she knew she'd have to pay for the repairs.

She put the envelope on the television set and cued up a recording on her CD player. Mozart, she thought. *The Marriage of Figaro*. At least in opera, love sometimes triumphs over all.

A long time later she opened the envelope. Inside was a handwritten note on Mitchell's stationery.

Laura—
I'm having a small party tonight to watch the election returns. Very small, since I didn't have time to send out invitations. If you come, that would make two.

She read it twice before noticing the tiny arrow on the bottom of the page, then turned the sheet over. On the back he'd written:

I'm a work in progress, Laura. The finished product might be worth the wait. I'll be up late.

A work in progress, Mitchell? Laura thought, feeling the tears. Damn it all, so am I. And if you're big enough to call, I'm big enough to answer.

But not tonight. Not so soon.

She was staring at the note with wet eyes when the doorbell rang, and she slowly went to answer it.

Outside her door was New York Police Lieutenant Carlo Maddalena, dressed to kill. A fine gray pinstripe suit, pink shirt with white collar and gold collar pin, silk tie. And in his hands, a dozen glorious red roses.

"Hello, Laura," he said. She looked at him in complete perplexity for a moment, feeling her mouth quiver, then put her head back and laughed loud and long. His pained expression made her stop. She waved him into the living room.

"Listen, Laura," Carlo said. "I know you think we're sort of a mismatch. Maybe you just can't imagine us together. But I can."

He's so *serious*, she thought. Dressed up like he's probably only dressed twice before in his life, speaking his rehearsed speech. It was so endearing she could barely stand it.

"I've moved out on my wife," he said. "Shoulda done that years ago. But better late than never. I, ah, I was hoping you'd be free for dinner tonight," he said.

Laura took the roses and led Carlo to a chair.

"You're sweet," she said, and thought she saw him blush. She looked at him a moment. He's not handsome, she thought. He'll never have Mitchell's money, or his style, or his intellect. Just a simple, solid, reliable man. Yet there was still the gap in her heart that cried out for Mitchell.

"Carlo," she said. "I've learned recently not to make any plans that aren't flexible. Thank you for the roses, but I can't go to dinner tonight. Give it some time, then try again?"

Carlo looked down at his shoes, then shrugged and said, "Sure, I can do that."

"I mean it," Laura said. He smiled a little, and Laura wrote her phone number on a slip of paper and shoved it into his breast pocket.

[243]

When he had gone, Laura closed the door behind her and suddenly gave in to a wave of giggles. Well, girl, she thought, how your problems can change in a matter of minutes. She picked up the phone and dialed Mitchell.

"Got your note," she said. "Can't do it tonight, sweetheart, but keep trying."

After she hung up she was alone, walking around the apartment giggling and crying at the same time.

"*Both* of them?" she said out loud, incredulous. "Laura doll, since you were in high school you never had two fish on the hook at once."

She heard the giddy curlicues of Mozart's finale on her stereo, six singers exclaiming, "What a crazy day!"

Then she called Cavanagh and begged off dinner.

"I'm taking myself out, Felix," she said. "For a big steak and some good wine. I'll see you later to watch the returns."

The returns. The election! She jumped up and checked the clock on her kitchen wall.

Yes, she thought. Still plenty of time to vote.